LUCINDA'S SUMMER VACATION

A DEVON GRAY NOVEL

LUCINDA'S SUMMER VACATION

ELIZABETH FACKLER

FIVE STAR

An imprint of Thomson Gale, a part of The Thomson Corporation

Detroit • New York • San Francisco • New Haven, Conn. • Waterville, Maine • London

LIBRARY OF CONGRESS CATALOGING-IN-PUBLICATION DATA

Fackler, Elizabeth.
    Lucinda's summer vacation : a Devon Gray novel / Elizabeth Fackler. — 1st ed.
        p. cm.
    ISBN-13: 978-1-59414-550-6 (alk. paper)
    ISBN-10: 1-59414-550-4 (alk. paper)
    I. Title.
PS3556.A28L83 2007
813'.54—dc22

2007011885

Published in 2007 in conjunction with Tekno Books and Ed Gorman.

Printed in the United States of America on permanent paper
10 9 8 7 6 5 4 3 2

Lucinda's Summer Vacation

CHAPTER ONE

Lucinda's luggage required five trips between house and car, which she thought was excessive even given that she was planning to stay two weeks and had brought some of Amy's stuff, too. Amy would be joining them on Monday, driving over from Cruces in time for supper. So Lucinda had almost four whole days with Devon to herself. She had relished the anticipation, and now that she was here, felt disappointed to find his house empty.

Impatiently she dropped the bags in Amy's room, intending to separate them later. After freshening up in the bathroom, combing the cap of her short auburn hair and using her palm to flatten the wrinkles from her yellow linen skirt so it fell more smoothly across her slender hips, she walked onto the deck and looked down the arroyo toward the pasture across the creek. Two horses—one black, one brown—grazed in the green field on the far side of the canyon, its creek bed lush with the pink blooms of salt cedar. Between her and the arroyo, three ten-acre properties had been fenced by their owners, the driveways leading to houses that faced away from Devon's, so his view was of their backyards. Other than the residents of those houses and their guests, no one drove on this road, not even a postman because the boxes were on the highway. Lucinda found that unsettling, that no one ever came here.

Uphill, barely visible through the piñon and juniper, was the pink adobe house of the woman newly widowed. Lucinda didn't know much more than that about Natalie Wieland. They had seen each other only once—across the meadow joining the south end of the two properties—had smiled and waved, neither of them taking a step to decrease the distance between them. Standing closer to the widow, Devon had been as gentle as if her bereavement crippled her gait and she required assistance to negotiate through a waist-high pile of rocks. But being as the path between the rocks appeared well-used, Lucinda saw not that Natalie needed help but that Devon seemed to be coaxing her closer. She retreated; the shy, sad widow. Lucinda had said later that she was sorry his neighbor couldn't join them for dinner, that Natalie seemed an interesting woman and must be so very lonely. But Lucinda wasn't sorry, always preferring to have Devon to herself.

Even sharing him with Amy wasn't as much fun, though Lucinda cherished every moment with her daughter. Her pleasure in their companionship compensated for losing Devon's purely romantic side. Days he would pull her into bed no matter how high the sun had risen. Mornings they would dawdle in the sheets. Midnights spent raiding the refrigerator without getting dressed. Standing nude in the cold light contemplating a possible snack, they often decided to savor each other instead. Having Amy in the house changed all that. Devon was circumspect, never allowing her to see anything explicitly sexual. He had a lock on his bedroom door and used it; nothing risqué transpired outside that room. Naturally modest, Lucinda approved of his discretion. But she also enjoyed the freedom to forget it when they could.

She heard his old truck at the front of the house. Not moving from where she stood, she followed in her mind's eye the progress of her dark, lean lover through the sun porch to the parlor, watched him glance into his bedroom as he entered the kitchen, then through the laundry room to the mud room and onto the deck, meeting her eyes as he came out the door. She smiled.

He took her in his arms and kissed her, broke the kiss, and smiled down into her face. "Good to see you."

"You, too." But she saw a distance in his eyes, a barrier, something withheld.

"Hungry?" he asked.

She shook her head. "Coffee sounds good."

He was gone, as if he had never come. Except she remembered his arms around her, his kisses, the most recent of the hundreds maybe thousands he had given her. One of his kisses would be her last, that was what lingered in her mind after he so quickly came and went, as he so often did. One day he wouldn't be back. It was her choice. She had made the decision that she couldn't live with him, thrive with him, feel safe. So he had moved here and was fair game for women like the widow uphill. Lucinda knew one of these days he would find a woman who chose not to live without him. She comforted herself with the belief that, until it happened, she had a chance to take him back. Though she recognized her chance diminished with each day that passed without her having restaked her exclusive claim, enough of her still rebelled at the fearful mindset of living with a fugitive to keep her quiet.

She found him in the kitchen and watched him push the button to start the coffee. The room was lit by one long, narrow window opposite the sink. The aged knotty-pine on the walls and ceiling mellowed the dim light into a becoming haze. The coffeemaker's red light came on as he leaned against the counter and slid his hands inside his jeans' pockets. A compact man of average height, brown hair and eyes, he was inconspicuously handsome. She smiled. "Hard not to love you when you look like that."

"Works both ways. You sure it's coffee you want?"

Remembering he had asked that the first time they had sex, she answered, "It's been weeks since I've seen you."

"Two. Seems longer, though." He smiled. "Is that why you're a day early?"

She laughed, girlishly embarrassed.

He nodded at the steaming, gurgling coffeemaker. "This'll take a minute. Why don't we sit down?"

She wasn't surprised when he led her through the door opening off the kitchen into his bedroom. She sat beside him on the bed, looking out at the dining room with its four chairs tucked neatly under the oblong table, all the legs like a forest of black walnut in the middle of the room. He pulled her to lie back close beside him, so she was staring up at the planks of knotty pine ceiling, old and seasoned, having been cut from the nearby forest eighty years before. His head propped on his hand, he asked about her days since he had last seen her. While she was answering, the coffeemaker beeped five times, but he made no move to get up. Not until the sky had long been dark did they return to the kitchen, scantily dressed, to dump the coffee and drink from beading bottles of sparkling water as they huddled together in the midnight breeze on his deck.

It was two-thirty before Devon left Lucinda asleep in bed. In the guest bathroom at the opposite end of the house, he washed and dressed in clean clothes. Though he didn't take time to shave, he had enough scruples not to go from one woman's bed to another's without washing in between. Wearing clothes he had stashed there earlier—jeans, black T-shirt, clean underwear, and socks—he stood on the front porch and stabbed his feet into his chilly sneakers. He crouched like a runner warming up, first above one knee and then the other, as he tied the laces. Pulling the last bow tight released him like an arrow. He shot over the steps to hit the ground running. Quickly clearing the flagstone walkway and crunching across the gravel, he leapt over the foot-high retaining wall that outlined his driveway— Anasazi pattern of stacked rocks in the moonlight—and jogged across the meadow to the next wall's defensive line. He gained that ascent without breaking stride. Listening to the breeze whisper in the tall summer grasses as he reached the rounded stack of boulders, he followed its well-worn path at an easy trot, crossed another landscaped terrace, and entered the widow's unfenced backyard. A squat, stone statue of a Pueblo woman holding a dripping jar above a shallow pond sat centered on the concrete patio in front of a dark sliding glass door. He slid it open and stepped inside.

Lucinda reached out in bed and missed him. Deciding he was in the bathroom, she stayed awake, wanting to snuggle before drifting back to sleep. The house was so silent, she sat up and listened, knowing the city was never this quiet. Not a single sound. The covers she folded out of her way thrashed through the air like a waterfall. Sitting on the side of the bed, she turned on the lamp. The shadows leapt into relief: the wicker dresser, on the wall above it the lithograph of a Navajo woman weaving beneath a tree. The black wrought iron lamp matching the curli-cued headboard, the little walnut table glistening beneath the fresh finish he himself had put on. The bed, its sheets blue Egyptian cotton, stiff though he used no starch. The goose down blanket, welcome even in June so high in the mountains. Beyond his closed bedroom door, the house loomed silent.

The door had been open when she went to sleep. She felt fairly certain she was right. Maybe he'd felt restless and had closed the door so as not to disturb her. But there was no light from beneath it. No light stealing through slivers around its edges. If he had gone to the far end of the house, would she be able to hear him, detect any light he might be using? She didn't know. She hadn't spent enough time in this house, not any time awake and alone in the middle of the night to know what sounds were normal, what lights real.

The house was old, the front room's long, narrow windows covered with neither curtains nor shades. With lights on at night, the bare glass reflected the room back at her. Devon said there was no one out there to see in, but she felt as if someone were watching. A habit, she supposed, learned from living in a city all her life. Well, at least a town. Berrendo was hardly a city, though compared to Salado it seemed like a metropolis. She couldn't understand why he wanted to live so isolated. After all his years in El Paso, she would have thought he'd wither out here with nothing but nature for company. But from what she could discover, he hadn't even gone to church or joined anything remotely social. His phone never rang! Beside his front door was a wooden bucket he habitually filled with mail he never bothered to look at. She had seen him nonchalantly toss it in numerous times. When he took her to the café in the village, people there knew him, but he always had eaten out more often than not. Even when she'd offered to cook his meals, he'd said he didn't like being committed to when and where he ate. She should have known then he wasn't husband material. Too many years as a homicide detective had spoiled him for domesticity. Sitting alone in his bed, a pool of light surrounding her from his black wrought iron lamp, she wondered where he was.

Devon stepped inside the living room of the widow's home, the entire wall behind him a window overlooking Sierra Blanca's snowy, moonlit peak. The wall in front of him held a balcony to the bedrooms. He climbed the white spiral staircase in the far corner and entered the upper hall in front of the first of two closed doors. The balcony was wide enough to accommodate the sofa and chairs of a sitting area between the doors, which he knew led to guestrooms. The next room down was hers.

No light shone under the door. He had expected her to be awake. But her games were so odd, it wasn't unlike her to be hiding under the covers waiting for him to peel them back in his search. On other nights he would have done it; tonight something felt wrong. Probably Lucinda asleep in his bed. He had never done this before, had always considered himself monogamous, when he had a relationship at all. Serial monogamy, he had heard it called. Smelling blood outside Natalie's closed door, he leaned close and listened. Slowly he turned the knob, swung the door open, a crack at first, then all the way. "Natalie?"

A moan from the bed.

He walked closer, whispering her name before saying, "I'm turning on a light." The click was loud. The rosy patina through her pink silk shade darkened the blood splattered over her face and oozing from a slash in her throat. Involuntarily, he took a step back, then forced himself forward again to pick up her bedside phone and punch in 9-1-1.

Lucinda got dressed when she heard the sirens. Nothing fancy. Mountain wear: jeans, heavy shirt, thick socks, and sturdy walking shoes. She wanted to look as though she belonged. She moved through Devon's house, turning on lights, assuring herself he wasn't there. Looking uphill from the deck, she knew he was with the men who belonged to the cars with rotating blue lights in the widow's front yard. The white light from an ambulance door standing wide open glared into the dark as she listened to a hubbub of indiscernible voices. She couldn't hear his, but where else would he be? She didn't let herself wonder why he would be in the widow's house at three o'clock in the morning. He could explain when he got back. For now, for hours, she stood on the deck drinking hot black coffee until her stomach hurt, waiting for him to come home.

When he did, he emerged from the widow's back door like a bandit, stood a moment looking down at where Lucinda was hidden in shadows, then disappeared in the trees. After a moment, he was on his own land, following a path he had cut from the wild grasses and lined with the ubiquitous red rocks. He had changed clothes since she had seen him last. Actually he had been naked then, but he had put on different clothes than those he took off before bed. She found that interesting in and of itself, that he had changed clothes in the wee hours of morning.

The moon was setting behind him when he climbed the few steps to the deck. She looked up at him, the top of her head reaching as high as his nose, so if she looked straight ahead she saw his throat, his pulse throbbing above the crew neck of his T-shirt, so black this must have been the first time he had worn it. She met his eyes, a mellow brown, hurt and hesitant, weary beyond measure. Suspecting then that he was sleeping with the widow, she looked uphill between the trees at the blue flashes of light strobing across the pink walls. "What happened?"

"Come inside," he said.

"Tell me first."

"Someone killed her."

CHAPTER TWO

She watched him make another pot of coffee though what she wanted was a stiff shot of bourbon. But Devon didn't drink, didn't keep liquor. She wished she had brought some for herself. They had talked about it once and he had agreed she could, that it wouldn't bother him. But she hadn't suspected she'd need it. She watched him finish with the coffee and join her at the table.

"That'll be ready in a minute," he said.

"I can't drink another cup."

They waited, watching each other through the breathing of the brewing machine. The five beeps announcing the end of the process trolled him to his feet. He filled a mug and brought it back to the table, sat down across from her, and watched her a moment through the steam rising from his cup. Uncharacteristically, he held his forehead and squeezed as if trying to force some knowledge into a discernable order. He dropped his hand, lifted his cup, sipped steadily a moment, then set the cup down.

"She was alive when I got there," he said in a flat monotone. "She'd been awake when someone cut her throat. The amount and scatter of blood indicated she put up a fight."

"My God," Lucinda whispered, unable to break her hold on his eyes, searching for any hint that it was a sick joke or she had misunderstood. "All that happened while we were asleep?"

"You were," he said. "Medic's opinion was she couldn't've lived more'n five minutes cut like that. So I was walking over there when it happened."

"You didn't hear or see anyone around her house?"

He shook his head.

"I guess the police asked you that."

He nodded.

"What else did they say? I mean, about you being there in the middle of the night?" She caught her voice rising toward hysteria and forced it back down. "Or more to the point, what do you have to say about it?"

"I saw her earlier today and she asked me over."

"At three o'clock in the morning?"

"Midnight was when she said, but three was the soonest I could get away."

She stared at him. "Were you sleeping with her?"

"She was a lonely lady still mourning her husband."

"You expect me to believe you visited her in the middle of the night but not for sex?"

"I'm telling you what I told the police."

"I think I deserve more."

"What do you want to know?"

"Whatever you're hiding."

He shook his head. "I tried to be her friend."

She knew that about him. More than once she'd had to curb her jealousy because his rendering of comfort involved physical touching. She had watched several women cry in his arms, others reach out to him when they were losing their emotional balance. He did befriend women and offer his masculine strength to assist them, but he had never slept with any of them for as long as he'd been sleeping with her. As far as she knew. Then there was the fact that she had no right to criticize his sexual activity. So why was he lying? Because the widow had been murdered, and a concerned neighbor sounded much more benign than a two-timing lover. Watching him finish his coffee, she realized he had told her what he'd told the police so she wouldn't contradict his answers if she were questioned. Getting your stories straight was part of the daily grind of living with a fugitive. Abruptly she asked, "Do the police suspect you?"

"I don't think so."

"Why not?"

"Why would I?"

"You're right. You have no reason."

"Do you think I did it?"

"No." She knew, however, that if she were still living with him, she would be terrified that this new murder would illuminate the one in his past. "Maybe I should go home."

He shuttered his face against the hurt she'd inflicted. "Might as well wait 'til dawn, no need to drive in the dark."

She laughed, easing the tension. "It would take me until dawn to repack the car."

He smiled. "Lot of work for such a short visit."

"You want any more of that coffee?"

He shook his head.

They didn't sleep. Lying side by side watching dawn slowly lighten the knotty pine ceiling, they didn't snuggle either, like she had wanted when she first discovered him missing. They held hands between their bodies, the most they could muster, both of them craving solitude. Not knowing when she had fallen asleep, she woke up alone. A note on the table said: GONE TO THE VILLAGE. BE BACK SOON. The absence of his signature made her wonder if he'd worn gloves while writing the note to avoid leaving fingerprints.

Pacing nervously, she kept finding herself on the deck looking up through the trees at the widow's pink house. It seemed abandoned, as if a hex were keeping everyone away. But then no one ever came to this neighborhood who didn't live here.

She walked the length of Devon's house half a dozen times: from the deck through the mud room, the huge laundry room with painted turquoise counter, into the knotty-pine kitchen and past the door to his bedroom, his bed made by her, and on into the parlor with its three, long, narrow windows barely lighting the all-wooden room. Into the hall, a square windowless space giving access to another bath, a small cubby-hole den, and the guest room with its long window overlooking the mountains. Watching the road through that window, hoping to see his old brown truck pull in beside her blue Chevy, she gave up and retraced her steps to the deck, where she watched the rock house of the murdered widow.

This time she walked into the yard, following the path uphill that Devon had walked the night before. The path meandered a gentle curve through wild grasses and the scrubby piñon until she could no longer see the yellow wood planks of Devon's house, only more of the pink walls above. The path came out of the trees and continued along the edge of Devon's land toward the road, but she stopped and stared into the widow's adjoining backyard, at the artistic rock groupings among spruce and aspen, the flagstone patio with its granite fountain of a bland-faced Pueblo woman resting a dripping jar on her thighs, beyond her the sliding glass door, its curtain not quite closed so that an alley of darkness beckoned from within.

She heard the rattle of Devon's truck on the first jag of the road. He came around the turn and his engine was louder, then the second jag was behind him and he was approaching his driveway. She cast a glance at the glass door before retreating back under his trees. By taking the path perpendicular to the first, she walked around the south side of Devon's house and came out in the driveway just as he shut off his truck.

Before he could open his door, she was close against it, her arms folded on his open window ledge as she leaned in to kiss his cheek, bristly with whiskers. "Take me to breakfast?"

"Get in." He turned the ignition and had the truck in gear before she had settled beside him on the bench seat. Belatedly she realized she had nothing with her, no purse, lipstick, money, not even a tissue. She folded the visor down and looked at herself in the clip-on mirror that she herself had put there as she flicked her auburn bangs to fall a little more smoothly over her forehead.

"You look fine," he said, pulling out of his driveway onto the road.

She pushed the mirror back and gave him a smile. "I'm not very dressed."

"We're not going anyplace fancy."

"I guess not," she said, "since you haven't shaved."

He raised his head to see himself in the rearview mirror. Leaning across her, he took a shaver from his glove box. He plugged it into the cigarette lighter and buzzed his whiskers off while he drove. She tried not to watch him but he completed the job so adeptly it was obvious he had shaved while driving many times. He even returned the shaver to the glove box without help. Admiring himself in the rearview, he asked, "Good enough?"

"Fine," she said, then turned away to watch the passing view of rugged red arroyos cutting through sweeping green meadows speckled with black Angus cattle. "I did your laundry," she said. The intensity of his gaze coerced her to face him. "I had some of my own, not quite a load, so I threw in what was in your hamper."

He stared at her a second longer before looking back at the road.

"I didn't know where to put them away," she said, "so I folded and left them on your dryer." She didn't want him thinking she had opened his closet or bureau.

He glanced at her again.

"I didn't do anything wrong, did I?" she asked in response to his stony silence. "Destroy evidence or anything?"

"It's too late if you did."

"What could have been there?"

"Being as the entire Salado police force know I was on the scene, nothing."

"Then why are we acting guilty?"

He downshifted and pulled into a viewpoint overlooking the panorama of the White Mountain Wilderness. They sat in the silence broken only by the ticking engine before he said, "Maybe you should go home."

She felt stunned. "You don't want me here?"

"Course I do. But you're taking it on yourself, which is what you said you couldn't handle and why I left Berrendo, remember? I act guilty 'cause I am. There's no statute of limitations on murder, and what happened in El Paso's not going away. But you're not guilty of anything. It's got nothing to do with you."

"Except I love you," she said softly.

He sighed, pulling her close to lean her back against his chest. Before them, the expanse of snow-encrusted peaks floated above the clouds, a mystical world beyond gravity.

The phone had already rung twice when they walked in, so the first they heard was Amy's voice through the answering machine: "Mom, are you there?"

Lucinda gave Devon a quick smile as she ran for the kitchen. She lifted the ivory receiver to her ear. "Amy?"

Devon walked on into his den. An extension phone was at his elbow, the light blinking to indicate Amy's message. He sat down behind his desk and looked at Sierra Blanca in the distance beyond the porch, remembering how he had fucked

Lucinda before they left the viewpoint. Acting like teenagers with nowhere to go. Or maybe flaunting himself in front of the law. Here, look, Officer, here's a grown man acting loose enough to lay his girl on the front seat of his truck in broad daylight at a public overlook. Why don't you check him out and see what else you can learn about him?

If that's what he wanted, he told himself, he should go back to El Paso and turn himself in. Then what? Serve ten, fifteen years in Huntsville to expiate his sin? No, thanks. He'd live with his conscience and count himself lucky. So why do it subconsciously, attract the authorities' attention? That was even more stupid. Especially after three years, with the case too cold to have goose bumps. Would have been a smoother ride if he'd stayed away from Natalie. What were the odds he would buy a house next door to a woman about to be murdered? That he would then begin an affair with her and would be in her bedroom the moment she died? He hadn't acted like any kind of cop then; retired, fired, or rogue. He had dialed 9-1-1, reported the address, and hung up. He knew she couldn't survive having lost that much blood. She knew it, too. They watched each other as she took her last breaths. He didn't question her. Maybe she could've told him who'd cut her, but he let her die in as much peace as he could give. He thought she looked grateful, but he obviously preferred thinking that. Maybe she hadn't even been able to see him, and what he took to be her focus had been a mirror showing him what he wanted to see. She died within a minute. He started to cover her face but left her as she was, walked out of the room and halfway downstairs before he turned around and went back. Wincing to see her staring at him from her bed, he picked the sheet up off the floor and covered her with a repetitious pattern of floral bouquets. He went all the way downstairs and stood in her open front door listening to the approaching sirens. No one else was there. His senses were raw and there was nothing else alive within range. If it were daytime, he could've looked for tracks. But it was dark, and besides, that wasn't his job.

Lucinda came and stood in the door of his den. "That was Amy," she said.

He nodded.

"She's coming on Monday night, as planned."

"Good," he said.

"Is it?"

"You didn't tell her not to, so you must want her here."

"I left it up to her."

"What'd she say?"

"She thinks you may need us"—Lucinda shot him an apologetic smile—"to help you look normal."

He laughed. "She's prob'ly right."

Later, while he was fine-tuning the timing on his truck, she took a book into the backyard, an old paperback *noir* novel by Keith Vining with a lurid cover of a nightclub singer in a blue sequin dress. Lucinda had always fantasized about being a nightclub singer having an affair with the homicide detective on the beat in El Paso. Never having been to the city, she imagined it dark and forbidding enough to pass for any asphalt jungle anywhere. The detective, of course, would be Devon, coming in after midnight to wash the grime of his job down with a couple of drinks. She ignored another part of reality by having him drink. Alcoholism and teetotalers didn't coexist with fantasies.

She settled in his backyard in an Adirondack chair in a sunny clearing. A round redwood table sat near the chair, so it was a place he often visited or at least had arranged for his comfort. She knew he liked to read. Being a librarian, she took note of people's habits in that regard. Sitting in the wooden chair, feeling the sun warm her as she watched a few fat nimbus clouds drift across the blue sky, she was nudged by the realization that this could have been their life, a string of moments like these, full of peace and contentment. Instead, as if El Paso were a template shaping their future, murder seemed to cry for his company. It had commandeered him in Berrendo, striking close to the heart of the family he'd found.

Amy's boyfriend had been kidnapped from school. Upon her entreaty, she, Lucinda, and Devon followed the suspect on an all-night manhunt across the prairies of southeast New Mexico. Devon's actions culminated in the suspect's arrest and eventual imprisonment, but the accomplice suddenly turned up murdered, his body found in a pecan orchard, his skull cracked by a moldy board discarded nearby. Lucinda couldn't help wonder if Devon hadn't been instrumental in achieving that, too. A compact of compassion had been wrought between him and Amy, so that often in the company of her lover and daughter, it was Lucinda who felt left out. What could pull two people together more powerfully than murder? And how else explain why Amy was coming now so eagerly to help defend him against this new brush with death? Lucinda tried not to reach the obvious conclusion—that Amy and Devon had conspired to eliminate the murderer's accomplice—so it floated around in her brain without being cataloged and tucked into place. Like the dead elephant in the middle of the room that everyone tried to ignore, the threat of their conspiracy blocked a lot of paths Lucinda might otherwise wander.

She listened to him working on his truck. The engine was racing, and she imagined him hearing how each cylinder rose and fell in sequence, listening for the one slightly off. Then the engine was quiet again, puttering at idle, and she heard a tool—a wrench or some such—fall with a clang to the gravel. She stood up, thinking maybe she'd go help, be a nurse to his surgeon, handing him scalpels. Shivering at that thought, she turned and found herself looking uphill at the house through the trees. She left her book on the chair and walked up the path.

CHAPTER THREE

At the edge of the widow's yard, Lucinda stopped and studied every detail. The bent-twig settee and chairs under the patio roof; a trickling fountain, water barely dripping from the Pueblo lady's jar into the pond; the clusters of burgundy flame grass against the wall, professional landscaping perfectly balanced. The curtain on the sliding glass door was open a crack, the latch silhouetted against the darkness inside so she could see it was down, the lock open. She stared at that protruding lever a long moment. Behind her, Devon's engine raced again, pushing the old machine to the limits of its endurance before he allowed it to slide back to an idle. The noise made her want to hurry, to slip in and out before he finished.

The Pueblo lady didn't watch her cross the patio; the statue's eyes were downcast as befitted a servant. Lucinda wondered why she assumed the widow was wealthy enough to employ servants. Well, the statue was a bit mammoth for the average yard. There was also the professional landscaping, though that wasn't terribly unusual in desert climates where maintenance was minimal. She slid the door open without hesitation and quickly stepped behind the curtain. Inside, the silence felt heavy. Of course she knew the homeowner had been murdered here, and information like that wasn't easily put aside to survey the surroundings with scientific indifference. But that she couldn't disregard it implied she was searching for an answer to a question she hadn't yet formulated except to know it was centered around what Devon had been doing here not only the night but the moment of the widow's death.

This was mid-morning and the light was astounding. Above the sliding door's draperies, the entire wall was a window. Bright sun filled the room with an exuberance of energy that struck Lucinda with her first personal knowledge of the widow: Natalie Wieland had rarefied taste. The white walls, splashed with colorful abstract weavings, were bleached wooden strips so fine as to suggest *latillas* reaching to the arched clerestory ceiling. White leather furniture and sleek glass tables; the floor, too, such a pale oak it seemed unsubstantial. Like the altar of a church, a stone hearth ascended the entire height of the wall at the north end of the room. To the south was a white wrought iron staircase leading to a balcony. Lucinda looked at the one open door on that sunlit corridor. Slowly she approached the staircase.

Devon had walked this route that night. Come in through that door, crossed this room, climbed these stairs. He had known where he was going, was expecting to be welcomed. Lucinda walked blind, not knowing what lay beyond her next step. She came out on the balcony and looked down at the pristine living room—not even a magazine out of place—then looked ahead, past a sitting area of mission furniture with indigo cushions, to the far open door across what seemed a mile of sunlight. The sun was wrong. Murder scenes should be gloomy. She forced herself forward, feeling dizzy so high above the living room, the open space a tugging force of gravity. With relief she turned into the room.

Blood was everywhere above the bed. A sunburst, a halo, a rounded pattern that had splattered as Natalie fought her killer with her artery slashed open. Lucinda turned away to find herself looking down into the depth of the living room. She had to grip the doorjamb to keep from falling. Forcing herself to focus on a window at the far end of the bedroom, the maroon drapes open, she watched gossamer curtains breathe with the breeze coming in the barely open casing. She took a deep breath and looked back at the bed. An immense amount of blood had soaked into the mattress, leaving an outline of a woman's body on the flowered sheet, as if the widow had lain there as a stencil for the blood to flow around. Lucinda imagined Devon standing next to the bed, closer than she was now because he had used the phone. She looked at it: beige, indistinct, merely a piece of plastic technology on a bedside table. She pictured him dialing 9-1-1, giving the operator the barest of facts before hanging up, not staying on the line as they wanted you to but following his own inclinations. To do what? He had said he went downstairs and waited at the front door. Where was he now? Unable to hear anything beyond the curtain buffeting the wall, she tried to discern something about the woman who had slept in this room, to intuit something Devon might have left behind, but she couldn't tear her eyes from the massive stain of blood on the pink-flowered sheet. She crossed the room and discovered the curtain didn't cover a window but French doors opening to a minuscule balcony, rust from its wrought iron fence staining the concrete floor. She could see part of Devon's driveway, and his truck with its hood up. He was checking the oil, pulling the dipstick out and wiping it on a rag, then sliding it all the way back in and pulling it out and reading the level on the notched gauge. She loved him dearly in that moment. Turning abruptly to escape this place of trouble, she brushed against the gossamer curtain and left a single strand of her auburn hair snagged in its filaments.

The police came early that afternoon. Lucinda had made tuna melts for lunch and she and Devon had eaten the toasted sandwiches at the picnic table on the deck, then moved to the swing under the tall juniper at the corner of the house. Their view was of the piñon forest interspersed with wild-grass meadows sloping slightly toward Magado Creek, a gash in the earth crowded with the festive pink blossoms of salt cedar. Devon lay with his head in her lap, his feet crossed above the far armrest as she gently rocked them in a lulling rhythm. He had his eyes closed, and she let her hand rest on his chest as she studied his face. He was handsome in a non-dramatic way. His features were regular, that was the gist of it, positioned well and of masculine proportion. His beard was heavy and dark; already it shadowed his cheeks though he had shaved four hours earlier. He would shave again before dinner. It was something he did automatically without having to be asked. In so many ways he was like that—a gentleman of the old school created by his Catholic upbringing—yet sometimes she suspected it was a mere protocol he had assumed because his manners allowed him to slide through almost any situation without causing a ripple of disturbance, which sometimes made him invisible. She could picture him on the mean streets of El Paso, opening doors for hookers and picking up checks for informants, riding on the gratitude they felt at being treated with respect. The honor with which he handled people sometimes seemed saintly, yet the flip side of that was a diminution of those people's worth in that he dealt with everyone the same. So rather than kindly, it could be interpreted as egocentric. Pushed to its extreme, the descriptive noun would be sociopath. If he were that, she wondered where she fit into what must be his distorted perceptions, and if perhaps murder had become an acceptable alternative in the perversion of his values. If that had even a remote chance of being true, she was risking not only her own safety but Amy's.

It was then she heard the car in the driveway. She was choosing her words to announce its arrival when Devon sat up. He cupped his chin a moment, noisily running rough fingertips across the beginning prickles of his beard, and she realized he shaved so often because he felt at a disadvantage being unshaven in company. She wondered if that meant he saw his natural state as something to be corrected; she could imagine such teachings being emphasized in Catholic schools. He dropped his hand and met her eyes. His were such a soft honey brown she trusted his heart to be as sweet.

From outside the gate a man's voice called, "Hello!"

"Chief Bright," Devon told her, standing up. "Shall I bring him back?"

"I'll make tea," she said.

He grinned, and she knew he was thinking something akin to—my! aren't we civilized, offering comfort to the enemy—so she returned what she hoped was a whimsical smile of camaraderie and walked away.

In the kitchen, pouring the morning's jug of sun tea into a blue glass pitcher, she wondered how many more times in their lives they would put on brave faces before being interrogated by the police. Any county deputy or city traffic cop held the power to take Devon away from her, maybe permanently, and the extreme length of the odds of that happening offered small reassurance because she knew luck and fate were quixotic. Neither she nor Devon could know which slip of tongue or trip of step would prove to be the spring of a trap. She tore a sprig of mint brought from her garden and dropped it to float on the tea. On a tray she balanced the pitcher and three glasses of ice cubes, along with three long spoons and a crock of sugar, and carried them toward the men's voices drifting in through the back door.

Gordon Bright was in his early thirties and seemed so pleased to be chief of police that his apple cheeks shone as if polished with pleasure. His small regular teeth lined his mouth like pickets guarding the writhing snake of his tongue as his gaze bounced back and forth between Devon and Lucinda with what appeared to be delight in their company. Lucinda looked down at the mint floating on the tea in her glass, hoping that when she again looked at the head of law enforcement for the village he would have assumed a more commanding appearance. She peeked at him from beneath her lashes and caught him watching her. His sandy thatch of hair was slicked back with mousse, his olive green eyes warm with affection, not for her but for his job. She looked at Devon, thinking that in some ways they were two of a kind. Seeing the heat in his eyes, the taut control of his posture, she realized he considered Chief Bright a worthy adversary. So she looked again at the man she had pegged a fool and saw his pupils dilate with acceptance of her newly exuded appreciation of his hidden talents.

"I've heard a few insinuations," he was saying, "but nothing more'n chatter on the airwaves. For the most part, Devon, you've made a good impression on the folks in these mountains. Not too many see it as wrong that you visited your widowed neighbor lady 'cause she asked for your help. What folks do wonder . . ." he paused to flick a smile at Lucinda that begged her forbearance of a little more time, "is what Mrs. Wieland needed your help with." He was smiling at Devon now, a disarming shrug belying the significance of what he was saying. "Most folks know you're a retired police officer. They think maybe the problem Mrs. Wieland was going to ask your help with was how to stop her killer but . . ." Bright shrugged again, this time with apparent sorrow. "He got there first."

Lucinda realized she had delayed Devon. If she hadn't arrived unannounced a day early, Natalie Wieland might still be alive. Quelling that thought, she reached to lift the pitcher above the tiny wicker table. "More tea, Chief Bright?"

"No, thanks. I gotta get going."

She refilled her glass, set the pitcher down, and leaned back in the swing. Devon allowed it to move a bit to accommodate her arrival. She felt the cooling breeze against her face, then it was gone. Bright had stood up, and Devon did, too. They walked toward the front of the house, leaving her alone. Belatedly she realized the chief had said goodbye and she had responded so automatically it might as well not have happened. She had echoed his goodbye, merely that. No invitation to come again or comment on how nice it had been to see him. But then she didn't suppose people said such things to an officer investigating a murder. She hoped he never returned, and rather than being nice, his visit had inserted a new wedge of guilt into her mind. Now she had to consider every move she made in relation to Devon by the light of what she might be interfering with in the rest of his life. If they lived together, that part wouldn't be so huge and she might stand a chance of making intelligent choices. But with most of his life unknown to her—she still didn't believe he hadn't been sleeping with the widow—every step she took was blind. She found herself in the crucible again of arguing for and against keeping Devon as her lover. Her weariness with the argument was itself a liability. On the positive side, he was only the second love she'd had, the first being Amy's father. Lucinda had experienced a few short-lived trysts so shallow they were easily discounted, but encompassing, passionate love she had felt only twice. She guessed she was doomed to bad luck with romance. First a man who had died before they learned she was pregnant, then a man whose past condemned their future. She remembered she had gained a daughter—the most precious part of her life—from her first love. Perhaps what she gained from Devon would be an equal treasure. The odds, though, were on the side of disaster.

She gathered the half-empty glasses on the tray and carried them with the pitcher, sloshing its remnants of tepid tea, toward the deck. Something caught her eye, then disappeared, down by the gate. She watched the spot as she walked, trying to discern what she had seen. All she saw now were the young apple trees abuzz with bees, the mountain juniper flopping like a comfortable floozy, the chain-link fence with its gate closed but unlocked. Beyond the fence, a vacant lot that was part of this property, a level parking place the former owner had used for his horse trailer; beyond that, the driveway to the neighbor's house, half-hidden behind the scrubby pines. Nothing seemed out of the ordinary, but in the next second everything changed.

A door slammed shut in her mind, a plane of awareness ceased to exist in her consciousness. She was a nebulous field of low-level reception, disembodied and unattached. Sounds swirled, the temperature of the air around her fell from torpid to chilled and back again, riding the thermometer like a seesaw of indecision. Unable to name what was happening, she floated in that sea while constantly striving to see a way through the murky waters to the air she needed to breathe to think to know who she was again. She opened her eyes to her daughter asleep in a chair beside her bed in a hospital room.

CHAPTER FOUR

Amy's once long, lustrous black hair had been cropped into a crewcut tinted an electric blue. She wore a gold hoop in her right eyebrow and a sapphire stud above the curve of her right nostril. Her left ear was adorned with a constellation of five stars pierced into the lobe, though her right ear was graced with the only remnant of her former hair, a swag of long black curls. She was wearing a baggy black sweatshirt over brightly printed capris that had been called beachcombers in Lucinda's day but now were called crop pants. The print was overlapping red and purple cubes on black linen, reminiscent of the Fifties. On Amy's feet were Earth Shoes, woven canvas sneakers that touted being made from no animal product. She was asleep, her head crooked onto her right shoulder, her plump body unabashedly collapsed into the chair, her green and blue eye shadow streaked like war paint, her eggplant-purple lips open to reveal a sliver of teeth and swab of pink tongue, the only aspect about her suggestive of the wholesome teenager she was.

Lucinda looked out the window, through the slanted miniblinds to the pale blue sky of early morning. She scanned the room for a clock but saw only hospital machines, sadistically ominous. A few of them hummed; one beeped intermittently. In her arm was an I.V. needle, its tube leading to a bag suspended above her bed. Something scratchy under her chin. She reached with her other hand to touch a bandage circling her neck. Her fingers explored until she felt the wound beneath them, the heat of blood and flaming tissue, a jagged cut running three inches at a diagonal from below the corner of her left jaw. Tears stung her eyes at the pain inflicted by her softest touch. She wished for a mirror, wanting to see what had happened to her. Trying to remember, she put it together slowly: Chief Bright's visit, the men leaving, she carrying the tray of glasses and pitcher of tea toward the deck. Something had distracted her and she hadn't watched her step. What could she have tripped over? And how very strange, to have cut her own throat. Lucinda laughed silently, thinking that, unlike the widow, she needed no help to incapacitate herself.

Amy raised her head and stared at her mother, smiling, then laughed and reached for Lucinda's hand. "Hi, Mom," she said, tenderly curling her fingers under Lucinda's.

"How long have you been here?" Her voice rusty, clogged with the fur of anesthesia.

"All night. After Devon called and told me you were in the hospital, I was out the door in ten minutes."

Lucinda raised her free hand toward the bandage on her neck. "Did the doctor say I'll have a scar?"

Amy's smile was scolding. "You almost died, you know that? Devon kept pressure on the wound to stanch the bleeding until the ambulance arrived."

Lucinda tried to picture that scene: she lying among the shards of glass, already having lost blood by the time he found her so he would be kneeling in it, holding her body closed so she wouldn't lose any more. Instead she saw him standing over a blood-splattered bed while the widow died without any attempt on his part to save her. Lucinda focused on her daughter. "How is Devon?"

Amy sat up straighter with a stalwart sigh and said, "He's drinking again."

"Why?" Lucinda whispered.

"Two women with their throats cut in his near proximity, the chief of police dogging him every time he leaves home. There's a coupla reasons for starters. Not that I think his drinking is a good idea, but it's definitely understandable."

"He'll throw everything away."

"Tell him that, Mom. I'll always be a kid in his eyes, and Devon doesn't take advice from children."

"No," she murmured, doubting he would take it from anyone.

After leaving the hospital, Amy drove east on Highway 70 to Wal-Mart. Not knowing what Devon had at home in the way of sickroom supplies, she stocked up on everything she could imagine needing, starting with a thermometer and bandages in the pharmacy and ending with chicken soup and ice cream from the grocery aisles. The June day was warm, and it was a solid thirty minutes from the south side of Ruidoso to Salado, so she triple-bagged the ice cream for the drive home. The countryside was just beginning to lose the bright green of spring thaw. She had been told precipitation would be scant until the monsoons hit in July, and strong winds would drive the temperatures up until then. Except for Ruidoso, whose humble beginnings as a flour mill evolved into a gambling haven that became a ski resort, Lincoln County had been a ranching community since Anglos began arriving after the Civil War.

Highway 48 wound around curves unfurling one spectacular mountain view after another. Running north toward the Bonito Valley, the rounded White Mountain Wilderness was crowned with Sierra Blanca, whose reach to thirteen thousand feet was soon behind her. Ahead, the rugged Capitán Mountains rose slightly more than ten thousand feet as they cut across the land east and west. Among their towering pine-clad peaks, the narrow canyons seemed snug and secretive. Between the mountains, plateaus of sprawling mesas provided short-grass prairie for the herds of black Angus and white-face Herefords seen from the road. They shared their forage with deer and elk, animals she also occasionally saw, especially deer. The elk were more elusive. Seeing horses and goats sharing the same corral, she remembered having heard the two animals were compatible and sometimes a goat would be bought to keep a horse company. But someone was always trying to unload a goat, so folks with room ended up with more. Same way with burros. Cute critters, they ate enough natural forage that keeping them wasn't expensive. She wished Devon would get one for his land. Two acres, after all, was enough to feed a goat or a burro with only a small supplement. Devon's answer was that animals tied you down; you couldn't leave without arranging for someone to feed and water them, which made weekend getaways problematic. But Amy suspected he was thinking more of leaving in a hurry with no intention to return.

She tried to imagine how she would feel if he weren't a fugitive, if she would find him so fascinating. His proximity almost hypnotically drew her closer, as if he would someday reveal some great truth and if she wasn't there she'd miss it. It wasn't a sexual attraction, though she conceded sex with him would probably be better than good; their relationship was more like that between a wise man and an aspiring apprentice. On television she sometimes saw ads for support groups for victims of homicides. The first time she'd seen such an ad, she was amazed that so many people had lost loved ones to murder. Then she lost Nathan, her boyfriend in high school, and witnessed the killing of the boy who had murdered him. Those events changed her. And because Devon had also witnessed just and unjust murders, she felt they were bonded beyond sex.

She had been away at college when he decided to move to the mountains. Although disappointed that he and Lucinda weren't getting married, Amy could understand that, without her at home to dilute the intimacy, Lucinda had become too intense for Devon. Lucinda had lived exclusively with Amy for eighteen years, and the first year her daughter went away to college was bound to leave her with an emotional vacuum begging to be filled. But Devon wasn't free to commit to marriage. Amy sometimes wondered if she herself would be able to, when the time came. Even having been a witness to murder changed a person, and the killing haunting Devon's past was like a first wife he kept locked in his attic.

Amy turned right off the highway, followed the gravel road uphill, swerved left around the first jag, right around the second, then turned left into Devon's driveway. The sight of her mother's blue Cavalier struck her with worry. She parked her white Focus behind Devon's old brown pickup, opened the gate in his unpainted picket fence, and followed the flagstone walk to his front porch.

Lucinda lay in her hospital bed seeing not the ceiling she was staring at but her daughter alone with Devon. Though she trusted both of them implicitly, she well knew how emotions could get the best of people, driving them to do things against their better judgment. If the two people happened to be a disgraced cop drinking to hide his shame and a teenager whose tragic first love had left her morbidly vulnerable, the collision of their needs could be volcanic. But Lucinda didn't think Devon would let anything inappropriate happen; he was so circumspect about sex around Amy, it didn't seem likely he would lose his caution just because he was drunk. But then, Lucinda had never seen him drunk. He had quit drinking when he left El Paso and just now, according to Amy, taken it up again. As for Amy's loyalty, Lucinda had always admired her daughter's precocious sense of fair play. Even with a reprobate like Zeb Mulroney, Amy had been discreet about the reason she quit seeing him.

His violent attack of another boy had happened in the lobby of Berrendo's only movie theater on a Saturday night, so rather than a secret it was the main topic of gossip in school all the next week, yet Amy had kept quiet, answering when asked only that she and Zeb were no longer dating.

Lucinda didn't suppose she was the first mother to envy her daughter. Not only the beauty and grace of youth, but also the opportunities that lay before Amy. Specifically, in this case, the chance to spend these days—however many they turned out to be—alone with Devon while Lucinda lay incapacitated in a hospital bed. Play house, that's what they would do. Amy would cook and wash the dishes, maybe even dust and vacuum, while Devon tinkered under the hood of his truck or worked on rebuilding his rock walls. After a supper he sloshed down with whiskey, while they sat on the front porch and watched the rosy hues of sunset stain Sierra Blanca crimson, how easy it would be for the daughter to take the mother's place.

Stop this nonsense! she told herself. Devon was an honorable man, and Amy, despite her youth, would not betray her mother. Not for the richest, most handsome Prince Charming any woman could conjure up. And Devon was far from fantasy. He had no income and scant savings, was pleasant looking instead of handsome, and rather than being a co-conspirator in the spinning of fairy tales was a hardboiled detective who had cut his teeth on homicide in one of the most violent cities in the country. He was no woman's dream, closer to most women's nightmare, actually. Lucinda wasn't sure why she wanted him, except to know that she generally felt unusually happy in his company. That would be enough if the world left them alone. But being the world, it impinged just then with the arrival of the police chief poking his head in the door. Smiling as he met her eyes, he asked, "Feel up to some company?"

"Come in," she murmured, wishing he wouldn't.

After the customary greeting and clucking over her accident, Chief Bright asked, "What can you tell me about how it happened?"

"Very little," she said. "The last thing I remember is being distracted by something at the gate."

"What?"

She shrugged, sending a sharp pain radiating from her wound, which made her wince. "I don't know."

"Don't remember, you mean?"

"I guess." Though it wasn't that she couldn't remember but that, even at the time, she had been unable to identify what had caught her attention.

"If you don't mind my saying so, Mrs. Sterling, your hair is an unusual color."

Lucinda stared at him, wondering if he was going to ask if the color came out of a bottle.

"It's very pretty. What do you call it?"

"Light auburn," she said.

"Your daughter has dark hair, doesn't she?"

"Yes. Her father had dark coloring."

"And so does Devon Gray, doesn't he?"

"And you have blond hair, Chief Bright. Why does it matter?"

"We found a hair similar to yours in Mrs. Wieland's bedroom. Did you know a lab can tell whether a hair has been dyed?"

"No, I didn't."

"Were you ever in her bedroom?"

She shook her head, more out of bewilderment than as an answer, though she realized he would interpret it as one. "I met her only once, in the yard."

"Did you like her?"

"We waved and called a hello, that's all. She seemed pleasant enough."

"Do you know if Mr. Gray was sleeping with Mrs. Wieland?"

"No."

"Do you know he wasn't, or do you not know?"

"He told me he wasn't."

"When was that?"

"After he found . . . after she died."

"As a way of explaining why he was in her bedroom at three o'clock in the morning?"

"Yes," she answered guardedly.

He stood up. "We've sent the hair for analysis along with everything else we found at the scene. It'll take a coupla weeks before the results come back from Santa Fe."

"Don't you need one of my hairs for comparison?" Lucinda asked.

Bright's smile was conniving. "Are you offering to give me one?"

Lucinda shook her head, wanting Devon's, or maybe a lawyer's, advice before saying more.

"Aren't you worried, Mrs. Sterling, about your daughter being alone with Mr. Gray?"

"Should I be?"

"If she were my daughter, I wouldn't want her staying alone in a house with an older man."

"Surely this is beyond the scope of your responsibilities as chief of police."

"Technically, but the well-being of my constituents is the umbrella of my responsibility"—he paused to smile—"so to speak."

She closed her eyes, not having to feign fatigue.

"One more question, Mrs. Sterling?"

She opened her eyes.

"Did Devon Gray contribute to the cause of your accident in any way?"

"No."

"Do you think he might have killed Mrs. Wieland?"

"That's two questions, Chief Bright. The answer to both is the same."

He smiled as if she had complimented rather than chastised him. "Thank you, Mrs. Sterling. We'll talk again, I'm sure."

She watched him leave, then listened to his footsteps receding down the hospital corridor. Thinking he was an evil man to stoke the doubt in her mind about Amy and Devon, she pushed the button for the nurse, intending to find out how soon she could go home.

"Hello!" Amy called, carrying her Wal-Mart bags through the shadowed living room to the kitchen. She set them on the floor and turned on the light, then stood listening to the silence. Despite his truck being in the driveway, Devon evidently wasn't home. She walked through the laundry room to the mud room and looked out the windows. Their glass was distorted with age, making the ridge and surrounding countryside look as wavy as if they were underwater. But no where in that oceanic landscape did she spot her mother's lover.

She returned to the kitchen and put the ice cream in the freezer. Her other purchases she took from their bags and spread on the counter, then threw the bags in the trash. Above the tall plastic bin, an ivory phone was attached to the wall. She picked up the receiver and punched in the number of her best friend in Salado. Sharon had still been in high school when she and Amy became friends the summer before; Amy had just graduated and Sharon was entering her senior year. Her brother answered the phone and said she was shooting hoops at school. Amy took a shiny Granny Smith from the basket on the dining room table and walked out the front door, locking it with the key Devon had given her. Munching her snack, she drove into the village to the basketball courts behind the high school. She parked and sat finishing her apple as she watched Sharon dribble and shoot.

Making every basket like the star player she was, Sharon had the grace of a natural athlete, the fluid movements of someone completely at ease inside her body. Her hair was a lusciously thick, dark hickory brown; even pulled straight back in a ponytail, it belied the mundane style to tumble in sensuous curls down her back. So displayed, her face was clean of makeup but no less interesting. Her dark eyes were placid, quick to note changes but withholding judgment, as if everything off a basketball court were equally inconsequential. Her nose was long with a faceted bone structure, her lips now petulant in thought as she bounced the ball, the muscles in her thighs quivering with impending action. Beneath her white short shorts, her long, tanned legs provided her height, five-ten being unusual for a girl but not enough to make her a freak. She looked like a colt not yet filled out, a filly yet to develop the apple butt of a mare, her lines boyish without being masculine, the sweep of her hickory hot ponytail across the sweaty back of her tee a touch of enticement above the lolling rhythm of her dribbling the ball toward the hoop. Her intention coiled and she became a feline mother pouncing on her child's supper, the indifference in her eyes replaced by a calculating drive toward success. Suddenly her arm projected outward, ejecting the ball from her fingers. She froze to watch it slip through the net and bounce once, then her knees laconically moved, her footsteps echoing the bounce, becoming one with it until she stopped, all of her twisting in unison, a spiral of action up her spine as she swiveled around to face the boy applauding from the bleachers.

Amy hadn't noticed him before: a pudgy blotch of dark clothes on the gray painted risers. Sharon was frowning, squinting her eyes against the sun behind his back. She touched her tongue to her lips in what Amy thought was an innocent recognition of the boy's sexual intent, then turned her back and dribbled the ball toward the door always open to the gym.

Amy got out of the car and ran after her. "Hey, girlfriend!" she called, catching up on the sidewalk.

Sharon turned around, lifting her T-shirt to wipe the sweat off her face, revealing her midriff to a cooling breeze that also carried the boy's lustful gaze.

Thinking Sharon seemed unaware of that, too, Amy turned around to stare at the cretin still on the bleachers. "Who is he?" she asked, studying the aura of hostility she could feel emanating from his vicinity. Amy considered herself psychic and paid close attention to people's nonverbal communications.

"Leroy Culler," Sharon answered. "When'd you get back?"

"This morning." She followed her friend into the gym. "My mom's in the hospital."

"I know. How's she doing?"

"Okay. Guess the whole town knows, huh?" She followed Sharon into the girls' changing room and watched her open her locker.

"I heard people talking about it in the post office," Sharon said. "Sounds creepy after what happened to Mrs. Wieland."

"What do you mean?"

Sharon turned around, her face crimped as if she didn't like saying what she was about to. "Someone killed her on Friday night."

Amy shrugged, unable to picture the woman, only her pink adobe house.

"Devon found the body at three o'clock in the morning on Friday night. On Saturday, your mother falls and cuts her throat."

"I know about my mother," Amy said impatiently.

"Mrs. Wieland's throat was cut. That's how she died. It's just

weird, don'cha think, both of them happening so close together?"

Amy felt chilled though the room was humid with heat. She
sank to sit heavily on the backless bench while Sharon peeled
off clothes and walked naked into the shower. Rather than seeing the steam curling beneath the ceiling she was staring at,
Amy was seeing Lucinda stumble on the flagstones and drop
the tray so the pitcher shattered into shards, one of which
projected upward enough to slash into her throat and nick an
artery. Unable to blame her mother's fall on anything other
than an accident, she forced her mind to remember the widow,
but all she could conjure up were prickles of desperation. The
sensation was like being slapped with a reed; the blade itself did
no harm but the jaws of tiny stickers embedded on its edges
dug in like lures. She wondered if that was how Devon had
been sucked into befriending the widow.

"How long's your mom gonna be in the hospital?" Sharon
asked, drying herself with a towel.

"I don't know."

"Will she go back to Devon's when she gets out?"

"Why not?"

Sharon raised her eyebrows as if to question Amy's sanity,
then wadded the towel into a ball and threw it into the laundry
cart across the room.

CHAPTER FIVE

Devon sat on a boulder atop Salado Peak, a modest precipice rising five hundred feet above the village. Thrust into the sky by an ancient earthquake, the face of the peak was a sheer drop. Behind that cliff, the mountain's spine descended only slightly into the rumple of ridges and arroyos rising toward Sierra Blanca, thirty miles distant and six thousand feet higher.

Centered below the cliff, the village sprawled in a ragged grid south of the highway. North of it, civilization's outermost edge was flung like a feathered fan on the few roads into the Capitáns. Twelve hundred people called Salado home, most of them retired or simply old and poor. The public school, which housed kindergarten through twelfth grade on one campus, was filled with kids off nearby ranches. Very few youngsters lived in town. Strung out along the highway, starting from the east, were the bird-viewing platform over the water treatment plant; the propane office; the Salado Police Station and Volunteer Fire Department; a barbecue restaurant, the Kickback, that served beer and had live music on weekends; the bookstore and the Farmers Country Market, across from each other; and then Lincoln County Mercantile, next to the market and across from the Endive, a vegetarian restaurant. Farther west, the post office was next to the Salado Café, the only restaurant in town open for breakfast; then the forest ranger station; Brewer's Shell Oil, with its convenience store; and a Mexican restaurant, all on the north side across from the school. Between the school and the police station lay four blocks laid out east-west as First through Fourth Streets intersected north-south by streets named for the county's founding fathers: Murphy, Dolan, Baca, and Dudley. Half the lots in the village were empty. There were three two-story houses, Victorians moved from a nearby mine when the railroad deemed the quality of the coal not worth its freight, several adobes dating back to the Thirties, and a few new homes glimmering behind their insulated windows. Everyone else lived in trailers. Some were well kept, their yards groomed; others neglected, their yards graveyards of past assets.

If Devon turned around, he could see his own house a mile away. The roof and part of the driveway, at least. Watching Amy arrive and carry her groceries inside, he had quickened his pace to the precipice. When he looked back again, her car was gone. He scanned the highway into town, saw her white Focus cresting the hill, and watched until she parked at the school. The girl shooting baskets he surmised to be Sharon Barela, Amy's best friend in Salado. He watched them walk into the gym, then saw another kid stand up from the bleachers. Devon hadn't noticed him before: a pudgy kid in dark clothes, probably a boy, though the body was so roly-poly it was hard to tell. The kid walked with a sauntering gait that Devon pinned as belonging to an adolescent male with an attitude. Small towns weren't different from cities, just smaller; the members of each class were fewer, but all classes were represented. Devon tried to imagine being chief of police in such a tiny jurisdiction. Given that he would know every citizen almost intimately, the constantly evolving configuration of personalities within neighborhoods would make society seethe like chicken shit turned by unseen worms under a coop.

He realized that was a negative image to describe his own kind, one which by extension reflected an unkind opinion of himself. He even recognized his low self-esteem as a symptom of depression. But he found it impossible to ameliorate the facts that he had watched a good friend die and was now suspected of her murder; had betrayed his lover and was keeping her around because he wanted her with him, not because she could gain anything from it; and was reeling into complicity his lover's daughter, whose huge heart and generous sensitivity didn't belong anywhere near the scene of a murder. How could he dismiss the shame he felt for all that as a simple symptom of depression? He reasoned they didn't have to negate each other; shame and depression could co-exist. The depression was his inability to act, to change the direction of things that had definitely taken a wrong turn. He had never felt so bereft of impetus. He felt as if his presence threatened the safety he wanted to provide Lucinda and Amy, yet he also knew that developing a habit of avoiding people could increase suspicion of his guilt. He had, after all, been the last person to see Natalie alive. Her wound was so new, her killer must have been in the house when he entered it, must have slunk out as he stole in, escaped while he watched her die. But he wasn't a cop anymore, and she was a friend he chose not to leave alone. Hoping Lucinda felt the same about him, he also wondered if she wouldn't go home after the hospital. There were many reasons she might prefer being back in Berrendo besides having lost the illusion of safety he could no longer provide.

Below, Amy's white Focus pulled out of the school's parking lot onto Fifth going east. Devon started home, confident of finding the solitude he craved. Halfway down the ridge, however, he saw Chief Bright's squad car in his driveway. Careless of his step, Devon studied his yard—what he could see of it through the trees as he walked—for a glimpse of the chief. If he wasn't in his car and he wasn't in the yard, he was in the house. Devon wondered if Amy hadn't locked the door, if the local law could be that casual about search warrants, and if there was anything incriminating to be found. He hadn't killed Natalie Wieland, but he was too damn close not to merit investigating, and the fact that he was guilty, not of this murder but another, was a scent any good lawman would pick up. Devon's opinion of Chief Bright was a rube hiding a hunter's instinct behind a polished vocabulary, but of the chief's ethics as a cop he had no evidence to make a judgment.

The last five minutes of his walk, he crossed from the far bank of the Magado, stepping from stone to stone among its dry pools, then ascended out of the arroyo to a juniper forest that hid his home from view. He broke into a jog and didn't break stride when he saw the silver squad car in his driveway. Turning in off the road, he met the eyes of Gordon Bright.

Salado's chief of police sat on Devon's front porch steps, watching him let himself in through the gate. "Nice view of the mountains," Bright said.

Devon looked across the intervening meadow and ridge to the range of Sierra Blanca and Monjeau Peak, their lesser brethren like a fleet of humpback whales surrounding an island in the sky. "You didn't come here to admire the view."

"Might've, if I'd noticed it last time I was here." He glanced uphill at the widow's pink house peeking through the trees. "I've just come from the hospital. They told me you haven't been there yet today."

"Did you see Lucinda?"

Bright nodded.

"How is she?"

"It'll take her a while to regain strength after losing so much blood, but she's recovering."

They studied each other a long moment, two pairs of brown eyes savvy and sharp. Devon didn't pick up any hostility coming from the lawman, not even so much as a twinge of dislike. Letting loose his breath as if he'd just surfaced from underwater, he asked the chief in for coffee.

"Don't mind if I do," Bright said eagerly.

Devon led him through the sun porch into the shadowed living room with its three long narrow windows, turned right through the dining room and past the open bedroom door adjacent to the kitchen. With only one of the narrow rectangular windows, the kitchen was dim until Devon turned on the overhead light.

Chief Bright leaned against the counter watching him put together a pot of coffee. "Do you expect Mrs. Sterling to return here or go home when she's released?"

Devon looked over his shoulder and said, "I don't know."

"I prefer she stay here," Bright said. "The paperwork piles up when we start extraditing folks between counties."

Devon punched the start button a little too hard. "Why would you do that?"

His voice deliberately soft and slow with a professional coercion toward calm, Bright said, "She's a witness."

Devon had used that tone many times in his career. It usually meant the interrogator knew more than the subject suspected. "Against who?"

"Perhaps more for than against. Your alibi, for instance. She gives some support to that. But I've been wondering if you could give her one."

"What do you mean?"

"Can you swear to Mrs. Sterling's whereabouts immediately prior to your arrival at Mrs. Wieland's?"

"Yeah, she was asleep in bed 'til the sirens woke her up."

"Is that what she told you?"

Thinking back, Devon couldn't remember that they had discussed it. When he had come home after the police let him go, Lucinda was waiting on the deck. He remembered she had been dressed, not wearing her nightgown and robe, which were still in her suitcase as she hadn't yet unpacked. Like two kids who couldn't wait, they had tumbled into bed undressing each other, then slept nude. He wondered if he should unpack her things so it seemed more likely she had slept in his bed. But if she was leaving anyway, it only mattered for these few hours, and he knew Chief Bright needed a warrant to search that far. "No, I guess not," he conceded. "I'm assuming the sirens woke her. It might have been something else."

Bright nodded. "She might have left the bed soon after you."

Devon laughed. "Are you suggesting she got there before I did, killed Natalie, then came back without my intercepting her?"

"It's theoretically possible."

"Not in the universe I live in."

"Why not?" Bright asked, amused.

"I would've seen her. This is my land. I live here. She doesn't."

"How much time elapsed between when you left her in bed and when you left the house?"

"Twelve, thirteen minutes."

"It took you that long to get dressed?"

"I washed."

Bright's amusement deepened his smile. "The gentlemanly thing to do between trysts."

"I didn't intend to have sex with Natalie."

"Perhaps Mrs. Sterling had other expectations."

Devon opened the cupboard and took out two coffee mugs, wondering if Bright could seriously suspect Lucinda.

"She could've dressed quickly," Bright argued, "run up there by a different path than the one you used, killed Mrs. Wieland, run back, thrown her clothes in the hamper, and been back in bed nude before you returned."

Remembering Lucinda had done laundry the next morning, Devon wondered how the chief knew she slept nude. "Without evidence, a theory's just words."

"The forensics team recovered a hair from the bedroom curtains," Bright crowed. "I sent it to Santa Fe for analysis, but from its color I feel fairly certain it came from Mrs. Sterling."

Lifting the quart of milk off the refrigerator's shelf, Devon didn't flinch.

"Do you know of any time when Mrs. Sterling was in Mrs. Wieland's bedroom?" Bright asked.

Devon set the milk on the counter. "No."

"Can you think of an alternative explanation?"

"Someone else could've carried it there," Devon said. "It might've even been blown on the wind."

"Those curtains were professionally cleaned the week before Mrs. Wieland was murdered. I found the ticket still in her car. Mrs. Sterling told me she arrived here about fourteen hours before the murder. And Friday wasn't windy."

Devon shrugged. "You're reaching so far, you're about to fall over backwards."

"Name another suspect," Bright said sharply. "Besides you, who else might've been in Mrs. Wieland's bedroom that night?"

CHAPTER SIX

Amy arrived at Devon's in the lavender twilight. Her mother's blue Chevy was now coated with dust. Cleaned at least by the wind of having been driven, Devon's brown truck was parked beside it, but she had learned that seeing it in the driveway didn't mean he was home. In the kitchen, she felt relieved to see the coffeepot half full, indicating he had at least been there. Since the coffee was cold, however, it could have been hours ago. She glanced through the open door to his bedroom, which seemed untouched. The rest of the house hovered with an almost palpable emptiness, so she continued through the laundry and mud rooms to the deck. He was sitting at the picnic table with a beading bottle of beer in front of him. "Hi," she said, flouncing herself down on the opposing bench.

With no smile of welcome, he asked, "How's your mother?"

"Worried about you."

"I missed visiting hours," he said, dropping his gaze in lieu of an apology.

She looked at her watch. "They start again in forty-five minutes."

He met her eyes, and she could see that he was blaming himself for everything. Maybe not Mrs. Wieland's murder, but its proximity to Lucinda and her subsequent accident he took to be his fault. Amy searched for the words to comfort him but felt too intimidated to argue against his version of reality. She was a student to his teacher; it wasn't her place to tell him he was wrong. She was also, in an emotional sense, his stepdaughter. Never having had a father, she was uncertain of her rights to critique his behavior. But as a friend, which she considered herself most of all, her need to speak up felt urgent. Too, she was studying psychology in school and very interested in techniques to get someone talking. She gave him a gently encouraging smile. "You saved her life. You should feel proud of yourself."

"I administered first aid. Any Red Cross volunteer could've done it."

Even though his anger was aimed inward, it bounced back with enough velocity to slap the air between them. Impatiently she asked, "Do you really think drinking will help?"

"I'm not drinking," he said, his deadpan voice dragged to a lower register by the disappointment of being misjudged. "This beer's nonalcoholic."

She looked at the label, then at him again.

He laughed, affection softening his disdain. "For being psychic, you sure blew that one."

She shrugged defensively. "So there're some things I don't know."

He nodded. "How's Sharon?"

Astonished, she asked, "How do you know I saw her?"

"I watched your car from the ridge. Saw you carry a slew of Wal-Mart bags into the house then drive to the school where she was shooting hoops. Saw you go into the gym and come out a little later and drive towards her house." He smiled. "That's when I knew the coast here would be clear for a while."

Hesitantly she asked, "Would you rather I go home?"

"Not until your mother's out of the hospital."

She sorted through her mind for why he had suddenly become uncomfortable in her company. "It's okay that we stay here together, Devon. No one's gonna think anything."

"I don't care what anyone thinks."

"Then what's wrong?"

"Let's just say I don't feel like I'm good company right now. More than that, I might even be dangerous company. And while I'm sorting it out, I'd just as soon not put you and your mother at risk 'cause, when you get right down to it, it's got nothing to do with you."

"Why does it have to do with you? Just because you bought a house next door to a woman who was murdered?"

"You have to admit it's an odd coincidence."

"It's a synchronicity," she said. "As long as you carry your past so close in your consciousness, you'll attract similar experiences. If you could let it go, things like this wouldn't impinge on the perimeters of your self-defense." She smiled, proud of her wording.

He laughed, but she suspected it was more in response to her smile than because he believed her. "I'm gonna visit your mother. Want to come?"

"Sure," she said.

She watched him driving his old truck, guiding the stick shift with a finesse not smudged by his anger. He needed a shave, his cheeks were darkly shadowed, and his dusty jeans and sweaty white T-shirt were the same ones he'd worn hiking the ridge. Picturing him sitting above the cliff watching her car on the highway, she wondered what emotions had flashed through his mind as he thought of her. That he felt wary of them spending a night alone meant he saw her as a sexual person. That surprised her. He had always treated her like a child, had insisted on it when she tried to broach those lines. Now she realized he didn't trust himself with her. That surprised her, too, because she had admired his strong self-control, the consistency of his discipline and steadfastness of his loyalty. Now he seemed vulnerable, capable of being lost, not only to her but himself as well. Because of what they shared from before, their bond was independent of whatever happened between him and her mother. That hadn't been articulated between them, but they both knew it was true.

At the hospital, he opened the door for her. Remembering how much her mother appreciated his old-school manners, she decided the novelty was annoying. Inside the elevator, she put herself in front of the buttons and punched the right one without his help. He didn't seem to notice that she had usurped his role. When the doors opened, she hurried ahead, suddenly wanting more than anything to be alone with her mother. Suddenly she realized that was exactly what he meant: their lives would be easier without him. Pushing that thought away, she shoved through the door of her mother's room. Lucinda's face beamed with joy, and she gingerly raised her arms for a hug. Amy leaned over the bed and held her mother as tightly as she dared. When they broke apart, Lucinda was watching Amy as if her daughter's sudden need of maternal care indicated something amiss. Lucinda looked beyond her. Amy stood up straight and turned around to look at Devon standing just inside the door.

"Come in," Lucinda coaxed. "Give me a kiss."

Amy moved closer to the window and watched him lean over the bed to kiss her mother. Lucinda's hand not tethered by the I.V. rose to his shoulder as he lingered in his kiss. Then he stood up and asked how she was in a voice husky with desire. Amy's ears burned at having witnessed the understated passion that seeped between her mother and Devon. She reached behind herself and touched the cord to the mini-blinds. They were open to the dark pines towering into the evening stars, the sky cobalt blue.

"There's a chair here somewhere," Lucinda said.

"I can't stay," he answered. "Just came to see that you're all right."

"Where are you going?" There was a note of desperation in Lucinda's voice, which she softened into a petition. "I need to talk to you."

Amy felt his gaze and raised her eyes to his. He said, "Why don't you bring us some coffee from the cafeteria?"

She didn't think that was allowed but she took the hint. Smiling at her mother on her way out, she said just beyond the door, "I'll be right back."

Neither of them said anything until the door thudded shut. Although Amy had been exiled, she didn't go far. She pinned her ears to the voices speaking in confidential tones inside the room. Corridor noises interfered. People walking in squeaky shoes, carts clinking by, telephones at the distant nurses' desk, the elevator periodically opening and closing. But what she heard of the conversation between her mother and Devon made her push back through the door. They both turned their heads to look at her, Devon from the far side of the bed where he sat holding her mother's hand.

"I'm sorry, I was eavesdropping," Amy said. She turned around to make sure the door was completely shut, then crossed to stand beside the bed and ask her mother in a near whisper, "Did I hear you say you're a suspect in Mrs. Wieland's murder?"

Lucinda sighed. "They found a hair similar to mine in her room."

Wanting to eliminate this scenario from the realm of possibility, Amy demanded stridently, "Were you ever there?"

Lucinda looked at Devon and nodded.

"When?" he scoffed.

"Yesterday. When you were working on your truck. I don't know why, I just felt curious, and I'd been up to the edge of her yard earlier and seen that the latch on the sliding glass door was unlocked, so later, when you were busy, I just walked in."

"What did you see?" Amy whispered.

Lucinda looked at her. "I wish I hadn't gone. It was awful, all that blood on the wall, and where she'd been on the bed, the shape of her body was outlined in blood."

They both looked at Devon. Amy thought it was as if they expected him to say such was often the case or something equally benign to deny the horror. But he said, "That was stupid, Lucinda. You just dealt yourself into a game you've got no business being anywhere near. I want you to go back to Berrendo as soon as you're released."

"And what'll happen to you?" she cried.

Amy shivered at the fear in her mother's voice. She saw it reflected in Devon's face as he closed his lips in a tight line of acceptance. Whatever happened, they were in it together, which was what Amy wanted, to keep them that way permanently. Tenderly intruding, she said, "I think we should all go home now. Back to Devon's, I mean."

"You're right," Lucinda said. "Bring me my clothes." She looked at Devon. "Will you find the nurse or whoever has whatever papers I need to sign to release myself?"

He didn't move. "You're sure this is what you want?"

Amy opened the closet and saw her mother's bloodstained sweatshirt on a hanger from the hospital laundry.

"Yes," Lucinda told Devon.

Amy listened to his footsteps cross the room behind her, felt him nearly brush against her on his way by, then heard the door thud shut. "Wish you had something else to wear," she said, carrying the stained clothes to her mother.

On Monday morning, Sharon came to visit. She and Amy walked the mile and a half length of Devon's road, Sharon bouncing a ball in syncopation to their footsteps as they talked about college at the end of summer. Sharon had won an athletic scholarship to NMSU and was worried she wasn't smart enough to earn good grades while playing on the basketball team. Amy could appreciate her friend's concern. She herself spent nearly every waking hour studying and sometimes felt she was barely comprehending what she was supposed to be learning.

The road suddenly dropped down toward the Magado and ended in a circle of three cedar houses. All of them had horses in pole corrals with lean-to stables. Amy and Sharon stood at the top of the hill and savored the view. Then Sharon bounced her ball and they turned around and started walking back. Halfway there, off to the right, a modest modular sat in a clearing free of trees, an older pickup and a small Jeep in its gravel driveway. A little farther, on the left, was a homemade A-frame, the principal construction material being unpainted plywood. Parked in its dusty driveway was an ancient Range Rover. Amy suddenly saw that a boy was sitting on the porch watching them. She recognized him as the kid who had watched Sharon practice at school. In a whisper, she said, "There's Leroy again."

Sharon followed her gaze and quickly looked away. "He's not playing with a full deck, know what I mean?"

Amy nodded, but it was more than inadequacy she felt coming from him; he exuded a tepid swamp of malice. "You should stay away from him."

Sharon laughed. "You're the one lives practically next door."

Amy shivered, not wanting Sharon to leave. "Can you stay for dinner?"

"Can't," she said. Her bicycle was in the driveway. She knocked the kickstand up and swung on. "See you tomorrow?"

Amy nodded. "I'll call you." She watched Sharon ride away, the basketball tucked under one arm, her long black hair spraying behind like a fountain in the wind. Turning, Amy had a vision of footprints in snow. A flash of the toes dug deep as the person ran through a pristine, untouched field. Then the vision was gone and she saw only the ridge rising above the Magado.

Sharon pedaled easily, holding the ball under one arm, her long legs smooth in their rhythm. She liked being tall and never had to think about moving; it just happened, usually with good results. But although she was a basketball star with ribbons and trophies in her room, she couldn't dance. She knew that sounded silly, but on the dance floor she was self-conscious in a way she never was on the ball court. Even when the boy was taller, she felt clumsy and inept. She worried that her pelvis would clash against his, her knees knock, her shoulder blades slice like knives beneath his hand. On the court she was comfortable with who she was, but on a dance floor she felt like a giraffe with three feet.

She figured it didn't much matter because her first love was basketball. She enjoyed making baskets, the finesse of a perfect shot, the glory of an impossible one, but she liked being on a team, too: the camaraderie before and after games, feeling like she was part of something important. She wanted the family she had with her future husband to be tight and work together as a team. Brimming with love surging to be expressed, she longed to give it to children. She loved animals and hoped to have lots of them, too. Not just dogs and cats but goats, cows, horses. She dreamed of opening a shelter for abused animals. To support her shelter, if she didn't marry, she intended to teach P.E. She felt that through sports she could teach kids how to live. Helping them achieve something worthwhile would be making a positive contribution, but in her heart she didn't want a job. She wanted to have a home full of kids and pets and for her job to be to take care of them all. Like the Good Shepherd at church; she wanted to be like Jesus and suffer the little children. She loved arranging flowers and growing vegetables and watching sports on TV. And she enjoyed visiting with her girlfriends, especially Amy when she was around, but Sharon didn't like boys much, considering it an unfortunate liability the way they always brought any conversation around to sex.

Her brother Josh, who was a year younger, had been a problem since middle school. It started when she went out for sports and discovered she was good at it. Track, volleyball, basketball, softball: she was a star player on all those teams. When her school won the state basketball championship and she was chosen MVP for the season, she looked into the stands and saw Josh give her a thumbs-up. She felt so proud. Later at home, though, he was back to his usual self, punching her arm as he passed her in the hall. "That hurt!" she yelled, but he didn't answer, just left her standing there rubbing what felt like a bruise spreading under her skin. She heard the screen door slam, then his Mustang rev and peel out of the yard. She went into the kitchen and helped her mother trim strawberries for a pie. Her mother didn't say anything about her yelling or the bruise on her arm. That was one thing Sharon could say for sure about her mother: Angela Barela was quiet.

From Amy's house, Sharon rode her bike to school and shot hoops for a while, slam-dunking the ball and taking pleasure in her success. Eventually she became aware of Leroy watching from the bleachers. She didn't trust Leroy. An odd gleam flickered behind his eyes sometimes. Having such a weird kid down the road was the only unpleasant thing, in her opinion, about Devon's neighborhood. Otherwise she loved it and would have lived there full time, if she'd been Amy. Sharon didn't understand the relationship between Devon and Amy's mother. She knew they were sleeping together, but Lucinda only came up every other weekend during the winter, sometimes less if the weather was bad.

Shot hard against the backboard, the ball returned in a spin to Sharon's hands.

She sometimes saw Devon around the village. Because of her friendship with Amy, he would stop and talk to her, an event that made her the envy of other girls at school. He had started out as a reclusive newcomer to their village, but after a year his elusiveness was sporadic and added to his mystique. The high school girls thought him handsome, and the fact that he was single made him more enticing. Having grown up thinking they must choose a husband from their peers, the girls of Salado were delighted to discover a new prospect in their vicinity. So every time Sharon talked with him on the street, she felt attention eddy around them like a whirlpool. Afterwards she would be questioned about what had been said, and envied with deeply drawn sighs. Most interesting of all was her suspicion that Devon was oblivious to the admiration he inspired. He seemed to slink from his den like a midnight raider forced out at noon, wary of the light and slightly grumpy about the disruption.

Chapter Seven

Lucinda walked the length of Devon's dark house to the guest-room at the south end. She knocked softly and pushed the door open, then stood a moment facing the less intense darkness. Covered only by bamboo shades, the long picture window allowed moonlight to fall as if through a forest. The bed's comforter was a pattern of ferns in varying shades of green, adding to the illusion. Beneath that leafy coverlet, Amy lay on her side, one hand tucked under her pillow, her eyes open as she smiled at her mother. "What are you doing here?" she whispered.

"It's cold," Lucinda whispered back. "May I come in under the covers?"

Amy lifted them high, allowing her mother to slide in unimpeded, and tucked them close around their nestled bodies. "Is Devon asleep?"

"He was when I left."

"What's it like, sleeping with him?"

"He snores," Lucinda said, and they both laughed.

"Does it keep you awake?"

Lucinda shook her head. "Not usually. I was worried about you."

"Why?"

"I don't like you being so close to something as terrible as what happened to Mrs. Wieland. I hate thinking of it myself, and I worry that it will affect you."

"I'm all right, Mom," Amy soothed in a remarkably adult tone. "It only affects me by what it does to you and Devon."

"Which isn't negligible. He starts drinking again and I cut my own throat."

"What happened was an accident."

"If there is such a thing. It's at least symbolic, don't you think?"

"Of what?"

"Maybe that a woman has to debilitate herself to love a man."

"That's an awful thought," Amy said. "Anyway, I was wrong about his drinking. His beer is the nonalcoholic kind."

Lucinda let this welcome knowledge sweep through her. Lying flat on her back, her daughter nestled beside her, the comfort she felt was accompanied by a strong sensation of *déjà vu* for the time she had surrendered to the illusion of being especially safe as Devon's lover. That was before they took that long lonely drive chasing a felon and Devon, almost as a way to fill time, had confessed to having committed a murder. His nonchalance shocked Lucinda as much as the fact, and her initial reaction was to want him out of her and Amy's lives. But she hadn't demanded his immediate departure, and then the autumn leaves fell and he set about raking them without being asked. After that, it seemed petty to evict him in winter. When she began sharing his bed again, all talk of his leaving had evaporated like steam from the radiators in her old house. Despite the melancholy that lingered over the death of Nathan Wheeler, that last year Amy was in high school and Devon was living in their garage apartment had been a happy one for Lucinda, marred only by the sudden whiplashes of reminders about his past. In those slashing moments, everything she valued felt threatened, Amy's safety most of all. But Devon's, too: the possibility that he could be arrested, taken from her, and so she would lose the second and no doubt last love of her life.

His move to the mountains had at first disconcerted her. She had hoped that despite her often expressed fear of living with a fugitive their intimacy would continue to escalate. That notion was quashed by his moving out of the garage apartment he had rented in her backyard, enabling her to accept a more realistic vision of their future. Expecting to eventually lose him, she compromised by vowing to enjoy his company with no strings attached. Since then, the degree of their mutual commitment had felt balanced until she began noticing a distance in his eyes, a reservation of affection, and she guessed he had taken another lover. To pin the widow as the culprit didn't require a great leap of logic. Now the widow was dead, and ostensibly both Lucinda and Devon were suspects. Though they hadn't discussed it, they had come to a mutual acceptance of the fact that they were in this together. Nothing, however, necessitated Amy's presence. Gently Lucinda said, "I think you should go back to school for the summer."

"No way!" Amy sat up so she was silhouetted against the bamboo blinds slit with moonlight. "The doctor wanted to keep you in the hospital but we insisted on you coming here. I'm not leaving until I'm sure you're okay."

Lucinda blinked back tears. "Devon can take care of me."

"He doesn't strike me as a very good nurse."

Lucinda laughed. "Ow! That hurts my neck."

"Let me look at it." Amy leaned toward the bedside lamp.

"No, it's okay."

Amy settled to sit cross-legged in the dark again. "Mom, what made you fall? Did you trip over something?"

Lucinda thought back. "Down by the gate, I saw something out of place. I don't know what but I was staring at it, puzzling over it, you know?" She sighed. "I stumbled, probably over my own feet, and fell."

"You're not clumsy, Mom."

"Thank you, sweetheart. Tomorrow we'll go look for what I found so interesting." She stood up. "I'm going back before Devon misses me."

Amy slid down into the warm groove where her mother had been. Lucinda tucked the covers close and kissed her cheek. They smiled at each other, both remembering the years Amy was growing up when they had only each other. Lucinda carried those years like a shawl she pulled close as she walked through the dark house to Devon's bedroom.

He was awake. She felt his attention as soon as she crossed the threshold. When she slid between the sheets, he welcomed her into his pocket of warmth. "Where'd you go?"

"I was worried about Amy."

"She okay?"

She pressed her face into the hard muscles of his chest. "I tried to send her back to school for the summer but she won't go, says she'll stay here and be my nurse 'til I'm better."

"I'm glad," he said. "I like having her around."

Lucinda stopped breathing a moment. "Don't you think she may be in harm's way?"

"No more'n in that student ghetto she lives in in Cruces."

"True," she sighed.

"If you're going to stay, I'd just as soon she be here too."

"Why?"

"She lightens up the place. The mood between us has gotten pretty heavy lately."

"Can we fix it?" she whispered, barely daring to hope.

He nuzzled her ear through the tousled curls of her hair. "I know a good way to start, if you feel up to it."

She opened her body to his, ignoring the twinges of pain from her wound to savor the much stronger and more sustaining pleasures he gave.

★ ★ ★ ★ ★

Amy was the first one awake the next morning. She liked having her own bathroom at the opposite end of the house from Devon's, but his bedroom's proximity to the kitchen discouraged her from making coffee or anything else while he and her mother were still asleep. She put on a green fleece jogging suit, black sneakers, and a Pirates baseball cap, quietly let herself out the front door and out his picket gate, then took off toward the arroyo. The creek bed was a thoroughfare of rounded boulders she skipped across. Following a deer trail up the bank, she came out by a dog's grave beside the barbed wire fence. The grave was an indentation filled with white rocks. At its head was a cross of rusty iron pipes decorated with a red velvet toy shaped like a foot-long Milk Bone. A few withered, purple mountain penstemon were stuck in the open ends of the pipes. Amy used the grave as her guiding point. She crawled on her belly under the fence and took off jogging across one of the many pastures of the immense Brewer Ranch. A dirt track led up a hill. At the top, panting hard, she stopped and looked back, seeing Devon's roof as patches of white showing through the pines.

Following the road into a valley, she thought only of her heartbeat's counterpoint to her footsteps, the bellows of her lungs, warmth of her muscles, rhythm of her stride. At five-foot-five and a hundred and thirty pounds, she was considered plump by modern standards. But no matter how often she ran, she couldn't lose weight unless she starved herself, something she had no intention of doing. She ate well. So she was big. Sometimes it seemed half her weight was in her breasts. She had worn a fifty-dollar minimizer bra since her junior year in high school. Not quite in competition with Dolly Parton's, her breasts were still the most noticeable aspect of her appearance. She had shaved half her head and pierced her eyebrow and nose in an effort to guide boys' eyes away from her cleavage. Her ploy only half worked. What it did achieve was to give most boys pause before approaching her, which suited her fine. Nathan was still in her thoughts. She filled her time studying and working a few hours a week in a local espresso bar. Anyway, she reasoned, with parents like Lucinda and Devon, she didn't have time to deal with the intricacies of bringing a whole new person into their delicately balanced family.

A small dark animal was suddenly running along the road in front of her. Startled, she stopped dead. The animal took the form of a cross and shrunk to nothing before she realized she was seeing the shadow of a raven flying above her. She watched the sleek black bird in the bright blue sky. He circled and came back, wafting his two-foot wingspan directly overhead. She shivered with the joy of being surprised by the world. As she retraced her path the way she'd come, aiming for the red velvet bone on the grave, she realized what an unusual event being surprised had become. She was so regulated by her school routine, nothing new seemed to pop up, and she had actually begun to consider herself a cynic. She inhaled deeply of the sharp, juniper-scented air, feeling its tonic rejuvenate her.

Arriving home, she walked along the shady length of the west side of the house, passing the three long narrow uncovered windows into the living room and the one into the kitchen. No light came from within. No noise or sensation of anyone awake. She stopped beside the steps to the deck and scanned the yard leading to the chain-link fence. A berm rose between the gate and the deck; low, sand-hugging grasses kept the hill from blowing away. Now hoping the people in the house would sleep a few minutes more, Amy walked around the deck to the back of the swing, then turned and surveyed the path her mother had taken the day she fell. It was ten, maybe fifteen steps from the swing to the deck, the only obstacles a few clumps of tall wild grass in the ground baked hard by the summer sun. Amy retraced her mother's steps, then stopped and looked at the gate, her eyes searching for something—in the term her mother had used—out of place. She let her gaze sweep back and forth like a searchlight along the metal fence, focused on the junipers just beyond the silver mesh, then on the weedy ground between the trees and the fence, seeing nothing remarkable.

But her mother had stood here at another time of day, which meant the sun had been in a different place in the sky and what it illuminated would have been different, too. If sunlight glinting off an object was what her mother had noticed, the object must be shiny to some degree. Amy walked forward slowly, watching for any hint of luminescence among the dry dusty weeds and hard-packed soil. She had to climb the berm to see it. Her mother's line of vision had been different but Amy knew she was seeing what had caught Lucinda's attention. It glittered like a diamond, almost blinding if she positioned herself at the right angle. As she slowly advanced closer, the glare became so intense she couldn't discern the object's shape. Standing directly above it, she hunkered on her heels and stared at the black handle of a knife impelled into the ground so that a mere inch of steel blade caught light above the dirt.

Amy stared at the knife for a long time. When she finally stood up and walked back to the top of the berm, the blade no longer reflected sunlight and the black handle was easily lost in the shadows cast by thick-stemmed lamb's quarter and purple prickly clover. She returned to where she had knelt and looked beyond the knife for footprints. There were dozens of them, many no doubt Devon's, perhaps some belonging to her mother. Anyone who had used that gate since the last rain would have left tracks. How long had that been? Weeks, she thought.

She let herself in the back door and made coffee in the kitchen, deliberately banging spoons and cups. When there was still no response from the adjoining bedroom, she knocked on the door. "Mom?" she called. "I need to talk to you." Need was too soft a word. She felt a desperate compulsion to share her discovery.

Lucinda's sleepy voice came muffled through the door: "I'll be right there."

"I need to see Devon, too," Amy said, shaky with suppressed tears.

"We're coming," Lucinda called as if from a great distance.

Amy retreated, having done all she could to summon them short of flinging open the door and inserting herself into their bedroom. She poured three cups of coffee, added milk to hers, and sipped it as she stared at the door from which they would emerge. Lucinda was first, tying her pastel-flowered silk robe tight at her waist.

"What is it?" she whispered. Coming close, she touched Amy's cheek as if to check for fever.

"I'll wait for Devon," Amy said.

Lucinda saw the two steaming cups, lifted one to her lips and sipped, watching her daughter.

Devon opened the door fully dressed in T-shirt and jeans. He hadn't shaved but he'd combed his hair. He looked at Amy, his eyes demanding that she explain without his having to ask.

"Come look," she said.

CHAPTER EIGHT

Devon hunkered as close to the knife as she had and stared just as long. Lucinda kept her distance, frowning at the black grip that had them all mesmerized. Finally Devon met Amy's eyes. "Did you touch it?"

She shook her head.

"Whose is it?" Lucinda asked.

"Could belong to Natalie's killer," he said.

They all looked again at what he had proclaimed a possible murder weapon. Now Amy could discern on the handle and blade a spatter of droplets the color of chocolate milk.

"Since none of us have touched it," he said slowly, his gaze sliding back and forth between them, "we should leave it that way."

"Leave it there?" Lucinda asked incredulously.

He nodded.

She sighed and looked at Amy. "This is what distracted me before I fell."

"Which means it's been there at least since Saturday," Amy said.

Lucinda looked at Devon. "Don't you think it," she paused to find the right word, "incriminates us?"

"Not if our fingerprints aren't on it."

"Know what I think?" Amy waited until they were both looking at her. "Whoever put it there wants us to find it. If we act like we haven't, it'll drive him so crazy, he'll blow his cover."

Devon smiled. "You may be right."

Lucinda argued weakly, "It doesn't seem wise to antagonize a murderer."

"We'll flush him out and be done with this," Devon said.

Amy and Lucinda looked at each other, trying to take courage from his prediction of success.

Just as they were finishing breakfast, they heard a car in the driveway. Amy watched Devon walk toward the front door, then Lucinda stand up and start clearing the table. Amy took the cruet of syrup and the lidded silver butter dish to the kitchen. When Devon had bought the dish at a yard sale, she'd teased him about his opulent taste. Now she appreciated how cold the metal kept the butter on the table in the middle of summer. She was pouring the leftover syrup back into its bottle when he returned with a rotund, red-haired man he introduced as Alex Wieland, Natalie's brother-in-law. Amy started a new pot of coffee as everyone else settled at the table. She joined them to flick the used napkins and odd spoon out of their way, then returned to the kitchen and leaned her elbows on the cool tile of the intervening counter while watching Mr. Wieland's pink face flush and blanch as he spoke.

"Forgive me for intruding," he began petulantly. "You knew Natalie, so I've presented myself here hoping you'll answer some questions I have."

"What do you want to know?" Devon drawled.

"Let me explain myself. I arrived in the village late last night and stopped first at the police station. Chief Bright was there, which surprised me. But I was glad to have the chance to talk with him without the constant interruptions usual during office hours, and he shared, I believe, fully all he knows about the case. I wanted to come see you last night, but as it was two-thirty when I left Chief Bright, I didn't presume to be so

inconsiderate. I waited in my car for the earliest hour appropri-
ate for my visit and," he smiled hopefully as his gaze scanned
their faces, not neglecting Amy in the kitchen, "I hope I'm not
intruding too terribly."

"Not at all," Lucinda said gently. "We're sorry for your loss.
Was Natalie's husband your brother?"

He nodded. "But I knew her before he did. And I knew her
after his death, so I knew her longer probably than anyone. She
was a fine woman."

"Yeah, she was," Devon murmured.

Alex stared at him a moment. "Chief Bright's investigation is
stymied. He has no motive, and apparently without one it's difficult to isolate a suspect."

Devon nodded.

"You were there when she died," Alex accused.

"She asked me to go see her," Devon replied dryly.

"At three o'clock in the morning?"

"Lucinda arrived from Berrendo earlier," Devon said without
rancor, "so that was the soonest I could get there."

"And Natalie was accustomed to receiving you at such an
hour?"

"She was an insomniac. I often saw her lights on in the
middle of the night and walked up to talk a while. She was
lonely." He shrugged. "So was I."

Lucinda looked out the window. From experience Amy knew
that gesture was her mother's way of distancing herself from
what she was hearing. To her credit, Lucinda didn't get up and
leave, she stayed and eventually returned to the conversation,
but her initial reaction to unpleasant news was always to
momentarily put herself somewhere else. Amy looked at Devon
and saw that he, too, was watching Lucinda with concern.

Alex Wieland said, "I invited Natalie to stay with me on the
coast. The ocean can be healing, you know, in the same way the

desert can but differently too. Ocean, desert, sky—they're all expressions of the same essence. I thought she would benefit from the change. She said she wasn't yet ready to leave the home she'd shared with Walter." Alex sighed. "If only she'd accepted my invitation."

"That line of thinking won't get you anywhere," Devon said.

"No," Alex mumbled. He looked at Amy standing in the kitchen. "Does that coffee happen to be done?"

"Almost," she said.

He smiled apologetically at Lucinda. "I'm afraid I didn't sleep much last night. I seem to be running down suddenly."

"Perhaps a nap will do you better than coffee," she answered kindly.

He shook his head. "Not yet. I need to feel some sort of resolution before I can quit enough to sleep."

"That's a dangerous way to operate," Devon said. "When it comes to murder, resolutions are sometimes hard to find."

"That's right, you were a detective, weren't you? Chief Bright told me. Also that you left your job rather abruptly under a cloud of some sort." Alex's smile was conciliatory. "It adds to your mystique in the village."

"I don't have any mystique," Devon said.

"You're wrong about that, at least." The coffeepot beeped five times. "Ah," Alex sighed. "I'm sure I'll be better company after a swallow or two of joe."

Amy brought them all cups, then returned with the pot and filled the cups with coffee. They were part of a set of yellow Fiestaware that Lucinda had given Devon as a housewarming gift. She had let Amy choose the color, and Amy had chosen yellow because she thought Devon needed more sun in his life. Chief Bright might think Devon left his job under a cloud, but the way Amy saw it, he'd brought the cloud with him. She longed to free him from what she was beginning to perceive as a subtle case of clinical depression.

Alex Wieland drank his coffee black. Amy had filled Lucinda's cup but wasn't finished filling Devon's before Alex held his up for a refill. Amy complied, then returned the pot to the kitchen and stayed there, watching from the shadows.

Alex visibly revived with the quick injection of caffeine. The pink of his face shone less mottled, and he smiled more often, revealing a jagged line of long white teeth. "I notice you didn't comment earlier," he said, carefully setting his cup back in its saucer, "on my saying I'd spent the night in my car." He paused to smile, coyly dimpling his cheeks, but his smile collapsed when neither Devon nor Lucinda responded. "In future I'll be staying at her house," Alex stated, sounding disappointed no one had inquired.

"At Natalie's?" Devon asked.

Alex nodded. "I'm next of kin. They didn't have any children, you know."

"So the house is yours?"

He nodded again. "I plan to sell it after a while. I'll stay in the meantime and savor the last remnants of her presence, then I'll take the pieces I want as mementoes and sell the house as is."

"I know a good cleaning woman in the village," Lucinda said. "You may want her to tidy up a bit before you go in."

"Natalie was always a meticulous housekeeper," Alex said, bristling with affront.

"I meant her room," Lucinda said gently.

He stared at her, his face slowly blanching until Amy, watching from the kitchen, thought he might tumble from his chair in a faint. "Oh, yes. Perhaps," he said.

Lucinda stood up and took a notepad and pencil from a drawer, wrote the woman's name and phone number on a page, and handed it to Alex. "Please warn her about what she'll have to clean."

Alex nodded, taking the paper. He looked at Devon. "I feel nervous approaching it alone. Will you accompany me?"

Devon stood up. "Let's go."

They drove in Alex's silver Lexus. The last year Devon had worked homicide in El Paso, the department began confiscating cars from arrested drug dealers and commandeering the cars when the dealers were convicted. Devon's superior had given him a new black Lexus to use. Before Devon tendered his resignation, that car had been beat to hell. He smiled now, remembering the garage mechanic's face when he turned the wreck back in to the fleet. Then, because he could sense Alex wanted to hear it, he said, "Nice car."

Alex beamed. "Natalie has a white one in the garage. Would you like to buy it?"

Devon shook his head. "Did she choose a car similar to yours or was that just a coincidence?"

"I gave it to her for her birthday last year."

"How'd Walter feel about you giving his wife a car?"

Alex sighed. "Walter wasn't truly with us then. He was in a coma, you know, fourteen months before he finally died."

Devon hadn't realized it had been that long that Natalie had nursed a vegetative husband. She had kept him at home with only a night nurse to help her. Admirable as that was, and desirable as it made her in the saintly wife competition, it was then she had started to drink. When the nurse arrived at six each evening, Natalie closed off that wing of the house and took her bottle and ice bucket out to the patio. Devon had sometimes seen her there but always shied away, not wanting to join her in drinking. So she'd been alone in her solitude. The nurse left at six each morning, assuming Natalie would soon rise to the call of her alarm clock so the patient would be untended no more than an hour. In truth, Natalie would show up in the sickroom sometimes as late as early afternoon. There was nothing she could do for him, she'd told Devon, except the cleaning chores normally reserved for infants. She couldn't stand it, she'd said, seeing her husband reduced to diapers and feeding tubes. So one afternoon she had smothered him with a pillow just before the nurse was due to arrive. The nurse found him dead and assumed it was natural causes. The doctor saw no reason to write otherwise on the death certificate. Officially and in the realm of gossip, Walter Wieland had succumbed to his stroke after nearly a year and a half of suffering. Within a month of his funeral, his widow began inviting her neighbor into her bed. A short time after that, she confessed, her face pressed against Devon's shirt, wet with her tears. She doubted that what she'd done was right, and begged him to absolve her of guilt. Devon stayed quiet, letting her work it out by simply allowing her to say everything she needed until finally it was expunged and she could rest easily in the official version: her husband had died of natural causes.

That resolution freed her to continue her life, and she developed an interest in Devon outside their midnight trysts in her bedroom. She discovered his other woman and began watching for when Lucinda came and went. The last day of her life, she had come to the café to frantically announce Lucinda's early arrival. He wondered why she had been so spooked that day. It was true she rarely left home other than to shop for groceries, but he couldn't credit her degree of distress when she had entered the café to the nervousness of a new widow going out in public again. He looked at Alex as the Lexus coasted to a stop in Natalie's driveway. "How long had it been since you talked to her?"

Alex turned off the engine and stared at the front door. The pink adobe house had an overhanging ledge of granite above its entry. On both sides of the door were tall stands of flame grass, rusty red against the walls. "I called her that morning," he said.

"Friday?"

Alex nodded. "I asked her to marry me."

Devon looked away from the glistening pink face, knowing Natalie had little regard for the small, piggish man. The photographs around the house of her husband showed him to be tall and dark gone gray, making Devon wonder if the two men were only half-brothers, or maybe not brothers at all. He had only Alex's word for the connection.

Yet Alex Wieland had a key to Natalie's front door. Devon followed him in and watched him look around with a beaming expression of approval. To Devon's taste, the decor was cold despite its tapestries' bright colors. Too much white and aluminum, too many angular lines directing the eye as if by command. The room felt like a straightjacket to him. After their first time, he had always made love to Natalie in her bed to avoid this room. But Alex seemed pleased with the authoritarian decor.

"I'll leave you here," Devon said.

Alex's pleasure paled. "I suppose I must be alone sometime."

"If you're going to stay."

"For a few days, I am." He looked up at the one open door on the balcony. "Until things are tidy, at least."

Devon walked the long way home, staying on the roads. It was a quarter mile of open country from Natalie's front door to his, a hundred yards of forest between their back doors. He wondered what she had said in response to Alex's newly issued proposal, if that was what had upset her so much she'd come into town to find him. The message she delivered concerned Lucinda's arrival, but maybe what she'd been trying to express was a plea not to be left alone. Did that mean she was afraid of her brother-in-law? Was that the fear that had rattled her so badly? Deciding to ask Chief Bright what he thought of Alex Wieland as a suspect, when Devon reached his driveway he got into his pickup and left again without speaking to anyone.

CHAPTER NINE

The Salado police station was a beige stucco box set next to the double-door garage of the volunteer fire department. Inside were four rooms: the reception desk area, the chief's office, a unisex bathroom, and a holding cell for prisoners waiting to be transported to the county jail in Carrizozo. Devon stood just inside the front door, letting the ambiance of a working police station settle over him. At one time, "cop" had been the sole word needed to describe who he was. Now it was the antithesis, and rather than having returned to where he belonged, he stood on the edge of what could potentially become enemy territory. The dispatch clerk—a young man with a blond crewcut and a red-on-black firefighter T-shirt—watched him with a curiosity too lethargic to merit speech. Devon watched him back a moment, their two gazes meshing on the same benign frequency, then he looked with dread at the open door of the holding tank, its walls lined with hard wooden benches, its floor a concrete saucer draining into a sewer, and suddenly his status vis-à-vis the clerk was no longer that of an equal but an adversary.

The chief's door jerked open and Bright strode across the threshold to the dispatch desk. His eyes noted Devon's presence but he spoke only to the clerk. "I'll call you in about ten minutes, Tom. If you gotta piss, do it now." Putting his peaked patrol cap on, he strode toward Devon. "Want to ride along?"

Devon got in on the cruiser's passenger side, his desire stronger than his aversion. He still enjoyed running hot with

79

lights and siren, watching the civilians scamper out of his way. In country like this, the roads were mostly empty, and Bright took the two-lane blacktop curves of Highway 380 West at maximum speed.

Neither of them spoke, though occasionally they would make eye contact. Devon saw a challenge in the chief's eyes, but he didn't know if it was merely the dare of a county cop flaunted in the face of a big-city detective, even an ex-detective, or the personal taunt of the investigating officer to his principal suspect.

Turning off his siren, Bright drove way beyond his jurisdiction before taking an unnamed dirt road that dipped around a dozen curves into mountains dark with ponderosa forests. Devon guessed this was BLM land under the county sheriff's jurisdiction. It was probably also patrolled by the state cops, but it definitely wasn't under the Village of Salado's chief of police. That meant whatever they were doing was apt to be illegal. Knowing it could be lethal for him to fall beneath the nit-picky glare of any investigation, Devon was about to bail out when Bright suddenly shut off his swirling emergency lights and swerved onto a rutted track leading through the wind-blown grasses of a mesa. He stopped beside the skeleton of a house that had been left unfinished. Its two-story windows were boarded up, its grand entries darkly forbidding. Taking his billy club, the chief said, "We'll circle the building. I'll go this way, you go that."

"Who're we looking for?"

"Whoever's there."

Bright slid out his door, closed it quietly, and disappeared behind the closest corner of the house. Devon glanced around the car for any kind of weapon, seeing only a shotgun locked in a rack. He stepped out and began walking the opposite direction Bright had taken, but he moved slow and kept his eyes sharp. When he turned the corner to the north side of the house, the sunlight was blocked and the shadow before him still held the cool of night. Having no reason to walk unarmed into the unknown, he hunkered against the wall, hoping that from a distance he looked like a lumpy abutment to the corner, and waited for the chief to herd their prey toward him.

For a long time there was no sound other than the delicate whisper of varmints crawling through the dry summer grasses. Then he heard running footsteps, awkward on the stony ground upheaved by the house's construction, followed by an echo of the chief in pursuit so the two men sounded like a four-footed creature charging toward him. He didn't move, not wanting to betray his presence. Now he could hear the labored breathing of the first man; wheezing, out of shape, probably blinded by sweat. Behind him, the chief was gaining fast, flaunting a surprising prowess. The first one began whimpering, his pudgy body propelled by the pump of his fat arms. When he looked back over his shoulder as he approached the corner, Devon stood up and tripped him. With a yelp, the teenager tumbled to the ground, crushing the tall grass he rolled through. Chief Bright jumped and handcuffed the kid on his belly with dirt on his face and mud in his mouth. Then the chief stood up and grinned at Devon.

Devon's smile was more guarded. Conceding they had succeeded, he still didn't know what they had done, but he helped the chief pull the fat kid to his feet. They all walked to the car, the chief put the panting kid in the back, and he and Devon got up front. As they listened to the kid gasping for breath, Bright looked at Devon and said, "This isn't my jurisdiction, but Leroy's one of ours so I always come get him."

Devon turned around and looked at Leroy. The kid's round face was shiny with sweat, his nose dripping snot. He leaned down and wiped it on the knee of his jeans, then sat up straight again.

Devon smiled and said, "That's an improvement."

The kid snickered. His brown eyes were placid, his fleshy cheeks slack, his body as loose as a sack of potatoes propped on the seat. He was wearing a dark blue velour jogging suit and black sneakers, a perfect burglar outfit except for the velour, a material that tended to either shed or pick up unwanted souvenirs.

"What were you doing out there?" Devon asked.

"Nothing," Leroy said.

Devon nodded, turned back around and fastened his seat belt as the chief pulled a U on the rutted track and headed toward the highway. In answer to Devon's question, Bright said, "He was trespassing." He looked at his prisoner in the rearview mirror. "Weren't you, Leroy?"

The kid had quit panting and was now only breathing hard. "Nobody lives there."

"That doesn't make it your playground. We've talked about this before." The chief looked in his rearview again. "Haven't we, Leroy?"

"Yes, sir," he mumbled.

"One of these days the sheriff won't call me. He'll send his deputies in there to get you. You know where you'll end up then, don't you?"

"Yeah."

"And how're your folks gonna feel about driving a whole hour to the county detention center to get you out and then another hour to bring you home? You think they're gonna be in a good mood when you get there?"

The kid stared in sullen silence.

"You know what I'm trying to prevent here, Leroy?" Bright asked. "I'm gonna tell you 'cause I don't think you truly do. I'm trying to prevent you getting a beating from your dad. Don't you think that's a good goal?"

"Yeah," he said.

The chief turned east on 380 and picked up speed.

Devon asked, "Does he walk way out there?"

"Hitchhikes."

"What's the attraction?"

"Used to belong to his dad. His real dad. He was killed in the first Gulf War before he finished the house. Mom remarried and the second husband sold it. New owners had a business setback and couldn't finish it like they'd planned, so it sits. But it's insured, and Leroy goes out there and lights fires." He looked in his rearview again. "Don't you, Leroy?"

"Only in the fireplace."

Bright grimaced at Devon in the chauvinistic camaraderie common among cops. Devon smiled back, but the exchange felt hollow at his end.

Bright picked up his cell phone and punched in a code number. "Bright," he said. "I'm en route with Leroy. E.T.A. twelve-ten." He dropped his phone on the seat and asked, "Want to get some lunch after I leave Leroy in the cooler?"

"Let's get takeout," Devon said. "I want to talk where we won't be overheard."

From the backseat, Leroy called, "Can I get something too 'fore you lock me up?"

Bright swerved onto the side of the road and stopped the car. He got out and walked around to open the door behind Devon. "C'mon, get out, Leroy."

"Jeez," the kid complained, pulling his bulk from the backseat.

Bright turned him around and took off the handcuffs. "Go on home 'fore I change my mind."

Leroy glanced at Devon watching through the open window,

then he turned and ran, pumping his elbows as he had when Bright was chasing him, as if maybe he thought the chief was playing a trick and might tackle him at any moment. A hundred yards up the highway, Hope Garden Road led south. Leroy cut the corner and was soon out of sight over a hill. Bright got back in and started his engine. "Barbecue okay?"

The first time Devon slept with Natalie Wieland, she had mentioned her husband's brother. It had been in March, during the last winter storm. Overnight a foot of snow had accumulated, and all the next day white flakes continued to fall from a low, gray sky congested with clouds. The roads were empty except for the Jeeps and trucks of the most stalwart workers; everyone else stayed home. In the long shadows of dusk, Natalie called asking to borrow enough wood to keep a fire burning through the night. Devon delivered it in his arms at her back door, making two trips from his woodpile to her hearth. When he stood with snow melting off his shoes as he brushed wood chips from his sweater, she offered him a glass of merlot. "I don't drink," he said with an easy smile, having learned how to handle being offered alcohol, "but I'll build your fire, if you like."

"Please," she said, then left him alone in the austere room with its towering ceiling. Needing warmth, he quickly laid kindling, balanced two quartered logs on the rack, and set them ablaze with newspaper. He hunkered on his heels, letting the fire's warmth soak his chest until she came back. Standing up to face her, he watched her sit on a white leather sofa as she carefully held a tulip glass of red wine. Her jumpsuit was ruby red satin, backless with a strap around her neck, her figure slender and pliable despite her fifty-nine years. In one of their earlier, less intimate conversations, she had credited her body to yoga and not having had children. Tonight she'd had her blond hair permed into loose chaotic curls framing a face whose only flaw was too much dark makeup around her blue eyes. Her voice raspy with disuse, she said, "Widowhood's more lonely than I had anticipated. I'm so afraid of being disconnected, I'm almost tempted to encourage my brother-in-law's crassly premature proposal."

Devon smiled from where he stood before the fire. "Almost?"

"I don't believe I could let him touch me. That'd be a problem, don't you think?"

"Pretty big one," he agreed.

"It's not how I feel about you," she said.

He let himself admire the lithe line of red satin she made on the white leather sofa before he said gently, "You're still mourning your husband. That's why you feel disconnected."

"But I can't reconnect by myself," she said smoothly. "I need the warmth of a man's touch. Will you do that for me? Hold me for a while?"

She was all bones in his hands. Cool dry skin attached with sinew but sporting neither muscle nor fat. He thought it was as if she had died with her husband and become mummified living in this house alone. Left to herself much longer, she might crumble into dust before anyone else could get close. If human touch would revive her, he could give her that. He hadn't been getting enough himself lately. And she was so compliant, opening her defenses like petals beneath him, the taste of wine on her tongue an aphrodisiac defeating his faint reluctance. They made love there in front of the fire he had given her, on the thunderbird pattern of a Navajo rug, with the ceiling soaring above them as if the sky itself were there instead of empty space collecting heat.

Afterwards, she said, "Thank you, Devon. May I call you again sometime?"

Realizing he was being dismissed, he pulled on his jeans as

he stood up. Buttoning them, he admired her pale body reflecting the flickering fire, then teased, "Next time I'll charge for the wood."

She laughed. "Repay yourself from my woodpile. I actually have a good supply. But do it tomorrow, will you, please?"

Pulling on his undershirt and sweater, he had decided she wouldn't welcome a good-night kiss. So he let himself out and walked through the moonlit snow, shivering with the sensation of having escaped something deadly. He stood on his deck watching the shifting shadows of horses corralled at the far bend in the Magado, almost hidden under the overhang of the ridge. Beyond it, the mountains slashed east-west across the sky, their forests dark and brooding in the moonlight. He told himself he shouldn't sleep with the widow again. But he did, and gradually, over the weeks, he realized that the length of time between her invitations was proportional to the minutes it took him to get dressed and out of her bedroom. Between stints of bachelor independence, the hours with Natalie passed as if he were drugged: sublime sensations building to a mutual combustion of pent-up loneliness that she extinguished as soon as her isolation became bearable again. Invariably he regained awareness with the realization that she wanted him gone. After hastily dressing and stumbling out into the cold, he would stand on his deck, shivering at again having escaped her while he put himself back on.

The process might have been easier if he had a clue as to who he was anymore. Having been a cop all his life, he didn't know what to do with himself now that he'd slammed that door. So he had bought a piece of land that needed constant shoring up to prevent it from sliding into the arroyo where it would cease to exist except as empty space. He thought it was funny that you could own land but, without it, the space above it, which is where you really lived, was no longer yours.

Chief Bright wiped barbecue sauce off his chin and asked, "What'd you think of Alex Wieland?"

"I was going to ask you that." Devon had finished his brisket sandwich and was sipping black coffee from a paper cup.

"My first impression was of a jovial gentleman caught in a tragedy."

"And your second?"

"After discovering he was a liar, I deleted 'gentleman' from my description."

Devon laughed. "What'd he lie about?"

"His story is he flew in after learning Natalie was dead, but he got here a week earlier and had been sleeping in his car all that time."

"Odd behavior for such an affluent man."

"Plus it puts him on the scene the night of the murder. Or at least presents the possibility."

"Did you give him a key to her house?"

"No," Bright said around the rib he was chewing on. He tossed its bone into his bag and wiped his hands on a paper napkin. "Did you have a key?"

Devon shook his head, recognizing that their conversation had turned the corner into interrogation.

"Did Mrs. Sterling know you were sleeping with Natalie?"

"Who says I was?"

Bright took the lid off his cup and blew on the steaming coffee as he stared out the windshield at the back of the rodeo arena's barn. Its wood was weathered gray, the surrounding corrals steel pipes; the stomped smooth ground shone under the early afternoon sun coming from almost straight overhead. Beyond the arena, the parched yellow valley stretched beneath the mountains, dark green under an immense, cloudless blue sky. "I'm having a hard time," Bright said, "picturing you and the widow in a platonic friendship. It just doesn't fall right in my world."

"Your world isn't mine."

Bright slurped his coffee. "I'm going along with what you're saying 'cause I have no evidence otherwise, Devon, but I'm sharing with you my doubt."

"Appreciate it," he drawled.

"Something else I'd like to share." Bright finished his coffee in a few swallows and dropped the cup in his bag. "As long as it's just between you and me."

"We agreed at the start this conversation's confidential."

Bright nodded. "Walter Wieland had an odd contingency to his will: the heirs changed according to the cause of death. If it was natural, Natalie got to keep the house 'til she died, then it went to his half-brother Alex. But if Walter died from an un-natural cause, the house goes to his illegitimate son, Matt Keller."

Devon nodded, a step ahead of the chief.

"I have reason to believe Natalie killed her husband as a form of euthanasia." Bright watched Devon's lack of reaction. "Did she tell you that?"

Devon nodded.

"I pretended I didn't know 'cause if I did know, I'd have to do something about it. Thing of it is, she deserved that house, it belonged to her as much as Walter. Now, by rights, it belongs to Matt Keller." Bright's smile was twisted. "Can you see how I've put myself in a hole by letting the euthanasia slide?"

"Doesn't the death certificate say natural causes?"

"Well, that's the thing, see. The doctor knew the truth and filed a preliminary report, but I haven't yet seen a death certificate. Nobody was demanding one so he hesitated to put his name to a lie. Natalie's murder, a'course, changes every-thing."

Devon nodded, though he didn't think a body could be buried without a death certificate.

Bright smiled more happily. "I wish I could blame you or Mrs. Sterling, laying the motive on a love triangle, but the more likely motive was money. It's more'n the house, you know. There's a sizeable trust fund goes with it."

"How sizeable?"

"Coupla million."

"Attached to the house?"

"Tight as blueing on metal."

"So Alex gets that, too?"

Bright shrugged. "If I let things stand and assuming the doc-tor or anyone else doesn't speak up. It bothers me for Alex to get it when he's not the rightful heir, but to stop him I have to accuse Natalie posthumously of murder, which is the only way Matt Keller could get it."

"Maybe someone else killed Walter."

"Unnatural cause of death by anyone's hand means Matt inherits."

"Sounds like Walt was worried."

"Yeah, he was so worried someone would kill him, he had a stroke that turned him into a vegetable, and the stress of deal-ing with that did drive his wife to kill him. Funny, ain't it?"

"Hilarious," Devon said. "Did he have cause to be worried?"

"Nah. He was cuckoo. Paranoid schizoid. He was a senile old man whose enemies, if he ever had any, had been riding wheelchairs in rest homes for decades. The only motive for murder was his money, and he set up his will so if he was knocked off, his son got it. Which would give Matt a motive—to bring out that Natalie had killed his old man—but if he killed her to do it, he'd be cutting himself into a fortune he had to look at from jail."

"Unless he thought he wouldn't get caught."

"Natalie told me she'd done it. I guess she told you. Can you think of any reason she'd lie?"

"Protecting somebody," Devon said. "Alex, maybe. Making sure Matt doesn't inherit."

"Once it's established that Walter was murdered, Alex is out no matter what happened to Natalie. I can't see either Alex or Matt killing her, which leads me back to your love triangle."

"That's a dead end."

"Actually, it could be a quadrangle." Bright grinned sheepishly. "The possibility exists that Amy might have done it on the misguided notion of protecting her mother."

"From what?"

"Losing you."

CHAPTER TEN

Sharon waved happily at Amy arriving in her little white car, then dribbled the basketball toward her, scooping a small backpack off the court by the gate. Her parents had taken Josh to Albuquerque to have his nasal septum realigned so he could breathe better, leaving her home alone. When Amy had invited her to spend the night, Sharon eagerly accepted, relishing the prospect of being among a much more interesting family than her own.

Lucinda was boiling pasta when they arrived. The kitchen was full of steam that the stove fan feebly wafted toward the open window. Amy waved at her mother from the living room then led Sharon in the other direction, through a small, square, knotty-pine room to the guestroom. Three of its walls were white plaster, the last a long window filled with a view of Sierra Blanca. An old, threadbare sofa was positioned to catch the view. At the far end of the room was a double bed with a comforter printed with green ferns. The two pictures on the walls were posters Amy had put there, one of Ammachi, the hugging saint, a rotund Indian woman in a purple dress that Sharon thought was probably a sari, and the other of Che Guevara, the Cuban revolutionary who had died before she was born.

Amy laid her purse and keys on top of a maple bureau beneath a small matching mirror and said, "Let's go help Mom." She left without waiting for an answer.

Sharon wondered about Amy's odd mood. She had barely spoken on the drive here from school, her expression tight with worry. Sharon left her bag at the foot of the bed and walked back toward the kitchen. She loved this house. All the knotty pine seemed so masculine, but maybe that was because she knew it had been built by a pioneer for his bride. At one time, these mountains had held many such homes built of native pine—ceiling, walls, and floor—but most of them had been bulldozed to make way for golf courses. Devon had lived here over a year without decorating more than to bring in the furniture he needed. The things on the living room walls—the John Nieto coyote print, a purple and red Guatemalan weaving, a green and yellow Tohono O'odham basket—had been hung by Lucinda.

In the kitchen, Amy sliced celery while her mother tossed the pasta in olive oil. Sharon sat on a stool and watched them prepare a dish they had obviously made many times. The chores had been divvied up and they each performed their tasks with efficient grace until suddenly there was a pink pasta salad, red with tomatoes, green with fresh basil, and black with ripe olives filling a clear glass bowl Lucinda was now covering with plastic wrap. "That looks delicious," Sharon said. Lucinda smiled, taking it to the refrigerator. "It has to chill three hours at least."

They all heard Devon's truck in the driveway. Lucinda hurried to wipe up the counter while Amy loaded the dishwasher. Sharon thought it a little funny the way they scurried to make the kitchen look as if no work had been done. She wondered if when they took the salad from the refrigerator they would act surprised to find it there.

Devon didn't look happy when he came in. For a moment his dark eyes fell hard on Amy, then looked appealingly at Lucinda. Sharon felt unwelcome, as if a trio of women were the last thing he wanted to see in his kitchen just then. Lucinda of-

fered him coffee or tea, sounding to Sharon like a waitress. All
three women waited for his answer. He stood looking at them,
then mumbled, "No thanks," and left the way he'd come. After
a moment, they heard him walking through the loose bark
beneath the aspen grove on the south side of the house.
Lucinda's gaze flitted to Sharon, lingered on Amy, then was
gone as she followed Devon. Sharon looked at Amy, who was
watching her. "Coffee or tea?" Amy mimicked. They both
laughed.

Amy took two bottles of water from the refrigerator and
handed one to Sharon, then led her out to the deck. They sat at
the picnic table watching the details of the horse ranch across
the far end of the arroyo gradually dissolve in the dusk.

From the swing around the corner, Devon said, "Maybe we
ought to run off to Mexico. He thinks any of the three of us
could've done it."

"I can't believe that," Lucinda scoffed.

"I wish I was making it up."

Amy rose and strode around the corner. Sharon followed her
hesitantly, arriving in time to see Amy straddle ground so close
in front of the swing that Devon had to stop it from moving lest
it hit her. Sharon sidled up along the wall, sheltering in its
warmth as she watched a chill fall between Amy and her parents.

"What do you mean," Amy asked, "he thinks we all three
could've done it?"

"Why don't you sit down," Devon said, more as a command
than a question.

Amy took a few steps back and sat on the bench against the
wall beneath the sun porch windows. She looked at Sharon and
patted the bench. "Come sit," she said, her tone apologetic.
Sharon joined her and found herself facing Amy's parents holding hands in the swing. She raised her gaze to meet Devon's
eyes. He was judging her, calculating and assessing her worth

and liabilities, and she thought this must be what it felt like to be bought. From beside her, Amy said, "You can trust her. Sharon's my friend." Devon glanced at Amy, then smiled at Sharon, and she felt herself blushing beneath his acceptance of her, at least for the moment, as one of the family.

"Bright suspects nearly everyone who had any contact with Natalie and some people who didn't," he said, his gaze wandering across the faces watching him. "The only way I can figure his thinking is that he's working on the elimination of suspects and has barely started. In fact, I can't think of anyone he's ruled out. Far as I know, he may suspect you, Sharon."

She giggled nervously. "Of what?"

"Killing Mrs. Wieland. Did you?"

"No!" she said, not sure he wasn't serious.

He smiled. "We've already gotten farther than Chief Bright 'cause we've eliminated somebody."

Sharon basked in the warmth of his smile until Amy's insistent voice intruded.

"When you said the chief suspects all three of us, I assume that includes me?"

Devon nodded.

"What did he say?" Her voice rising.

"That you have a motive, is all," Devon answered, maintaining his calm.

"Which is?" she demanded.

"Protecting your mother. That you saw Natalie as a threat to her."

"That's absurd! Besides I was in Cruces. When did she die?"

"Three a.m. Saturday morning."

"I was asleep."

"Alone?"

"Yes!"

"How long was it between when you saw or spoke with

someone before you went to bed and after you got up the next morning?"

Amy thought. "I left Sally in the cafeteria at six, went home and studied 'til one, then went to bed. The next morning, I met Paula for breakfast at seven, so that'd be about thirteen hours."

"Plenty of time to drive here and back without being missed."

Amy looked at her mother, who was frowning at Devon. Amy asked him, "Do you think I did it?"

"Did you?"

"No!"

He smiled. "We're two ahead of Chief Bright."

"What about you?" Amy asked, sounding peeved. "Did you do it?"

He shook his head.

Amy looked at her mother. "You?"

"No," Lucinda scoffed.

Amy looked back at Devon. "Why does he suspect us?"

" 'Cause he doesn't have anyone else," Devon said.

Lucinda asked, "What about the brother-in-law, Alex Wieland? Maybe he has a motive."

"He was in love with her," Devon said. "I don't think he'd harm her, but she had just turned down his proposal so maybe he got mad and lost control. Doesn't ring true but it's possible, I guess."

"How do you know he was in love with her?" Lucinda asked.

"She told me about the proposal, that she'd turned him down."

Lucinda looked off across the road toward the arroyo. Amy had told Sharon about her mother's habit of looking away when she didn't want to hear what was being said. Figuring Lucinda was avoiding thinking about Devon with Natalie, Sharon decided if he hadn't been sleeping with Mrs. Wieland, she wouldn't still be such a point of contention between them. She was, after all, dead. Sharon looked at Amy, thinking she had probably reached the same conclusion. It subdued their mood with a melancholy that was almost sweet.

Devon started moving the swing in a lulling rhythm, and after a while Lucinda retrieved her attention from the mountains and mentally rejoined them. Sharon listened to the wind in the trees, the chitter of birds, wind chimes on the distant front porch, and far off above the ridge, the lonely cry of ravens. Sitting there with her friend's untraditional parents, she knew they were a family in the truest sense, and she didn't feel outside of that when they finally rose to make supper. She helped slice bread and pour tea and carry the food to the picnic table on the deck, where they ate under the cobalt sky of twilight before moonrise.

Devon and Lucinda were back on the swing, sitting so close they were merged into one silhouette, when Sharon followed Amy through the dark house to the bedroom whose windows could be covered only with gaping slats of bamboo. "Can't someone see through?" she asked.

"Devon says there's no one out there to see in." Amy pulled her T-shirt off over her head, unhooked her bra—breathing a sigh with the release of her ample breasts from confinement—and walked across the room to drop her clothes in a dark wicker basket. "Go change in the bathroom if you're worried."

"That's all right," Sharon said. But she sat on the bed, below the window's line of vision, until she had pulled her nightie over her head.

Amy put an Alison Krause CD on the player and flopped onto the couch. "Sorry things are a little weird around here."

Sharon gave her a smile of forgiveness. "It's not every day your neighbor gets murdered."

"And we get suspected! I can't believe the chief's serious, can you? I mean, do you think he'd frame innocent people just to make an arrest?"

"There's a theory in business management called OMF: Others Must Fail. That way you don't have to do anything except make other people look bad, so you win by default. I guess it could apply to law enforcement, too."

"That sucks." Amy shook her head and stood up. "Dance with me?"

"I can't dance," Sharon said.

"Come on," Amy coaxed. "No one's gonna see."

"Except you," Sharon said, standing up.

"Yeah, and I'm gonna pick you to shreds. Come on, you can do it."

Sharon shifted her hips and flopped her elbows to what she hoped was the beat.

"That's right," Amy said. "Look, I'm gonna shut my eyes so you don't have to worry about being watched." She closed her eyes and swayed her arms as her feet followed the intricate rhythm of the song about a lucky one.

Sharon watched her, trying to mimic her steps, to feel comfortable moving to the music. She spun and twirled, doing things she knew she'd never do on the dance floor but feeling free enough to exaggerate her gestures, to cross the boundaries then reel herself back in and become reserved again, more precise because she had let herself go. She laughed, feeling she was getting the hang of it, and was just about to tell Amy she was having fun when she saw a face in the window. It floated disembodied, as if not even a skull lay beneath its skin, like a death mask she had seen once in a book, its bloated features supported by nothing but air. She screamed.

Chapter Eleven

Amy followed her friend's gaze and saw the face, pale and flat as if on a platter, the eyes and mouth visible through slits in the shades, the nose blocked behind one. A flabby face of indeterminate sex except for the masculine lust in the ravenous eyes. Amy opened her mouth to scream, too, but refused to give him satisfaction. Instead she yelped, "Come on, Sharon!" and ran from the room, through the empty square hall to the living room.

Devon was coming toward her from the kitchen. He took hold of her shoulders and watched Sharon crowd close. "What?"

"A face!" Sharon sobbed. "In the window."

Amy nodded when Devon looked at her, then he ran through the sun porch and out the front door. She started after him, but her mother called her back.

"Amy!" Lucinda scolded. "You're not dressed."

She looked down at her baby-doll nightgown, white cotton with a print of red strawberries. Since it wasn't see-through, she thought it acceptable and overrode her mother's command. She was nineteen, after all; a full year older than the age of majority for a girl, and she had been on her own for over a year. She gave her mother a smile of regret at the necessity of disobedience and ran after Devon. Inside the front door lay a collection of shoes too funky to wear in the house. She stepped into a pair of sling-back sneakers and pushed through the screen door.

Hearing it bang closed behind her, she saw neither Devon

nor the peeping Tom in front of the window. The light falling through the bamboo slats striped the ground as if with slivered bars, their intervals empty. She looked at the open gate in the picket fence, then heard their running footsteps on the gravel. She took off after them.

They were on the road when she hit the driveway. She couldn't hear them anymore, only her own footsteps, not as fast as she could've run with tie-on shoes. Hers kept threatening to fly off her toes if she strode too fast. She heard voices, indistinct but male, out of breath so coming ragged, the words staccato against the quiet night. She slowed down, wanting to hear what was being said.

"What's your story?" Devon asked in an exasperated tone. "You spend your time doing what you're not s'posed to?"

"Ow," a boy said, gasping for breath. "You're hurting me."

"This is nothing compared to what's ahead if you don't change your ways."

Amy stopped as they came into relief, both of them wearing dark clothes silhouetted against the pale caliche road leading toward the arroyo's chasm. The boy had his back to her, the hood of his sweatshirt pulled up so she couldn't see even an outline of his head. His body was squat and pudgy, his shoulders heaving. Devon saw her. His gaze raked down from the scoop neck of her nightie above the erect nipples of her generous breasts to her legs, bare from her mid-thigh hem to her floppy shoes. Rather than censorious, he seemed amazed she would come out dressed as she was. He looked at the boy. "Let's go back to the house so I can call Chief Bright to come get you."

The boy turned around and Amy recognized Leroy. His sweaty face still gasping for air, he seemed to stop breathing when he saw before him what he had peeked at from behind the blinds.

"Yeah, you got what you came for," Devon said, jerking him

roughly by the arm to propel him forward.

She stood up straight, telling herself the fact that men were aggravated by seeing a woman's body didn't mean she had to accommodate them. Devon looked at her as they passed as if to say he was way ahead of her, but she doubted he was even halfway capable of understanding what she had been thinking. Their exchange ended, however, with a teasing smile shared between them, a smile that she would have run into the night nude to gain.

Both Lucinda and Sharon were dressed when Amy followed Devon and Leroy into the living room. Lucinda's frown sent Amy scurrying to her room so she'd be back before she missed too much. Squashing her breasts into her minimizer bra, she suspected that if it had been flat-chested Sharon who ran after him, Devon wouldn't have been so bothered; it was these melons hanging off the front of her chest that made men hot to see her naked. She had often thought about having her breasts surgically reduced, not wanting to go through life as a pair of boobs in men's eyes, but she always ended by wondering why she had to change herself because they had a problem. She pulled on jeans and a baggy yellow T-shirt and walked back into the living room barefoot.

Leroy was standing in the kitchen leaning his forehead against the closed laundry-room door while Devon stood beside him talking on the wall phone. "That's what I'm saying," Devon said. Then, after listening a moment, "Thanks." He hung up and told Leroy, "Go sit at the table."

Leroy slunk into the dining room and sat with his back to the wall.

"I've made coffee," Lucinda said.

Devon leaned against the end of the counter and folded his arms, his gaze still on Leroy. "I'll take a cup."

Amy whispered to Sharon, "Never a dull moment in Devon's

house, huh?"

Sharon laughed, and Amy was glad to see her spirits had revived, thinking it boded well for her success at college. The boys there were capable of such rude behavior it made peeping seem bland. She hadn't mentioned that to Sharon, who still held out hope that the males of their generation could be gentlemen without being condescending chauvinists too. Tugging her toward the sofa, Amy pulled her down to sit close.

"Has this ever happened before?" Sharon asked.

"Not that I've seen him," Amy answered, still whispering.

"Do you think he was here 'cause of me?"

Amy remembered Leroy watching Sharon at the basketball courts, and how slimy she'd felt when he'd seen them walking in front of his home. She shrugged. "He's going to jail now, so it won't happen again."

"Will we have to testify against him?"

"Maybe." Amy watched her friend closely.

"I don't think I could do that," Sharon said. "I mean, he's not right in the head, you know? Jail wouldn't be good for him."

"I don't think it's good for anyone, but I get your point."

"Sharon?" Lucinda called from the kitchen. "Would you like coffee?"

She raised her voice. "No thanks, Mrs. Sterling." Whispering to Amy, she said, "I wouldn't mind a beer."

"There's none in the house," Amy commiserated. "Devon quit, so Mom doesn't keep it around."

"Why'd he quit?"

Amy looked at him, standing with his arms folded watching his captive. Knowing his reason involved the murder he'd committed in El Paso, that his heavy consumption back then had muddied his thinking and he'd decided not to risk that again, she recognized this as one of those moments she could betray him. It could be an inadvertent slip or a sharing inspired by trust similar to what she now felt for her friend, but either way it would be a mistake. That was the razor's edge of living with a fugitive. "He thought he was getting a paunch," she said.

Sharon giggled. "Sometimes I like men with beer bellies. They can be kinda charming, know what I mean?"

Amy nodded and laughed, too. When she looked back at Devon, she saw both him and Lucinda watching her and Sharon with envy, for their youth she supposed.

They all heard Chief Bright's car in the driveway. Lucinda walked out to let him in. Coming through the door, he looked first at Amy and Sharon sitting close on the sofa, which Amy thought was odd, then at Leroy hunched over the dining room table. Finally Bright looked at Devon and said, "Tell me what happened."

"Best let the girls tell it," Devon said, not hiding his surprise that he'd been the one Bright asked.

The chief listened without interruption to their jagged and somewhat desultory recounting of the event. When they were again quiet, he looked at Leroy. "What were you doing out there, boy?"

Leroy raised his head, his face pinched with what Amy took to be misery. "Jus' looking," he mumbled.

"It's not nice to look into other people's windows," Bright said. "You know that, Leroy, don't you."

"Yes, sir," he said.

"You walk here from home?"

Leroy nodded.

"Come through the back?"

"Through the gate, yeah," the kid muttered.

"Why don't you show me?"

Devon set his coffee cup down and stood up away from the wall. "I don't see that as necessary."

Bright hooked his thumbs in his gun belt. "You have a

problem with me looking at your back gate?"

"You've got no cause," Devon said.

"By calling 9-1-1, you gave me permission to search your property."

Devon shrugged, still frowning.

Bright glanced at Amy watching, then told him, "I'm gonna look at your back gate. I'd rather you come with me."

Devon nodded at Leroy. "You gonna leave him here?"

"No, he can come with us." Bright smiled at the kid. "Maybe he'll even show us his tracks."

Amy asked hopefully, "Can we come?"

"I don't know why you bother to ask," Devon said gruffly.

She felt rebuffed but refused to be left out. Apparently unwilling to stay behind alone, Sharon stuck close as they and Lucinda followed the men and Leroy tromping through the laundry and mud rooms to the deck and down the two steps to the hard-packed dirt.

The motion light came on under the eaves, illuminating the yard. Beyond the berm, the chain-link fence shone while the surrounding junipers sheltered darkness in their hearts. The dry grasses on top of the berm rustled in the breeze, and below its hump the blade of the knife glimmered discretely. Amy quickly looked away lest the chief follow her gaze. She looked at Devon, who was watching Leroy, then at the chief, who asked the kid, "Why don't you retrace your path?"

Leroy looked at the ground, his cheeks hollowed by shame. "I came in the front."

Bright spread his arms wide and took several steps backward, descending the berm. When he stopped, the heel of his left boot was only a few inches from the black grip of the knife. "This was the shorter way," he said. "You live right over there, almost directly catty-corner to this gate. Why walk clear around to the front?"

"He lives over where?" Devon asked.

Amy was surprised he didn't know. She wished she had mentioned how she felt about the kid before now, so Devon would've had some history behind what was happening. She felt off balance going into a situation knowing more than he did.

"In that makeshift A-frame down the road," Bright said. "I'm still waiting for your answer, Leroy."

" 'Cause of him." The kid barely jerked his head toward Devon.

"What about him?" Bright asked.

"I would've had to walk past his window." Leroy shrugged. "Figured he'd prob'ly hear me."

"So you've done this before?" Devon asked sharply.

"Once." Whining with his head down. "I only did it once."

Lucinda tched. "I knew we needed drapes."

Amy looked at Devon, thinking he seemed to be losing ground. First he hadn't known Leroy lived nearby, now he had misjudged the innocence of his neighborhood. Guessing that was what happened when a person kept himself isolated—he lacked the information to make sound judgments—she watched the chief's heel in the sand mere inches from the knife. Looking at Sharon, Amy saw her watching it, too.

Devon asked the chief, "You through now?"

Bright seemed amused at the question.

Lucinda said stridently, "I think we should all go to bed. I mean, I think we should say good night, Chief Bright. It's been a long day."

He nodded and took a step away from the knife.

Lucinda sighed.

"I'll come back in the morning to discuss charges," Bright said. "You do plan to press them, don't you?"

Devon looked at Amy, who shook her head. "We'll talk about it in the morning," he said.

The chief looked around the circle of faces, lingering longer on Amy's than she liked. "I'll need you all here at, shall we say, eight o'clock?"

Not waiting for anyone's agreement, he said no more except to urge Leroy to accompany him as they walked along the south yard, through the aspen grove illuminated by light from within the house, to the driveway. No one else moved until his engine disappeared in the quiet night.

"First thing tomorrow," Devon told Sharon, "you're going home. This isn't anything you have to be anywhere near."

"What isn't?" she asked.

Amy slid her arm around Sharon's waist. "Come on," she whispered. "Let's go to sleep now." But she didn't expect any of them to sleep. So far their plan to flush the killer out by ignoring the knife he'd planted had brought forth the chief of police and a peeping Tom, neither of whom Amy could credit as a candidate for murder.

Devon hunkered on his heels to stare at the knife, wondering if it held Leroy's fingerprints. The kid carried a grudge against the world that he used to justify trespassing, and Devon knew from experience that grudges like that tended to expand into a justification for general mayhem. If Leroy had the nerve to peep at young women, he had probably peeped at Natalie, too. It could be an easy next step to actually enter her house. And if he was as mentally messed up as he appeared to be, cutting her throat might fall in line with his sick fantasies. As feasible as all that potentially was, hiding the murder weapon in her neighbor's yard suggested malice toward the neighbor, but Devon hadn't met the kid when Natalie was alive. He wondered if Amy had, and if Leroy could have planted the knife as an act against her. Chief Bright claimed to suspect her of the murder on the flimsy motive of protecting her mother. Devon had to admit that maybe he couldn't countenance that possibility because he didn't want to. They had never discussed her involvement in the death of Zeb Mulroney, the kid who had killed her high school boyfriend, though Devon suspected she had at least witnessed it. If she had even helped cause it, she might make the leap to thinking she was not only invincible but justified in delivering retribution. He could concede the possibility of all that, albeit reluctantly, but to murder the other lover of your mother's boyfriend didn't seem the act of a sane person. Despite her newly acquired, and in Devon's opinion, bizarre facial piercings, and even considering her claim of psychic precognition, Amy was as sane as anyone. Unable to fathom why the chief would suspect her, Devon wondered if that, like the knife, wasn't a ploy to lead him into making a mistake. Which meant the chief thought he had killed Natalie. The stickler was the motive. Nobody had one, at least none that he could believe. He looked up at the lights from Natalie's house shining through the trees like a beacon drawing him back.

CHAPTER TWELVE

As soon as Amy closed the bedroom door, Sharon asked, "What's going on?"

Amy sighed, recognizing that she was at another crossroad rife with opportunities to betray Devon. "I'm not sure I can explain it."

"What was that black thing Chief Bright almost stepped on? The thing you were all pretending you didn't see. The way you were acting was like a skit on Comedy Central."

"Were we that obvious?" Amy asked miserably.

"I almost cracked up when your mother suggested we go to bed. My first thought was, together?" Sharon laughed. "I think that was the chief's first thought, too."

"Do you think he knew the thing he nearly stepped on was there?"

"I don't know. What is it?"

Amy hesitated, but her desire to be forthright with her friend demanded her honesty. "A knife," she whispered. "Devon thinks it's the one used to kill Mrs. Wieland."

Sharon's eyes widened. "Who put it in your yard?" she whispered back.

Amy shrugged. "We decided whoever did wants us to react when we find it. If we don't, he won't be able to stand it and will blow his cover by making a mistake."

Sharon leaned back against the bed. They were both on the floor, though Amy couldn't remember sitting down. She supposed they felt protected being below any line of sight from the window. Even though the odds of another peeping Tom appearing tonight were minuscule, the dark beyond the glass now seemed threatening with danger.

"Mrs. Wieland came from somewhere else, you know," Sharon said. "She lived here for over twenty years, but she went home to visit a lot. So the person who killed her could be someone from somewhere else that nobody around here has met."

"And this stranger," Amy said with growing enthusiasm, "planted the knife in our yard on a whim, knowing he'd be back in LA or wherever before it's found and not caring what repercussions it causes."

"And everybody here dies because of that one thing he did without really thinking."

They laughed a moment at the potentially absurd chain of events, then their smiles fell into disarray and finally became frowns. "Except it isn't funny," Amy said, " 'cause it's us."

The next morning, Devon called Chief Bright and told him not to come because the girls wouldn't press charges.

"You can do it," Bright argued. "You're the property owner."

"Sharon thinks the kid has mental problems and she doesn't want to add to them," Devon said.

"He's going to jail sooner or later if he doesn't change his ways. An early taste of incarceration may wake him up."

"Might," Devon conceded. "But the girls won't testify."

Bright sighed. "His mother bailed him out last night. You might want to warn the girls who won't testify that he doesn't know they won't."

"Yeah, thanks," Devon had said.

He stood now on the edge of the widow's yard in the soft light of mid-morning. Everything appeared the same though its essence was gone, leaving the fountain and furniture looking like props abandoned after a hastily broken down set. He wondered what he would think if he didn't know, if he had been on vacation and was making his first visit after his return, if he could guess that she was gone. Metal, stone, and plants indigenous to high desert mountains, each piece seemed unchangeable except that it no longer glowed with that passion of life dependent on its mistress. Now the house was occupied by Alex, a man Devon didn't care to spend time with. If he was to learn anything, though, it would be inside. He figured he had two choices: he could pretend to like Alex and befriend him as a turncoat, or he could steal in like a burglar and owe no one an apology. He had waited until he saw Alex leave before making his move.

The sliding glass door was still unlocked. He thought it odd that a man from the West Coast, where such doors were common, wouldn't have noticed it was open. Using his handkerchief, Devon lifted the lever to latch the lock, but as soon as he let go it fell open again. He tried to remember if it had been broken the night she was killed. It had been unlocked, that's all he knew. He hadn't detected anything amiss. Not even all the way to the door of her room. At the very moment her killer was backing away from his work, Devon was advancing closer, and it amazed him that he had been so oblivious to such proximity of evil. A lot was amazing him lately, like not knowing Leroy lived down the road, and also his assumption that the dark outside his windows was always empty. For himself it didn't matter, but he should have been more protective of the women. He decided he had to quit riding the fence between bachelor independence and taking care of the women he loved.

In Natalie's soaring living room, he stood looking up at her open door. As he had that night, he crossed the pale oak floor quietly in his sneakers, climbed the steel stairs gently so they made no sound, and silently walked the carpeted length of the balcony. Casting one last glance over the empty living room below, he quickly crossed the threshold into her bedroom.

The arcing splatter pattern and her outline on the bed were still there. The amount of blood meant her killer must have been drenched in it, too. Studying the carpet without seeing any footprints or path of fallen droplets, Devon remembered he had picked up a sheet to cover her. The sheet was gone, perhaps wrapped around her corpse. He wondered why it had been on the floor, who had put it there and when. He walked closer to the bed and studied each fold and crevice for any hint of another occupant, squatted in front of the bedside table and peered with his eyes level to its polished surface, searching for what might be a masculine fingerprint. The table top was clean. He opened her closet door. Not having time to search everything, he followed his instincts and checked skirts and jackets he had seen her wear. The sensation of sliding his hands into the satin linings of her pockets felt like a violation he could not have stomached if his motive were other than finding her killer. What he found were folded Post-its of shopping lists. He closed the closet and scanned the top of her bureau: a china pink ballerina in a net tutu reigned alone on its gleaming surface. Though the illusion of movement was strong, the painted porcelain face was consummately incapable of testifying to anything it had witnessed.

He went into Natalie's bathroom and looked at her makeup strewn across the alabaster counter like an abstract portrait of a woman in a hurry. He stared into her mirror, trying to imagine her standing here looking into it for the last time. That would have been long after she'd come home from the village café. She would have cleaned her face for bed if she hadn't been waiting for him. Self-conscious about the age etched into her skin, she never saw him without makeup. So there she would have stood, fully painted, in the nightgown she died in but which he couldn't remember because, by the time he saw it, it was soaked in her blood. Having to admit that he saw only himself in the mirror, he focused on his image: his body compact, a little trimmer since he quit drinking; a man not far past his prime, freshly shaven and wearing clean clothes; maybe needing a haircut but not much could be done about the hurt in his face. When he'd been a cop, the victims he'd dealt with were strangers.

Concentrating on not seeing what he was touching, he ransacked her drawers, letting his eyes respond only in recognition of something that didn't belong; like an arrowhead among stones, it would be an artifact of another echelon. In the top drawer of her lingerie chest, hidden in a stack of perfumed, silk nightgowns, he found her passport inside a red leather envelope also holding two one-way airline tickets from Albuquerque to Rome. Behind them in the leather envelope were ten one-thousand dollar bills. He had never seen a thousand-dollar bill so couldn't vouch for their authenticity, but they looked real. Returning the envelope, his hand stopped in mid-air. The tickets didn't have anyone's name on them. Visiting Rome had always been an ambition of his. He could even make the argument that Natalie would have liked for him to have this money. Maybe she even intended to invite him on the trip. He buried the leather envelope where he had found it, slid the drawer closed, and watched the ghostly curtain flutter against the window at the far end of the room. Could that have been why she wanted to see him so urgently? A trip she needed to embark on immediately, perhaps to avoid brother Alex coming to visit? But Alex had been driving around the county, sleeping in his car, all that last week. Had Natalie known that? Had he threatened her? With what? Why? Devon heard the automatic garage door begin to rattle open.

Running from the room, down the spiral stairs, and across the soulless shell of a living room, he was on the patio before he heard the garage door clang to a stop and the hum of Alex's Lexus poke its nose inside. Devon trotted across Natalie's yard to the tree line and under the shadows on his own land.

He found Lucinda in bed on top of the covers, a fresh bandage on her wound. Wincing that they had brought her home from the hospital only to leave her alone—he had no idea where Amy had gone—he stopped on the threshold and asked, "Feeling bad?"

She drowsily opened her eyes, then let them slide shut. "Headache, is all."

He approached a few steps closer. "Did you take something for it?"

"Tylenol. Where've you been?"

"Natalie's house."

"How's Alex?"

"He wasn't there."

She opened her eyes. "What did you find?"

"Two tickets to Europe along with ten thousand in cash."

He slid his hands in his pockets as they watched each other a moment. Then she closed her eyes and said, "Too bad you're not a thief."

He chuckled in self-deprecation, knowing how close he had come. Or maybe he hadn't even been in the ballpark, but he'd felt a moment's empathy for how easily it was done. Once having been at bat, maybe next time he'd swing. There would have to be a next time before he'd know for sure.

"Who was she going with?" Lucinda asked.

"The only person I heard her mention was Alex, but what she said didn't make me think she'd go traveling with him."

"No girlfriend or old school chum?"

"None that I remember."

"What about her telephone book? Maybe we could call her friends and ask."

"I'll pick it up," Devon said, "next time I'm there."

She opened her eyes. "It's dangerous."

"Yeah. But I owe it to her to catch her killer."

"Why?"

"I should've asked when I sent her home from the café what the hell was wrong, but I let it slide 'til later 'cause I . . ." He stopped, not wanting to shift blame.

"Knew I was here," she said.

"I wanted to see you," he admitted.

She smiled. "I should've warned you I was coming a day early."

He shook his head. "How'd you manage to get off work?"

"A policeman was killed and the mayor closed all the city offices."

Devon winced. "Who was it?"

"Lieutenant Saavedra. I think you met him?"

He nodded, stunned by the news.

"He was shot in a robbery," she said. "But he managed to kill the robber before he died. The robber had a little girl held hostage. Saavedra's a hero."

Devon started to leave, then turned back to belatedly ask, "Is there anything I can get you?"

"If I lie here quietly, my headache'll be gone in a few minutes."

"I'll be outside," he said, walking away without looking back.

He returned to rebuilding his rock wall, lifting the fallen stones and resetting them in place, finding others to fill gaps, the consistent repetitive thrust of labor that dulled the sadness he felt to know Saavedra was dead. He had been young enough that his best years were in front of him, which wasn't true of Natalie. But someone had taken her last years without her consent, and that rankled Devon while what he felt for Saavedra was sorrow. The sacrifice that saved a child's life had been his choice; it hadn't been Natalie's, and no one was saved by her dying.

Devon was soon slick with sweat from toting stones, cracking them into position, rocking them to settle deep, then doing it all again until, as if from another life, he heard Lucinda calling him for lunch. He tossed his last stone uselessly into the dust and headed toward the house's cool shower and accommodating woman waiting in the kitchen.

"There's Leroy again," Amy said, spotting the kid in her rear-view mirror as she and Sharon sipped Cokes through straws from ice-filled cups. They were parked outside Brewer's, the only gas station and convenience store in the village. Everyone hit Brewer's once or twice a week, if for no other reason than to buy the *Ruidoso News* on Wednesdays and Fridays. This was Wednesday, and the paper lay unread on the backseat.

Sharon twisted to catch sight of the fat kid in her side mirror. "I thought he was in jail."

"Bailed out," Amy said as if with droll boredom. "What he did is just a misdemeanor." She sucked noisily on her straw. "Devon said Leroy gets caught trespassing on a place that used to belong to his father."

"Yeah, he was killed in Desert Storm," Sharon said sadly.

"Do you know where the house is?" Amy turned the key in her ignition. "Let's go see it."

Sharon slumped down out of sight as they passed Leroy. Amy looked straight at him. Seeping from his eyes was a swamp of pain, his pudgy body slack and weak, but as she held his gaze, he assumed his angry pose, rigid and snapping with a danger she couldn't ignore. She glanced at the scant traffic and accelerated onto the highway. "Am I going the right direction?"

"Yeah," Sharon mumbled, peering back over the top of the seat. She sat up straight and sucked on her Coke again. "I don't think I can find the house, Amy. It's back off a lot of dirt roads that twist and wind around. Why do you want to see it anyway?"

"I thought maybe I could pick up something about what he needs by feeling whatever it was his father left behind."

"You're talking about being psychic again."

"Sometimes I get insights, is all," Amy said. "Like with you, I keep getting this image of footsteps left by someone running through snow." She glanced at her friend. "I'm not sure what it means, but it keeps coming back."

Sharon laughed. "We're months away from snow, so I'm not gonna worry about it."

"No, that's best," Amy agreed, though she knew by the intensity of the vision that what it foretold was eminent. Balancing between a subject's need to know and his or her desire to know wasn't easy. Most people took affront at being warned, as if Amy were trying to ruin their day by gloomy predictions instead of trying to save them from something unpleasant and irrevocable. So she had learned to keep her impressions to herself. This vision about Sharon was stronger than most. The very fact that Amy knew it was associated with Sharon spoke to its urgency, since the vision itself was nothing more than anonymous footprints in snow. But in addition to Sharon, Amy felt the vision concerned Leroy, so she struggled to decipher its meaning. Philosophically, she didn't believe in predestination. What could be foreseen could be prevented. She decided a step in that direction might be keeping Sharon and Leroy apart. "Let's go down to the Outpost and get a burger," she suggested.

"All the way to Carrizozo?" Sharon asked with pleased surprise.

Amy accelerated on 380 West into the mountains. Dark green

and heavily shadowed, deep, narrow canyons opened off on both sides of the road. Indian Divide was a hump they rolled across to begin their descent. At mile marker 77, the road rounded a sweeping curve and the Tularosa Basin sprawled into view, a brown, dusty expanse stretching to the distant blue ledge of the Oscura Mountains. Along the descent, the pines diminished in size and number, became scarce, then disappeared altogether on the barren foothills towering over sand drifts of their own erosion. Rolling down the long decline into the Tularosa Basin, Amy drove past the gates to the Saddle Ridge Ranch, which was newly divided into ranchettes for sale, and the O-Bar-O, for sale intact. A broad concrete bridge spanned the railroad tracks. At its apex, interrupting the grandeur of the view, a billboard advertised the Apache resort at Mescalero by promising a room with every view. At the bottom of the bridge, Amy coasted into the crossroads of Highways 380 and 54, marked by a blinking red stop light and the Four Winds Motel. Turning left toward the famous old saloon that was now renowned for its green chili cheeseburgers, she felt Sharon was safe in this village, which was also the county seat, headquarters of the county sheriff and modern location of the once-infamous Lincoln County Courthouse. The new town was quaint, boasting a few ruins and the old bar.

The Outpost was dark inside, its shadows lurking with stuffed heads of slain animals. Not just deer and elk, but javelina, fox, wolf, coyote, even a buffalo. A six-foot rattlesnake skin stretching above the bar completed the motif of death decorating the room. The jukebox gleamed across the dark dance floor puddled with reflected neon, and a pool table held its rack ready for absent players. The only other customers on this mid-week afternoon were a tourist family in a far booth, two plump parents and three chubby kids, two girls and one boy, all with flaxen hair in identical bowl haircuts. Sipping a fresh Coke while waiting for her burger and fries to come out of the kitchen, Amy watched Leroy sidle in from the bright sun outside.

CHAPTER THIRTEEN

Lucinda lay naked in bed beside Devon behind his locked bedroom door, enjoying the smooth slide of his hand gliding up the curve of her waist to just brush her breast with the back of his thumb, then down the curve again to the ascent of her hip and over that to her thigh. She snuggled her face deeper into his chest as if he were a blanket of comfort, but too soon he pulled away and asked, "Where's Amy?"

"With Sharon," she said, watching him now.

His eyes were dark. "I warned her Leroy's mother bailed him out."

She pulled back. "Surely he won't bother them?"

Devon stood up and stepped into his jeans. He buttoned them as he walked to the window, and buckled his belt while peering out through the green calico curtains that were hanging there when he bought the house. Lucinda had washed them during her first visit.

"Think I'll go look for her," he said.

"And say what?" She watched him open the closet and take out a long-sleeved blue shirt.

He faced her as he buttoned it. "Maybe nothing. I only need to see her to make sure she's okay."

She sat up, holding the sheet to cover her breasts. "Why do you think she wouldn't be?"

He sat on the edge of the bed to put on clean socks. "Kids like Leroy are usually harmless. Their crimes are passive—peeping, trespassing—nothing that puts them at much risk." He yanked his shoelace tight. "I'm just a little worried Amy might take more on herself than she should."

Suspecting the conversation she had wanted for so long was about to happen, she asked, "What do you mean?"

Devon tied his other shoe and turned on the bed to face her. "I don't know if she's psychic or not, but she believes it and sometimes it seems she thinks she has a responsibility to right the wrongs only she can see. I also suspect it's made her feel protected to some degree. I'm afraid she'll insert herself into the Wieland investigation and find it hard to get out. Chief Bright already suspects her."

"So you've said, but I don't see how he could."

"Maybe she was in Natalie's room and left something behind, like you did."

"Even if we were all there, he can't seriously think any of us killed her."

"Hard to think of another reason we'd all be there."

"We're her neighbors. Why shouldn't we visit?"

"You met her once in the yard. Amy never did."

"Bright doesn't know that."

He smiled. "Be careful you don't get so tangled in your secrets they trip you up."

Encouraged by the warmth of his smile, she grabbed the opportunity to ask, whispering though they were alone in the house, "Do you think she had anything to do with Zeb Mulroney's death?"

Devon nodded. "I think she was there and saw it."

Trying to picture that scene in her mind, she again felt sad that Amy had lost her innocence so young. "Wouldn't that make her an accomplice?"

"Only because she didn't come forward."

Barely daring to breathe, she asked, "Do you think she did

more than keep quiet?"

"I don't know." He smiled again, looking handsome in the filtered light. "Why don't you ask her?"

"I'm waiting for her to tell me of her own accord."

He leaned close and gently kissed her cheek on the far side of her wound.

She watched him walk out, listened to his truck start and then its engine drone into silence. In his absence, she felt lighter than she had since her accident, because she now believed he was no longer unwilling to share his knowledge of her daughter. She felt the expansion of their deepening commitment like a sensation of space opening around her. His former avoidance of the subject had barricaded paths her thoughts couldn't travel. Now the barricades were down and she was free to pursue any thought that presented itself. She wondered what it would mean—if she were writing a fairy tale—that the heroine fell and cut her own throat when faced with a competitor who'd had it done for her. Had she placed herself in the role of victim and imitated the woman she feared was stealing her lover? Shouldn't it be enough that her competitor was dead, or did she need to guarantee her dependence on Devon by crippling herself? Could it be possible that her fall had been a mere accident, totally meaningless? Was anything? It had to be one or the other: either all was meaningful or nothing was. If life were preordained, it could have been predicted that at three in the afternoon on Saturday, June 18th, Lucinda Sterling would fall and cut her throat on broken glass, but the fact that Natalie Wieland would have her throat cut approximately twelve hours earlier and a mere hundred yards away was probably just the intertwining of two separate and distinct fates, implying nothing beyond coincidence.

"I don't believe in coincidences," Amy said. "Leroy's here 'cause he followed us."

Sharon shrugged, noisily sipping Coke through her straw as she watched Leroy standing just inside the door of the Outpost in Carrizozo.

"Something that's bothered me," Amy said, "is why Devon didn't know Leroy lives right down the road."

"He lived with his mother on the other side of town 'til a coupla weeks ago," Sharon said softly, as if wary of being overheard. "She remarried and her new husband didn't want Leroy around, so he was sent back to his first stepfather's to finish school. Now he's s'posed to make it on his own 'cause he's eighteen, you know?"

"Which means do what?" Amy asked, thinking of the scant jobs outside of ranching or waiting tables that existed in the mountains.

"That's something everybody has to figure out on their own. Thing of it is, some things are hard to figure even if you're smart." She glanced across the room at Leroy still standing by the door. "He's not right in the head but I'm pretty sure he's harmless. We should invite him to join us."

Amy looked at the fat kid staring at them morosely. Her lack of pity was enough to start him walking toward their booth. Quickly she whispered, "Come over here so neither of us'll have to sit by him."

Sharon quickly slid over and snuggled close.

Leroy sunk his weight onto the bare bench. "Hi," he said shyly, glancing back and forth between them. "I want to apologize about peeping last night. I shouldn't've done it. Sorry."

"Just don't do it again, okay?" Sharon said sharply. "You're gonna have to grow up someday, Leroy. Ain't no reward for putting it off."

He leaned back, his scowl pinching his piggy eyes as he stared at her. The waitress brought their burgers and a basket of fries.

Leroy ordered a glass of water. He kept looking at the fries until finally Sharon offered him some, after which he hungrily emptied the huge basket. Amy kept working on eating her burger, not wanting to leave any he might snatch off her plate. The green chili and melted cheese dripped through her fingers, and she had to wipe her hands and mouth after every bite. He alternately watched her and Sharon as intently as if hoping to catch a dribble off their chins.

Sharon took a break with her burger half finished. She drank some Coke and burped discreetly. "So what're you gonna do, Leroy, now you're out of school? You gonna get a job?"

"Might."

"Doing what?"

"Maybe I'll be a cop like your friend Devon was."

Sharon glanced at Amy, then picked up her burger and began eating again.

"I seen you talking to him around the village," Leroy said. "Seen how he leaned close to hear what you were saying 'cause you talked soft so nobody else'd hear you. He leaned close like he wanted to touch you but wouldn't let himself 'cause you were jailbait."

Chewing furiously, Sharon looked at Amy.

"Devon's in love with my mother," Amy stated flatly. "He doesn't play around."

Leroy snickered. "He was doing the widow. I seen him coming and going myself."

"That's none of your business," she retorted.

"I watched him come out of her house lots of times late at night. But he wasn't the only one."

"Only one what?" she asked more softly.

"Men visiting the widow at night."

"Who else?"

"That fat guy who's staying there now."

"He's her brother-in-law," Amy scoffed.

"I seen Chief Bright around sometimes." Leroy grinned. "But the one stayed longest was your mother's boyfriend. That's all he is 'til he marries her, so don't give me any of that stepfather shit."

"You're rude," Amy said, dropping the soggy remnant of her burger. She wiped her fingers. "There are connections between people more important than legal definitions, but I don't expect someone as crass as you to understand that."

"As stupid," he accused. "That's what you mean. Why don't you say it?"

"Don't tell me what I mean." She looked at Sharon. "You ready to go?"

Sharon was already standing up. Amy slid across the booth, then stopped, astonished, when Leroy asked plaintively, "Can I have a ride home?"

"You're kidding," she muttered, walking away.

Hurrying beside her, Sharon said, "He's not right, Amy. We should give him a ride."

She stopped in the middle of the neon-lit dance floor. "How'd he get here?"

"Hitchhiked, probably. But it's later now, and the guys who pick him up will be cowboys coming in for a beer, and they won't be nice to him."

Amy looked at Leroy in the booth watching them earnestly. More than empty, their plates had been wiped clean. "Okay," she said, sighing with pity. "But he rides shotgun. There's no way I want him behind me."

Driving up the long gradual ascent from the desert floor of the Tularosa Basin into the piney foothills of the Capitáns, Amy felt a combustion of emotions simmering under Leroy's facade. As the road began its winding approach to Indian Divide, she felt his lethargic inertia gain impetus. Coasting around the curves of their gentle descent into the Bonito Valley, he compressed himself into such a tight wad of anger she halfway expected him to occupy less space on the seat. But he was still as pudgy as before, flaccid and flabby, his complexion an unhealthy pallor as if lit from inside with the blue bulb of a television screen.

"What's your problem?" she asked sympathetically. "I mean your overall situation that you're finding so tough to handle?"

He stared at her like an escaping felon caught in the beam of her searchlight.

"You can tell me," she coaxed. "Sometimes just naming a problem takes away some of its power."

"I don't have any problems," he muttered.

"Everybody's got problems," Sharon said from the backseat.

Amy smiled at her in the rearview.

Leroy's smile was snide. "I don't get any pussy."

Amy and Sharon looked at each other with disgust before Sharon jibed, "Why do you think that is, Leroy?"

He stared out his window and said, "I'm fat."

"Why don't you go on a diet? Take up a sport? You'd lose a lot of weight playing football."

"School's over."

"Yeah," she said, looking at Amy again. "Sometimes it's hard to believe high school is behind us. Seems my whole life I looked forward to it, and now it's over."

"You're starting college in August," Amy said.

"Sometimes I think I won't go."

"What do you mean?"

"I've never been out of this village 'cept for little day trips."

"All the more reason to see some of the world!"

"Want to see my house?" Leroy asked, butting in.

Amy glanced at him, looking away from the winding mountain road only a few seconds before she said, "We were talking about that on our way over, but neither of us knows where it is."

"Take the next right," Leroy said.

Amy met Sharon's eyes in the rearview without picking up any hint of a vote against going. So she made the turn and followed Leroy's directions to make a dozen more, all of them onto dirt tracks seldom traveled. She was beginning to doubt she could find her way out when he told her to turn into a driveway she couldn't see for the sagebrush until she was on top of it. Puttering at ten miles an hour, she easily caught the turn. The driveway was rutted from someone having gouged out tracks when the ground was deep in mud. Ahead she saw the silhouette of a building. When she stopped her car, Leroy got out and walked away, leaving his door open, as she stared at the house.

The hulk was two stories of black insulation, its arched windows covered with long rectangles of plywood, the cavernous side entry a tunnel into darkness. She scanned the lot, appreciating the view of both Carrizo and Diamond Peaks. The meadow around the house was green with grama grass, sotol, and piñon, but it was the unfinished home that held her attention. Boarded up and all its walls tacked over with funerary black, it seemed a monument to what would have been if the builder had come home from war: a world of self-assurance, of belonging on this land, being centered in a purpose. Leroy had not inherited that; his patrimony was the lonely pride bestowed on a Purple Heart instead of the love of a living father. She watched the orphan circling around to the front of his father's former home. Awkward in his baggy pants, his worn out sneakers stumbling because he didn't watch his feet, he stared at the house as if at a shrine, his face hopeful of a miracle.

"Have you ever been inside?" Amy asked Sharon.

She shook her head.

"Want to go?"

125

Amy watched Leroy as she waited for an answer. His belly hung down over the front of his legs like a gargantuan fanny pack, making her suspect that when he walked his thighs had to lift the weight with each step. She tried to imagine how ponderous that would be; maybe if her breasts grew from between her hips, instead of her shoulders, the burden of their weight would be borne by her legs when she walked.

"Okay, why not?" Sharon said flippantly though she had pondered her answer a while.

CHAPTER FOURTEEN

They climbed out of the car just as Leroy disappeared around the far side of the house. Feeling nimble after watching his clumsy gait, Amy trotted after him. Sharon stayed one step behind. When they turned the corner, Leroy was nowhere to be seen. In the middle of that side of the house, they found a door standing open. Intricately carved of an originally dark wood, it had been left exposed to the weather and was now dull and cracked. Amy saw no sign of forced entry, which made her wonder if after all this time Leroy still had a key. She stopped on the threshold and peered in but saw only a dark void. "Think I'll get my flashlight."

"Good idea." Sharon backed away from the door and stared at it as if she didn't trust what might emerge.

Amy jogged toward her car. Reaching in through the window to open the glove box, she felt drawn to the car's comfortable familiarity. For a moment she thought about getting in, calling Sharon, and driving away. Leroy could get a ride to wherever he wanted on his own. He'd proven that many times. But she felt intrigued by the house and wanted to see inside. Walking back to her friend, she reminded herself that twice in her past she had done something equally impetuous: she had once hidden in the car of a murder suspect in order to talk to him, and later she had met his accomplice alone in an orchard. Both of those had been rewarding in the long run, and both were much more dangerous than what she was doing now. Grinning at Sharon, she asked, "You game?"

Sharon laughed the dry cough of gallows humor. "Whenever you are."

Amy turned her flashlight on and crossed the threshold. "Leroy?" Her voice echoed in the empty room but no one answered. Standing in the last circle of daylight falling through the door, she leaned close to whisper in Sharon's ear, "You know he's going to try'n scare us, don't you?"

Sharon nodded as they met each other's eyes with a promise they wouldn't let him do that. Holding hands, they followed Amy's beam of light through the foyer into the dark. They stood inside the living room, the beam scanning the ceiling-high rise of the river-stone fireplace. The floor was wood, dull with dust but otherwise unmarred by the house's long-lasting emptiness. At both ends of the room were doorways leading deeper into darkness. Amy played the beam across the dust on the floor, trying to see where Leroy had most recently disturbed it. The area in front of the hearth was wiped clean, the hearth itself black with soot and charred wood. Other than that, a path led to the right of the front door, the dust kicked into balls that collected along the edges of the disturbance like brush along a creek bed. She aimed her beam of light into the tunnel of the hall.

No end was discernable. The walls were white plasterboard with the nails gleaming at regular intervals. The floor was cement. "Leroy?" she called.

From far away she heard his diminished voice: "Down here."

She looked at Sharon, who shrugged. Together they advanced into the seemingly endless, pitch-black corridor. When Sharon slid her arm around Amy's waist, her welcome warmth cuddling close told Amy they were equally scared. The end of the hall was in sight, a flat panel of drywall, cracked and crumbling. They stopped at the T of the hall and Amy shone her flashlight down the narrower passages leading right and left. At the end of each was a wooden, switchbacking staircase. She shone the light on the floor, revealing scuff marks leading in both directions.

"Guess he wants us to split up," she whispered.

"Guess we won't, huh?"

"No way. Right or left?"

"We could go back," Sharon said.

Amy turned around and shone her light the way they had come. It was as dark as a nightmare, only her beam illuminating a corridor of safety. Holding hands, she led Sharon toward the place they thought led outside.

Devon drove into the village and stopped at Brewer's for a newspaper. Even though Amy had promised to bring one home, it was a good excuse to go inside. Chester, the rotund middle-aged clerk, remembered seeing Amy and Sharon earlier but knew nothing about where they had gone. Devon drove the five-block length of Main Street, from the school to the Kickback, without seeing either the girls or Amy's white Focus. He turned around and drove east on 380 four miles to the Fort Stanton road. Another few minutes and he was at the Rio Bonito trailhead. A popular starting point for horseback riders and hikers, the parking lot was empty.

Devon sat a moment looking at the snowy peaks of the Sierra Blanca range. The spectacular scenery had become so commonplace he barely saw it anymore. He wondered if marriage to Lucinda would be like living with the mountains: an inspiration that after a while he took for granted, weakening his ability to appreciate her gifts. When he truly thought about it, he was surprised she had bothered to stick with him at all. Yet in so many ways she sustained him. Her warmth between the sheets at night, not just sex, but the heat of another human sharing his sleep. Her receptiveness to whatever he had to say. Her logical assimilation of his meaning, a rational response honed by decades of serving the public's curiosity as a librarian, concentrating not on what she wished to hear but on what the patron was trying to say. He even admired her for expecting more from her future than life with a fugitive. In spite of that, she couldn't stay away. He smiled, appreciating the luminous white peaks against the brilliant blue sky. But recognizing that he had been blessed with love despite his wicked ways did nothing toward finding Amy.

Odds were she was safe and having fun somewhere he would never think to look. And though it was true Leroy had been released from jail after posting bail on the misdemeanor charge of window peeping, Devon didn't think the kid was dangerous. The girls could be scared, and he didn't want that, but he didn't think Leroy would harm them otherwise. Someone in the village would, though. The someone who had killed Natalie and planted the knife. Almost certainly it was a man; most women wouldn't have the strength to cut the throat of a person fighting back. Neither would a lot of men. An athlete might. A football player. Devon considered the possibility of Natalie having other lovers. She was newly widowed and shy in his hands. Having assumed she wouldn't be like that with more than one man, he scolded himself for making such an egotistical assumption.

It could explain Alex hovering around the flame but never quite going in. After twice having his marriage proposal rejected, he could have watched men coming and going from Natalie's. Unable to sleep, he hadn't bothered renting a room. When he wasn't watching her, he was probably cruising the county. Devon started his engine and pulled out of the trailhead onto the road toward Fort Stanton.

When he'd been a cop in El Paso, he spent a good part of his life cruising the streets. He'd grown up there and knew the city. Sometimes he missed it, though it wasn't El Paso he was missing but the life he'd had, expecting to retire and live out his old age being doted on by grand-nieces and -nephews. The latter part might still happen—El Paso was only three hours away—but he wouldn't be retiring from that or any other police force. One impetuous act had derailed the entire thrust of his life.

Downshifting his old truck for the sharp turn toward the airport, he calculated he had six months left before he would have to face employment or homelessness. He had hoped taking on a house—he bought it from the owner so no banks were involved—would motivate him to generate an income but so far he hadn't done more than read the want ads. Most employment in the mountains consisted of service jobs in restaurants or stores. He couldn't see himself doing that. His brother and nephew were eager to start a private detective agency, but Devon had no inclination to investigate people involved in bitter divorces, which most of that work was touted to be.

As he drove past the small airport—the private craft parked inside closed hangars, their owners' SUVs beneath metal awnings across the road—he wondered what answer he would have given if Natalie had offered him one of those tickets to Rome. Could he be a paid companion, a gigolo? How about a bodyguard who was sleeping with his boss? That would be akin to marriage if the woman had all the money. He wondered how women let themselves be financially dependent, then realized none of the women he'd taken as lovers were like that. They all had professional positions requiring college degrees. He hadn't gone to college unless, as Clark Gable used to say, you counted the School of Hard Knocks. He'd joined the army after high school, spent two years in the swamps of Georgia on duty as an M.P., went back to El Paso and was hired as a traffic cop. Because he could think on his feet, knew the city, and spoke a passable Spanish, he was soon promoted to Crimes Against Persons and not long after that became a detective working homicide. He'd had the best conviction rate in the department. Pride in his job had sustained him through unsatisfying romances and a less than amiable home life with his brother's family. At the end, he'd been contemplating marriage to a woman who was a librarian like Lucinda, but unlike her lived in a fantasy world devoid of rational thought. Devon laughed, guessing he had exaggerated Samantha's naiveté.

He approached and passed the soaring wings of the Spencer Theater, a white concrete swan on the high mesa below the Sierra Blancas, then sped by the shell of Mrs. Spencer's mansion. Her estate was tangled in lawsuits between her children and her last, much younger husband, so the house sat unfinished. Like the house Leroy's dad had left when he went to war, the building seemed doomed. Others might own it, as they had bought and sold Leroy's house, but no one could override the ghosts long enough to live in it. Devon wondered if it wasn't the same with him, if the man he'd been in El Paso hadn't become a shell inhabited by ghosts.

Splicing through the affluent neighborhood of Sonterra, the road wound down toward Highway 48. Devon turned north, heading back toward Salado. But when he reached 380, he turned west, thinking Leroy might be at his father's house, and if anyone knew who had come and gone from the widow's late at night, it would likely be the neighborhood's peeping Tom.

Lucinda stood naked in front of the steamy bathroom mirror and looked at her wound. Puckered around the stitches, the gash was closed in an otherwise straight line. The scar would be thin. At least for now. Who knew how it would age. She considered letting her hair grow. A feathery cut curving in toward her chin might hide the scar most of the time. If she dyed her hair blond instead of its natural auburn, its color wouldn't bring out the red of the wound. Raising her fingers to gently touch where her flesh had been cut and her artery nicked, she imagined her blood soaking into the ground. Devon had held her body closed until the ambulance arrived. If not for him, she would be dead. Her daughter would be an orphan. Wondering how Amy would do on her own, Lucinda looked away from the mirror, down at the sink, and saw it was dirty.

She wrapped herself in a towel and walked through Devon's bedroom to the kitchen where she made two calls on the wall phone. First she called Loretta to come clean the house, then she called Gayle and asked about an appointment to have her hair done. Gayle had a cancellation so Lucinda was out the door in fifteen minutes, leaving a note on the table beside his: GONE TO THE VILLAGE. BE BACK LATER.

"I warned her you can't treat men like that." Gayle shook her scissors at Lucinda in the mirror. "But that Natalie, she never was one for listening."

Gayle was big-boned and lantern-jawed, her hair a rooster comb of metallic ruby red. Although forty-eight, she was lithe and slim and had kept her looks up to date. "It ain't no secret I play around," she said, meeting Lucinda's eyes in the mirror. "Any man spends a night in my bed knows he's not the first who's been there. Natalie played the virgin queen to half a dozen men. Said it fed their ego to think she'd chosen them to break her mourning, as if they offered something special she couldn't get from anyone else." She concentrated on Lucinda's hair, snipping strays behind her comb.

Gingerly, Lucinda asked, "Do you know who she was seeing?"

"She wouldn't tell me. Said I'd know 'em if she did but it was better if nobody knew. I told her that folks'd find out. You can't keep secrets in this town, 'specially if any of the parties involved are married."

"Were they?"

"Most folks are. Being single myself, I take note of the eligible men in my vicinity, and if you don't count ranch hands, of which there are many but forget any kinda future, you're left with half a dozen, one of which is your Devon and I don't guess he hardly counts."

Lucinda noted the qualifier ascribing less than certainty to Devon's standing. "So who are they, other than Devon?"

"Chief Bright, he's probably the most promising. Chester, but he works twelve-hour shifts at Brewer's and nearly always works weekends, so he's not often available, though he's funny." She laughed. "Hank and Gil are two old cowboys retired off the mineral rights on their families' homesteads. They're pretty beat up from cowboying for forty years and not much good on a dance floor, but they're both good sports and willing to listen if you don't need a whole lot of comprehension coming back. Now you go a little younger and there's Matt Keller. He owns a construction company and worked himself up from scratch to being a millionaire. One of these days he'll choose a bride and start a family. But it won't be me, though we've tangoed in bed a coupla times. There's Buffalo Joe, the leather man, if you don't mind that kinda smell 'tween the sheets. He lives with his sister and prob'ly won't ever marry. Out of all of 'em, the only one I could see Natalie with was Chief Bright."

"What about Matt?" Lucinda asked, easily able to imagine the widow with a younger man.

"He's her stepson from Walter's wild oats." Gayle picked up the hair dryer and blasted its high heat on Lucinda's hair, tossing it this way and that. After she turned it off again, she said, "That woman died under peculiar circumstances, too."

"Matt Keller's mother?" Lucinda asked.

"Yeah. It was so long ago, I'm not sure I remember exactly how it happened." She worked on a knot with her comb. "She drowned, falling off a boat, I think, in Grindstone Lake, but it wasn't ruled to be any kinda foul play."

"Alex told us Natalie and Walter didn't have any children."

"They didn't, together, but everyone knew Matt was Walter's boy. They had a falling out a long time ago and Walter left everything to Natalie. Now it seems it belongs to Alex rather than Matt." She smiled into the mirror. "How do like yourself as a blond?"

They had chosen a light ash hue, wanting it to be more subtle than flamboyant. The new cut curled toward her chin but wasn't quite long enough to cover the scar.

"In another coupla weeks," Gayle said, reading her thoughts, "it'll get there. Come back and I'll trim it up free of charge."

"Thanks," Lucinda said. "It helps that it's not red anymore."

Gayle whisked the black plastic cape off Lucinda's shoulders. "Kinda creepy, your accident and her murder coming so close together like that."

"There's no connection." Lucinda opened her purse for her wallet.

"Except Devon," Gayle murmured, busying herself with straightening the counter's collection of brushes.

Snapping her purse shut, Lucinda clutched the two twenty-dollar bills in her fist and asked, "Do you think he was sleeping with her?"

Gayle stood up straight. "He sure hasn't warmed up to anyone else, but maybe Natalie seemed safer to him, or maybe more needy. She was good at milking sympathy."

Lucinda looked at the money she had crumpled into a tight ball. She unfolded and flattened it on the counter, thinking Devon would respond to a widow's need. But would he be so easily fooled by a fake? If Gayle's portrait was halfway correct, the widow had been a user enticing men into her nest only to kick them out when she finished. Lucinda handed over the money. "Thanks," she said, "for everything."

CHAPTER FIFTEEN

Amy couldn't find the door. Her flashlight scanned the walls in front of her, smooth and straight as far as the beam could reach. Not even a crack in the plaster, a seam in the drywall. No nails or screws visible, no evident means of construction, as if the house were organic and had grown as seamlessly from this land as a tumor on the brain. Not even cobwebs or dust balls. She remembered that previously she had seen tracks on the floor. Now she couldn't see the floor. The light wouldn't penetrate below her knees. The support under her feet felt solid but she could only assume from the lines of the room that the beams weren't warped or wouldn't suddenly disappear. She stopped to listen. The huge house hovered above and around her, forty empty rooms drained of purpose. Dry as old bones, the air stale. Ahead she saw a mirror aimed to the side. She quickened her step, eager to see the face reflected there, expecting to see the resident of this dead shell of a home. Facing the mirror, she saw no one. She shone her light straight at the leaded glass and saw only a sunburst that hurt her eyes. She blinked and the door opened and Devon stood on the front porch, his expression one of pleasant surprise.

She looked down at Sharon's hand holding onto her arm, at the flashlight beam disappearing into daylight beyond Devon's hip. Hearing Sharon laugh, Amy smiled, wanting to hide how confused she felt at being jerked out of her vision so abruptly. She tried to catch the tail end of it and see the face in the mirror. But after the glare, she had seen Devon, and his presence overpowered what had come before. Realizing he was watching her, she looked at Sharon, who was watching her, too. She guessed they both knew something had happened, and supposed that to them it would seem like a fit, something aberrant that should be controlled. Only later, after she had sorted it out, could she try to explain it, and then it would be to Lucinda. So she smiled again and said, "We were just on our way home." Devon stepped out of her way as she walked into the sunlight's welcome relief.

"What about Leroy?" Sharon asked, following her.

Devon looked into the house. "You two run on. I'll bring him back."

"No!" Amy said, too quick and too loud.

He looked his question at her.

Softly she said, "That house isn't healthy for you, Devon."

He laughed. "You mean there's a spook in there out to get me?"

"More like a spirit of yourself," she mumbled.

He frowned. "I can't live in fear of your world, Amy. You two go home. I wanted to talk to Leroy anyway." He put a hand on each girl's shoulder and gently propelled them forward while he followed a step behind.

Sharon whispered, "You know he's not right in the head, don't you?"

Devon shrugged. "What's wrong with him?"

"I heard one teacher call him a case of arrested development. It's like he quit growing when his father died. Mentally, I mean. He's still that little kid."

"Sounds like a choice he made," Devon said. "Which means he can make another one."

As he opened her car door, Amy said, "You make the world seem so simple."

"That's 'cause I don't give credence to spirits and ghosts," he teased gently. "They tend to complicate the picture considerably."

"Or define it more sharply," she said.

He merely smiled with forbearance, tempting her to kiss his cheek. If he were her stepfather she could, but as her mother's boyfriend he was off limits. She got in and waited for Sharon to get settled before she started her engine. Maneuvering the rutted driveway, she glanced back to give him a last wave, but he was leaning inside his truck getting something from the glove box. A flashlight, she presumed. As she pulled off the rutted drive onto the dirt road, she looked over at Sharon. "That was weird, him appearing like that. I didn't hear his truck, did you?"

Sharon nodded. "I mentioned it, but you didn't say anything."

"I didn't hear you," Amy said.

"We were holding hands," Sharon scoffed, "and I didn't whisper."

"I must've been deep in thought," Amy said, laughing apologetically.

"I'll say," Sharon said. "What do you s'pose Devon wants with Leroy?"

Amy looked into her rearview but all she saw were the overbearing mountains stained red in the late afternoon light. She stopped her car. "I don't think I should leave them there."

"Why not?"

"I can't explain," she said, looking straight ahead at the highway and the green hills behind it.

"He told us to go home," Sharon said. "And Devon strikes me as a man who can take care of himself."

Again Amy looked in her rearview, but this time she remembered the mirror slashed by a light that revealed Devon's face. Knowing that in dreams a house symbolized the human mind, she wondered if it were possible that she had slipped inside his for those few moments, and if it could be as bleak and empty as that house. Blinking against the glare of sun on the pale caliche road in front of her, she shifted her Focus into park and told Sharon, "I think you should drive."

On her way home from Gayle's beauty shop, Lucinda stopped at the widow's house to visit Alex. She intended to offer her help in arranging Natalie's funeral, hoping to get a glance at the guest list or perhaps even make a few calls to people who should be notified. Surely Alex would find doing it alone to be taxing, emotionally as well as simply logistically. Disposing of the dead wasn't easily done. There were a myriad of tiny details to be seen to. She wondered if the police had released the body yet, and what funeral home Alex had chosen.

She turned off the highway onto Magado Creek Road and followed its serpentine matriculations toward Devon's house. But she turned into the driveway before his and parked her little blue Chevy in front of the widow's imposing front door. Suddenly she felt frightened. This woman whom Devon had been seeing—Lucinda felt almost certain they'd been having an affair—was wealthy beyond her imaginings. Wealthy enough to keep ten thousand dollars in cash in a dresser drawer. That was as much as Lucinda's entire savings account, which was tied up in a six-month CD. She wondered if Natalie had intended to invite Devon on that trip to Rome. Wondered if he would have gone. Other than his relationship with her, Lucinda couldn't see any reason he was especially tied to this part of the world. And having been raised Catholic, he might feel that Rome held a special appeal, maybe even a spiritual one touching something she was unable to reach.

Impatiently she jerked open her car door and got out. The widow was dead. Devon wasn't going anywhere with her so it was useless to conjecture on what might have happened. Lucinda tugged the ends of her hair toward the center of her neck in an effort to hide her wound as she rang the doorbell and waited for Alex to open the door. She rang the bell a second time but still no one came. Taking a step back, she frowned at the door, disappointed to be stymied in her purpose. Reluctantly she returned to her car and drove to Devon's.

Leaving her purse and keys on the dining room table as she walked by, she continued through the house to the back door. Outside she looked up at the pink adobe glimmering through the dark forest. Urgently, she skipped down the steps and jogged up the path toward the widow's backyard. A quick glance told her the yard was empty. The sliding glass door still wasn't locked. Lucinda stepped inside and stood still and listened. The house was silent. She walked into the kitchen and opened the door to the garage. One car, a white Lexus with white interior, pristine in the gloom. Lucinda remembered that Alex's car was silver. Gently closing the door, as if the house were quiet out of respect for the dead, she looked at the view from this new perspective, thinking Natalie had seen it every time she came home.

The living room was visible only as a sliver of white light. Predominantly what lay before her was the shadowed passage beneath the balcony, an alley of sepia leading to the even darker foyer of the front door. From here, the house looked industrial, or at least corporate: beige and brown against the startling white, the vibrant tapestries not visible, neither the soothing river-stone hearth nor the finely honed ash latillas rising like wings up the walls, only this dim corridor leading to a darker entrance, the white metal spiral staircase ascending to light. She climbed the stairs and came out on the balcony. The mission furniture with its azure cushions looked undisturbed since her last visit. As then, the doors along the hall were all closed save one. Slowly she walked toward the open door, watching its blazing sunlight for a hint of someone moving inside and throwing a shadow into the hall. Nothing like that happened. She kept glancing at the living room below and listening for an engine in the garage, but nothing changed there either. She stopped on the threshold and looked into the widow's bedroom.

The room had not been cleaned. The blood was still on the bed and the wall above it. One of the French doors was still open at the far end; hung between heavy maroon drapes, the curtain still bumped against the casing in the breeze. Lucinda knew that Devon had been in this room since her last visit, but she couldn't discern that anything had changed. She wondered if Alex had been unable to come farther than the door or even that far, wondered why he hadn't called someone to clean up, if maybe the police wanted it left intact. But there was no tape on the door. Shouldn't there be yellow tape if this were a protected crime scene? She scanned the perimeter of the room, the bureau and dresser and vanity, wondering why she had come, then remembered: the telephone book, the list of the widow's friends. The obvious place was in the drawer beneath the telephone next to the bed.

Hesitantly, Lucinda approached the nightstand. She looked down at the phone, trying to avert her eyes from the outline of the woman's body etched in blood, and thought about how Devon had stood in this exact spot and watched the widow die. Natalie Wieland. Slowly Lucinda pulled open the drawer. It was empty. She stared at it a long moment. Not even a bobby pin or rubber band. Nothing. Someone had taken the contents. The police, probably. Thinking they might have dropped something, she knelt to look under the bed. Not knowing what she hoped to find, she peered into the dark under the dust ruffle and caught a tiny flash of reflected light. She dropped the ruffle and sat up straight. The flash reminded her of the knife she had seen catching sunlight and which had puzzled her so much she had tripped and nearly died. Reassuring herself that this wasn't the same, she took a deep breath, trying to calm her racing heart, and leaned down to look again.

A small metal box dangled from a string tied to the bottom rail of the brass headboard. She slid under the bed on her back until she was beside the metal box and saw a tape recorder and a little black velvet bag suspended on the string. Its knot was above the mattress beyond her reach. She considered coming at it from above but the thought of leaning across all that blood stopped her. When the string proved too strong to break, she leaned close and bit it in half, catching the metal box, no larger than a pack of cigarettes, and its velvet sack. Scuttling back out from under the bed, she sat on the carpet and looked at the tape. It was at the very end. She tried to rewind it, but the battery was dead. Inside the velvet bag were several more tapes. Standing up, she slid the machine inside the bag, too. The house was still silent, though the bloody bed behind her seemed loud with the widow's right to be heard.

Through the open front door, Devon let sunlight illuminate the foyer of the unfinished house that sheltered Leroy. Studs defined the space, the gaps between them open to a darkness deepening with distance from the door. He clicked on his flashlight and let the door fall closed, diminishing his vision to a tunnel of light through the dark. Raising his voice, he called the kid's name: "Leroy!" He hadn't expected an answer and didn't receive one. The kid might not even know the girls were gone, might still be planning a trap he hoped they would fall into; if so, hearing a man's voice would confuse him into retreat. Devon followed the scuff marks in the dust to the hall that led the length of the house and stopped at a T. He saw the floor was scuffed in both directions but returned only from the left. Figuring the kid would eventually be backed against a wall, Devon turned right.

At the end of the hall, he climbed a narrow, switchbacking staircase and came out on the second-floor hall. Only the exterior walls were solid, the others were merely studs, filling the floor like a forest of sticks. He was reminded of the pecan orchard in winter. The severely pruned trees stood in perfect lines stretching from any point as if to eternity. He had visited the scene of Zeb Mulroney's murder there by the seventeenth sluice. Lieutenant Saavendra had taken him and pointed out the position of the corpse. No one had any theories. The cops had found no clues, no evidence, no hint that anyone else had been there. Backing away from where the corpse had lain, Devon bumped into a tree. Tangled in the crevices of the bark he found a yellow thread, so short it had obviously been missed by the investigating officers. The color matched his windbreaker, and he remembered a time he'd had to search for the jacket because it hadn't been hanging in his closet in the place where he usually kept it. That had happened right around the time the Mulroney boy had been killed, though at the time Devon hadn't put the two together.

"What've you got?" Saavedra had asked.

Devon gave the thread to Saavedra, who studied it before looking at the yellow jacket Devon was wearing. They watched each other a moment, then Saavedra dropped the thread and let it blow away. "No good would come of that," was all he said.

Devon thought of Saavedra being gunned down in the heat of a shootout and having the stamina to send one last bullet to meet its mark. That was a fitting death for a cop. Devon often wished he'd died in the line of duty. Retirement might be okay at its proper time, but this idleness in midlife was a living limbo he couldn't seem to escape. Like the forest of studs in front of him now, all opportunities looked equally thin. Smiling at his simile, he played his beam across the far end of the floor. It appeared a small space had been partitioned off, perhaps for a furnace. He wasn't quite sure, but the enclosure beyond the door seemed roomy enough to hide someone. Anyway, Leroy had nowhere else to go.

"Leroy!" Devon shouted, wishing the kid would surrender so they could sit outside and have a pleasant conversation in the sun. But no one answered from the darkness surrounding him.

Taking his first tentative steps away from the wall, Devon listened to the wood floor complain beneath his weight. Yet Leroy weighed at least thirty pounds more, and the disturbed dust in the flashlight's beam indicated someone had been here. Devon didn't think anyone but Leroy would come, certainly not upstairs on this unreliable floor. He was beginning to feel foolish himself for risking it, thinking he should go back to his truck and wait for the kid to come out without endangering himself like this. The floor cracked and shifted a few inches downward. Devon retreated to where he'd come in. "Leroy! Why the fuck don't you answer me?" He listened hard but heard no hint of anyone else being there. "Leroy!" he called again, not wanting to leave the kid up there alone. "I don't think this floor's safe. Is there a way down from your end?"

He heard a faint shuffle in dust, then the kid appeared in the doorway at the far reach of the flashlight's beam. Devon smiled before realizing the kid couldn't see him. "How you doing, Leroy?"

"Where're the girls?"

"They went home."

"How'd you get here?"

"In my truck. Want a ride?"

Leroy looked at the floor between them.

"Is there another way down?" Devon asked.

Leroy shook his head.

Devon lowered his flashlight to directly in front of the kid's feet. "Take it slow, it'll prob'ly hold one more time."

Carefully the kid inched forward. The floor moaned and cracked as if being twisted by an earthquake. Leroy stopped. "Why'd you come here?"

"Wanted to talk to you," Devon said, wishing the kid wouldn't stop, that there was another way down, that this attempt was behind them.

"About what?"

"Let's go sit in the sun. I'm cold."

Leroy laughed. The floor cracked and he jumped ahead as the wood he'd just stood on split and dropped to the floor below. He scrambled forward, the rotten plywood splintering into strips beneath his weight. Suddenly it fell out from under him. He was caught hard, straddling a rafter, and he cried, blowing bubbles from his nose as he yelped with fear. When he was quiet again, he wiped his nose with his sleeve and searched for Devon in the dim light.

"Think you better stay there," Devon said. "I'll go for help."

"Don't leave me!"

"I've got a cell phone in my car. Firemen'll get you out."

"They'll condemn the house," Leroy argued frantically, "maybe tear it down."

Devon let the flashlight's beam fall through the hole at the kid's feet to the floor below. He supposed the boy had attached his hope for a father to this house, and probably thought as long as the house remained standing there was a chance the man would return. But that man was only a memory in the minds of people who had known him, an ache in the hearts of those who loved him. He no longer existed except as this boy who carried his genes. Devon studied the fat, miserable kid. "If I was your father," he said, "I'd rather you let go of this house and live your life to make me proud."

"I don't remember him," Leroy said. "How can I know what would make him proud?"

"You know he was a soldier. And a builder. That means he believed in the future. Maybe that's enough."

"You think I should join the army? Would that make him proud?"

"How would it make you feel?"

The rafter creaked beneath the kid. "Would you do it?"

"I did." Devon winced, hearing the wood crack deep in its core. Quickly but quietly, he said, "I think you should move back, Leroy. Do it slow but don't take too long."

"You joined the army after high school?" he asked.

"Yeah, but those were different times. We weren't at war."

The rafter split in two, dumping Leroy to the first floor in a shower of dust, wood chips, and broken plaster. The last Devon saw of him was the startled O of his mouth as he slid down the rail feet first.

Devon ran back through the upstairs hall and down the stairs, listening as he ran but hearing no human voice. In the living room, he found Leroy sitting on the floor with his legs stretched straight, a humbled expression on his face. "You okay?" Devon asked, offering a hand to help him.

Leroy awkwardly stood up on his own, looked around at the debris, and laughed. "Wow," he said.

"That's an understatement," Devon said, laughing too. "You sure you're okay?"

Leroy patted himself, his arms and legs, torso and butt, earnestly concentrating on checking for anything amiss. He shrugged at Devon. "Everything seems okay."

"I'm gonna have you checked at the hospital. Come on, I want to talk to you anyway, and driving over there'll give us a good forty minutes."

Leroy shuffled forward, limping a little on his right ankle. The way the kid walked in front of him made Devon feel as if his flashlight were a gun. When he opened the door, the sunset seared his eyes, the horizon a scarlet inferno directly in front of him. He looked down, shielding his eyes until they adjusted as he walked toward his truck, hearing Leroy stumbling along behind him now. They had turned the corner and were protected from the sunset's glare when Devon looked up and saw Chief Bright leaning against the hood of his squad car.

Bright grinned and said, "You can turn your flashlight off now, Devon."

CHAPTER SIXTEEN

Lucinda's hands shook as she replaced the battery in the widow's tiny tape recorder. Afraid of what she was about to hear, she went into Devon's bedroom and closed the door even though no one else was home. She rewound the tape and, trembling, pushed the play button. She heard a few clunks and bumps and surmised they were caused by Natalie hanging the recorder under the bed. What followed was a long stretch of silence, then a door opened and a woman could be heard crying. Metal clanged loudly enough to have been striking the headboard before she heard Natalie's voice, tight with suppressed tears and smothered anger:

"Can't I have a nightgown?"

A man laughed. "Lucinda sleeps nude so I guess that's how Devon likes his women."

Lucinda felt certain the man was Chief Bright, and his knowledge of how she slept chilled her.

"How do you know that?" Natalie scoffed.

"Leroy isn't the only peeping Tom in this neighborhood." His voice came closer. "See you later, sweetheart." His breathing dominated the tape, then a whimper from Natalie followed by a door closing.

Lucinda hugged herself, feeling repulsed but unable to stop listening. After another moment of empty tape, Natalie began speaking, her voice low and secretive, thick with fear and assertive with determination: *I'm afraid this will be my last recording. Bright was here. Chief of Police Gordon Bright. He handcuffed me to my bed and stripped me naked and left me in a draft from the open door. Then he left the house. I've been listening and haven't heard him return. Devon promised to come. It's so late, though, he probably won't. Lucinda's there. If these are my last words and anyone finds and hears this tape, please tell Lucinda I'm terribly sorry to have involved Devon in my wickedness. He's such a good person, he could never do anything seriously wrong. I'm afraid though . . .*

Bright's gonna be surprised when these tapes are found and he learns I've recorded every moment we've been together in this bed starting with the second time it happened. I wasn't prepared for the first time. Which is too bad because it was the worst. But I've told about it here.

This is a ninety-minute tape. When I heard his key in the front door, I put a new one in. Someone told him I saw Devon in the café this morning. He figures Devon will come sooner or later. I don't think it'll be tonight, it's already so late, but if it is, I hope it happens before the tape runs out. Bright has something evil planned. When I hear Devon, I'll yell a warning. I don't know why Bright didn't gag me like the first time, but my scream will stop Devon from coming up. No, it won't. He'll hurry to help me. Then, hurry, Devon. Get here before the tape's gone.

A long silence ensued filled only with the hissing of empty tape. Lucinda heard a car in the yard and turned the machine off. Sliding it with its velvet bag under her pillow, she hurried into the kitchen and quickly began cooking supper. She was cubing potatoes when Amy came in looking as dusty as if she had rolled in a grave.

Leaning in through the side window of his truck, Devon put his flashlight in the glove box, then stood up and looked at Chief Bright, who was watching Leroy, an oddly playful light in his eyes. Devon could feel an unusual combustion of energy inside the chief, and he worried for its consequences.

"You two running a demolition derby inside?" Bright asked. "Thought for a minute you were blowing the place up."

"Floor collapsed under Leroy," Devon said. "I'm taking him to the hospital to get checked over."

Bright assessed the kid as if with X-ray vision. "Looks okay to me."

The edge in the chief's voice made Devon worry for Leroy's safety. Bright was standing between them, and the sudden tension reminded Devon of crime scenes where two opposing officers wanted credit for the arrest. But the only crime committed here was trespassing, which hardly warranted the heat of Bright's aggression, and his was the only badge. Not wanting to escalate matters the least degree, Devon kept quiet.

Leroy caught on that a contest was being waged for his custody. "My back kinda hurts," he said weakly.

"Fell through the floor, did'ya?" Bright teased. "Bound to happen, as fat as you are."

Leroy hung his head.

"What'd you expect," Bright continued, "you keep climbing around inside an abandoned house? Things rot, you know?" He took a step closer to the kid. "Did'ya think this house was in heaven with your daddy and not subject to the laws of nature? Huh? Answer me, boy!"

Leroy's head bobbed up, his face indignant, as if he were about to protest.

Bright's fist smacked him in the jaw. Leroy staggered back a few steps and sat down hard. Devon took a step closer, his own fist loose by his leg, then stopped. Bright looked over his shoulder and asked, "You want in?"

"I'm here," Devon said.

Bright turned to face him. "Isn't your business, though. I'm a police officer dealing with a lawbreaker."

"You're outside your jurisdiction," Devon said.

"The county sheriff gave me leeway to watch this property and do what I can toward controlling this particular kid. You're new here, Devon. You don't have any authority at all."

"I have the authority of any citizen against police brutality."

"A slap in the face is hardly brutal," Bright scoffed.

"It was a punch in the jaw and it knocked him on his tail after he already fell through the floor. You could've aggravated something serious."

Devon glanced at Leroy, who was still sitting on the ground. The kid looked apprehensive but alert, so probably not badly injured. His layers of fat might have protected his bones. But he showed no inclination to stand up between two men facing each other with clenched fists. His only weapon, Devon's fist hung tight by his thigh. Bright's was suspended in front of his holster, which for the moment was still snapped shut. Both men had been cops long enough to know there were situations when a badge was worth only the will of the person behind it. This was one of those moments. A gun, however, was always a wild card. Devon knew Bright could get away with killing him and Leroy. Even if an investigation ensued, if it brought out what Devon had done in El Paso, Bright would be commended for nailing a cop killer. No one would miss Leroy. The world was crowded with cannon fodder like him, victims of kingpins high and low. Devon had seen so many fall before a strongman's ego, it made him question the definition of strength. Ability to inflict one's will on others was the way he'd always defined it. Now, after three years off the job, he could see that allowing others to flow around without changing you was a more subtle kind of strength. But unlike the typical practitioner of passive resistance, he could back his up with violence if need be. In a conciliatory tone, he asked, "You gonna let me take him to the hospital?"

"You gonna mention what just happened?"

"How about it, Leroy? You gonna press charges against him

for assault?"

After a moment, the kid asked in a squeaky voice, "You mean like have him arrested?"

Bright spit air at the absurdity.

"At least slapped on the wrist," Devon said.

"I don't want any more trouble," the kid said.

Bright grinned. "That's smart, Leroy. For once you're showing some brains."

"Can you get up?" Devon asked him.

"I guess," Leroy said, clumsily doing it.

Devon watched impatiently, wishing he hadn't volunteered to drive the kid, that he'd pushed him off on Bright, whose job it was, after all. But suspecting the chief would take a few more frustrations out on the kid, Devon remembered he wanted to talk with Leroy anyway. It was why he'd come out here in the first place.

Leroy pulled himself to his feet and trundled over to stand by the truck, slapping dust out of his jeans.

"Get in," Devon told him, then waited, watching Bright, until he heard the door slam shut. Loath to lose sight of Bright, he couldn't bring himself to stoop to the melodrama of walking backward. He pinned his ears for movement behind him and crossed the short stretch of open prairie to the driver's door. Leroy was staring dumbly at Bright, and Devon hoped he could read a change by the kid's reaction.

Devon got in and started the engine, then met Bright's eyes as he shifted into reverse. Only to glance into the rearview mirror did he take his eyes off the chief, who still stood with his fist clenched in front of his gut. Out on the road, Devon watched the cop in his rearview until all he could see was a billowing blanket of dust flapping in his wake. Settling the truck into third, he said, "Now, about that talk I wanted to have with you, Leroy."

The kid didn't answer, and when Devon looked at him, he had either very abruptly fallen asleep or unconscious. Cursing his luck, Devon stepped on the accelerator.

Lucinda sat on the swing in the falling dark waiting for Devon to come home. Amy had said she'd left him at some abandoned house about five. It was now nearly eight and he hadn't called. She struggled with acknowledging that the parameters she herself had laid down for their relationship gave her no right to expect him to report to her, with balancing that against feeling hurt that he had so little concern for her worries. If she hadn't already been nearly fatally wounded on this visit, she might have gone in search of the abandoned house to see if he was still there. Her accident made her feel vulnerable. She argued the opposite was more likely; the odds of being severely injured twice in a short span of time were infinitesimal, so that rather than being exposed to risk she was protected, statistically speaking. But she didn't move from the swing, taking comfort in its gentle rocking.

Amy had come home alone. After reacting with shock to her mother's blond hair, she had tried to explain the vision she'd had concerning Devon. "You know, Mom," she'd begun in the slow voice of reason, "in dream analysis, it's generally agreed that when you dream about a house, you're dreaming about your mind. Did you know that?"

Looking up from cubing potatoes for the green chili stew she was making, Lucinda shook her head.

"Do you believe it?"

"Sounds reasonable." She scraped the potatoes off the cutting board into the pot of simmering chilies and chicken.

"When we were leaving Leroy's," Amy said, watching her intently, "I had a vision of being inside an abandoned house, but it had forty rooms so wasn't the one we were in. In my vision, I saw a mirror at the end of a hall, and I knew when I got there I'd see the face of the person who lived in that house. I'd see the face in their mirror, you know?"

Lucinda nodded, watching her without moving.

"When I got there the mirror was blank. I shone my flashlight into it and it like exploded with light, then the door opened and the sunlight was blinding but when I could see again, I saw Devon's face."

"He was at the door?"

"Yeah, but I think he was in the mirror, too. The house had forty rooms, and he's forty years old, so I think it was his mind I was in."

Lucinda smiled. "I don't think Devon has abandoned his mind, Amy."

"How about the life he could be living if he would recalculate his decision? It's like the focus of a camera. When it's slightly off, things are distorted so you're not seeing a fair representation of reality. But if you adjust it just a tad, everything's sharp and clear again."

Lucinda smiled with more forbearance. "Assuming things ever were sharp and clear."

"Don't you believe what I'm trying to tell you?" Amy asked.

"I believe you experienced it," Lucinda said, wanting to hug her but afraid Amy would construe that as being babied. "Maybe your interpretation's not quite right. After all, you never did actually see Devon in the mirror. You said it was empty, then he opened the real door and your dream was gone, so you stuck him onto the tail end of it when in reality he was on the other side. Maybe?"

"Whatever feels right in a dream is right," Amy said stubbornly. "And I feel it was Devon in the mirror, or would've been if he hadn't opened the door."

"So you're saying he's abandoned his mind?"

"His life," Amy said. "The one he should be living."

Hours later, sitting on the swing and hearing the sad music of Norah Jones flowing faintly from Amy's room, Lucinda ached for her daughter. Amy felt all of life so deeply, she seemed in danger of wearing herself out. During that conversation while Lucinda finished chopping carrots and snipping cilantro, Amy told of the sensations of hostility and malice she felt emanating from Leroy and of her recurring vision of running footprints in snow that she associated with Sharon. Lucinda empathized with the difficulty of juggling those visions with what everyone else agreed was reality. She had in the past suggested to Amy that perhaps a psychotherapist could help, but when Amy retorted that she wasn't mentally ill, Lucinda had quickly agreed. When she tried to bring it up again using another term—counselor— Amy replied she was being advised by a professor at school. The only other information she would share was that the professor was a woman, old and single and close to retirement, and that Amy felt lucky to have caught the last years of her career. Lucinda felt pleased that Amy was having a positive experience in college and let it go, though she was terribly curious. She assumed Amy would tell her someday, and that she had to be patient and wait.

As she was trying to do now, sitting in the swing waiting for Devon. She wondered where he could possibly be, and why he wouldn't think she'd want to know where he was. Lately when they were together, she had felt closer than ever before, yet times like this made her admit their relationship was in crisis. All because his neighbor had been murdered, a tragic event that should have intruded only superficially into their lives and only that because of its proximity. Instead it had changed everything. Devon was acting like the fugitive he was instead of the ordinary citizen he had so successfully become. Lucinda clung to him when he was around because she feared he was imminently leaving. Perhaps in consequence to her clinging, his absences were becoming longer and unexplained. Ruefully she conceded that Amy's vision of an abandoned house could apply to his relationship with the two women who so dearly wanted him in their lives. Maybe he truly didn't want them. A man didn't reach forty as a bachelor without a large part of him liking to be on his own.

Lucinda heard his truck in the driveway. She forced herself to stay where she was, wanting him to find her of his own volition. Not having listened to any more of the tape, she wasn't certain she cared to know what it might reveal. It could be that Natalie's fear had been realized and the tape had run out before Devon arrived. But had it run out before she was murdered? Did it record the struggle culminating in the slashing of her throat? Then the removal of the handcuffs as mere clinks of metal, the thud of a door signifying the killer's escape into oblivion? Or had he spoken, had she called his name? If she had, what would it turn out to be?

Lucinda heard Devon's and Amy's voices coming through the open windows, soft homey greetings without resentment, and she hoped she could make her own voice as blameless. The refrigerator door opened and closed, then a bottle hissed with the release of carbonation. She heard his footsteps on the deck and soft soil behind her. He came around the end of the swing and stood before her, sipping his nonalcoholic beer while watching her face to read her mood.

She smiled. "Welcome home."

"You've changed your hair."

"You don't like it."

"I'll have to see it in daylight." He dropped down beside her. "Stew smells great."

"Thanks," she said, disappointed.

He moved the swing in a faster rhythm, his gaze scanning the horizon of jagged black mountains against a dark sky prickled with stars. "I went looking for Leroy," he said.

"Amy told me."

"He fell through the floor. Didn't seem hurt but I took him to the medical center in Ruidoso to have him checked out." He turned on the swing to face her. "I forgot I wasn't on anybody's expense account. First thing they wanted to know was who would pay for it."

She nodded.

"I told 'em to charge it to the Salado Police. They called and Bright backed me up. Prob'ly 'cause he punched Leroy and knocked him on his ass after he'd already fallen on it through the second-story floor. Kid slept all the way there, which had me a little worried, but he came out all right. X-rays didn't show any broken bones."

"Why did Bright hit him?"

Devon sipped his beer. "He's frustrated and the kid's a helpless target."

"Why do you think he's frustrated?"

"He hasn't found Natalie's killer. I can't imagine he's thinking about much else these days."

"My hairdresser thinks he was sleeping with Natalie," she said, watching him in the dim light falling from a distant window.

"Bright was?" His face noncommittal.

She nodded. "Gayle said Natalie would brag about sleeping with half a dozen men but wouldn't tell her their names."

"Did Gayle mention any other suspects?"

"Only as candidates because they were single. Except for you, it sounded like a sorry lot."

"She mentioned me?"

"As one of the single men in town."

He looked up at the mountains and she watched him struggle

with telling her the truth. She remembered Amy accusing her of looking away when she didn't want to deal with what was being said, but with him it was different. He changed his focus to eliminate her from consideration as he decided what he should honorably do, no matter who was on the receiving end. It was times like this when she felt most exchangeable. He returned his gaze to her and she smiled, wondering what verdict he'd reached.

"I was sleeping with Natalie," he said.

Hearing him say it, she felt newly wounded.

"I'm sorry," he said.

"Are you?"

"Very much so since she was murdered. But that aside, what I think you and I've been sharing these last days makes me sorry I broke our stretch of being only with each other."

"What do you think we've been sharing?" she asked, wishing he would touch her.

"I've been feeling the kind of loyalty I haven't felt since I was living with my brother's family. I don't know if that makes sense to you, but to me it means we are family, you and me, and it won't do us any good to deny it."

She laughed softly, covering her face with her hands, needing that privacy because his declaration was so unexpected. She had expected to avoid an argument, to sound accusing when she was trying so hard not to, to end at best in a stalemate of appeasement that allowed them to try and regain their intimacy in the dark under the covers. Instead he was laying his love at her feet. How could she refuse the gift she had coveted for so long? Before when she decided she couldn't handle sharing his life as a fugitive, he hadn't offered marriage. She had never been married. Amy's father had died before they knew Lucinda was pregnant. In all those intervening years, no man had moved her as deeply as Devon did. She dropped her hands and looked at him. "Are you asking me to marry you?"

"Never thought I'd propose to a blond," he teased. "Are you saying yes?"

She nodded, feeling as if she had stepped off a cliff into free-fall.

He leaned close and kissed her. "This is how you always seal this kind of deal," he said. "Not that I've done it before, but it's what I've heard."

"Me, too," she said, leaning close to catch another kiss. From behind them, she heard Amy's footsteps crossing the deck as the motion light abruptly threw a blue glare across the swing.

"Devon?" Amy called, quietly intruding. "Chief Bright's here with a warrant."

CHAPTER SEVENTEEN

"What kind of warrant?" Devon asked, letting go of Lucinda as he faced Amy over the back of the swing.

Bright stepped out of the shadows behind her. "Search warrant for the premises," he said, his face amused at interrupting what he probably thought was an ordinarily cozy evening.

Devon stood up. "Pursuant to what?"

"A knife capable of inflicting the wound that killed Natalie Wieland."

Devon plumbed the chief's eyes, trying to guess what was motivating this now. Finally he asked, "May I see it?"

Bright handed over the legal paper folded in thirds. "I don't need your permission, but I'd like it."

Devon unfolded the warrant without reading it. "Mind if I take this inside for better light?"

"Go ahead," Bright answered, stepping out of his way.

Devon turned on the lights in the mud and laundry rooms as he passed through, figuring if they were going to be searched he might as well appear cooperative. The chief would be hard put to make a case, though, without a motive to kill the widow. If Devon had killed her, it was unlikely he would have called 9-1-1 before she died. What if the EMS techs revived her? It would've been smarter to simply leave. Even if Bright thought all that had been done to decoy him away from the truth, the chances of its working were so slim as to discourage the attempt. In the kitchen, Devon spread the warrant on the counter and skimmed the pertinent paragraph: ". . . to search for such weapon in and on the premises of . . ."

He watched Bright come in followed by Lucinda and Amy. The women were scared, probably thinking the chief could arrest him, which of course could happen. Glad he was able to tell the truth, Devon said, "Except for a pocket knife in a jacket in the coat closet and a utility knife in my toolbox in the shed, every knife I own is in this room."

Bright let his gaze flit around the closed cupboards and drawers. "Course, if you were guilty, you'd lie."

Devon folded his arms across his chest and leaned back against the counter. "You gonna search this whole place by yourself?"

"I was hoping you'd point the way."

"You're fishing," he scoffed, "without any bait."

"I got a tip the knife was on your grounds."

"From who?"

"That's confidential."

"What'd he say?"

"That I'd find it here."

"Go ahead and look."

Bright glanced around. "I don't want to tear your house up, Devon. Why don't you just tell me where it is?"

"What makes you think I know where it is?"

"My informant said you do."

"Why don't you ask him where it is?"

"I'd rather you show me."

Devon laughed softly. "Your informant's gotta be Leroy. Who else has been around here enough to say anything?"

Bright shrugged. "Could be Alex. He lives next door now."

"You don't have an informant," Devon said. "You made all this up and got a judge to believe you. Go ahead and search. You'll prob'ly plant what you want to find anyway."

162

"You're impugning my search before I've started."

"I don't have the power to impugn anything, but I'm not gonna let your fingers out of my sight."

Bright looked at Lucinda and Amy watching. "Do either of you know where it is?"

"You don't have to answer him," Devon said quickly. "I'd like it if you left us alone." He gave them both a smile he hoped communicated that being polite wasn't the point, it was playing the game, and at that he was consummately more experienced than they were. Relieved, he watched them put their arms around each other's waists and walk with downcast eyes across the living room toward the hall and Amy's room beyond. He looked back at Bright and said, "They're guests. Nothing that happened here is their fault."

"Perhaps," the chief said. "Can I borrow a flashlight? My informant told me the general area to look."

"And where was that?"

"Your backyard."

"There's a motion light out there, as you well know."

"You're the one who brought us inside. For the light, you said."

Devon stared at him. "Why don't you go on out and look?"

Bright lifted his hand toward the door. "After you."

Walking back through the brightly lit laundry and mud rooms, Devon realized he felt angrier than he had walking in just a short time before. He warned himself not to let it escalate but to keep the cool he'd maintained in the kitchen. The trick was to pull Bright into the camaraderie of the police brotherhood, allowing either of them to admit mistakes without undue chagrin. But whether Bright found the knife or not, Devon knew his own position would be considerably more complicated after the next few minutes. He walked to the edge of the deck, his presence activating the motion light, and turned his back to the rail as he watched Bright follow him out.

The chief walked down the steps and halfway to the berm before stopping. He let his gaze survey the yard, slowly pivoting in place. When he was facing the house again, he raised his palm to shade his eyes from the light.

"Would be easier in daytime," Devon said, knowing he was only a silhouette to the chief.

"Too late for that," Bright said. "If I leave now, you'll hide it." He walked to the top of the berm and looked down toward the fence. "Did Mrs. Sterling ever remember what distracted her just before she fell?"

Not yet having lied in this conversation, Devon kept quiet. But watching the chief stand still without even breathing, he knew Bright had spotted the knife. Analyzing himself, Devon felt a collected calm. He hadn't put the knife there and the fingerprints of no one in his home were on it, therefore the fact that it was in his yard was merely circumstantial and not extraordinary given that his yard was next to the victim's. He watched the chief approach the weapon and hunker down on his heels.

"Come look at this, Devon," Bright said as if he had found an interesting insect.

Devon strolled across the yard to hunker next to Bright and stare at the black hilt above the exposed inch of steel catching light. "Looks like a knife," he said.

"The one used to kill Natalie Wieland," Bright crowed.

"Maybe."

"Maybe hell! What else would it be doing here?"

"That's supposition. You gotta prove it."

Bright pulled latex gloves from one pocket and a plastic zippered bag from another. He put the gloves on and held the open bag ready as he reached for the knife. Slowly he drew it from the dirt, the abrasion of the soil enough to wipe the blade clean. But the speckles on the exposed steel and black grip remained.

"Let's take it inside," Devon said, "where we can see it."

Bright studied him a moment before silently agreeing. Together they walked back to the kitchen and laid the bagged knife on the counter. Devon turned on the indirect light to complement the overhead as he and Bright stood staring down at the weapon. Its blade was eight inches long, flatly curved so as to resemble a scimitar.

"Handle's bone," Bright said.

"Not your common knife," Devon said.

"Shouldn't be hard to trace."

"Not something Leroy'd be likely to have."

"Do you suspect him?" Bright asked in a teasing tone.

"Not really, but he might've graduated from peeping in windows to climbing through 'em. Once he was inside, anything's possible."

"Could belong to Alex," Bright said, as if thinking aloud. "You can buy everything on the West Coast." He looked up from the knife to smile at Devon. "I've heard the same's true of El Paso, being next to Juárez."

"You're thinking circumstantial again, Gordon. We've prob'ly all been somewhere we could buy a knife like that if we wanted to but that doesn't mean we did. Forensics will give you concrete answers to build a case on."

"Can you give me some examples of what they might come up with?"

"Matching the cut with the blade, for one thing," Devon said, wondering if Bright hadn't been trained in homicide investigation. "If this is the murder weapon, the killer didn't push in more than the tip 'cause of the way the blade widens so fast. I remember the wound being kinda small. Then, of course, there may be fingerprints."

"You think the killer didn't wipe the weapon clean?" Bright scoffed.

"Might've missed one. Or something else. Maybe he cut himself and left a drop of his own blood along with hers. Or maybe his hand was sweaty and it's all over the grip." Devon smiled. "Those lab boys are good at what they do."

Bright nodded. "What made you quit?"

"I got burned out."

"You also get burned out on Natalie?"

"If I had, I wouldn't have killed her."

"What would you have done?"

"Prob'ly no more'n you, Gordon. I heard you were banging the same drum."

Bright stared hard.

Devon smiled sympathetically. "I thought I was the only one, too. But Lucinda's hairdresser was also Natalie's, and apparently Natalie used to boast about sleeping with half the bachelors in the county. Did she say you were the only one she'd let touch her so soon after she was widowed?"

"I knew you were seeing her," Bright said. "Did you use a condom?"

"I thought she was a chaste widow who hadn't been with anyone but her husband for the last thirty years, not the village hussy reeling in any man fool enough to go."

Bright stared at him without smiling.

"No sense getting jealous," Devon said, surprised Bright was so openly taking it hard. "The chick's flown the coop."

"One of you killed her."

"One of them, maybe."

Bright nodded at the knife. "I could arrest you on that alone. I won't if you promise not to go anywhere 'til I get an indictment."

"I don't have any plans," Devon said, wondering if the chief noticed he was hedging.

If he did, Bright let it pass. He picked up the knife and held out his hand. "Thanks for your cooperation, Devon. I'll be in touch."

Devon shook his hand and walked him to the front door, then stood on the porch and watched him drive away.

Lucinda came out and snuggled close, sliding her arm around his waist. "Is it gone?" she asked.

"Yes," he said, surprised at her choice of pronoun, then realizing she meant the knife.

Amy came out and snuggled against his other side. He raised his arms and held them both, sheltering in their warmth. They stood in silence a few minutes, just their breath moving among them, before Amy said, "How could it have happened that our neighbor is murdered and the killer plants his weapon in our backyard? I mean, statistically, what are the odds of that happening?"

No one answered her. They all three stood staring at the snow-tipped mountains in the moonlit distance.

"I know why," she said softly. "It's 'cause you're always thinking about it, Devon. By keeping it in your mind, you're attracting it from the universe. It's like when you get a cold, it's not because the germs are suddenly there—they're always there!—it's 'cause your resistance is weak and allows the germs to attack you. It's the same with what's happening now. Because you feel guilty, guilt-inducing events are attracted to you, and because you feel guilty, you look and act guilty, and the whole thing spirals down into a vat of guilt you can't get out of."

"Are you saying," he asked, humoring her, "that Natalie was killed because her neighbor's guilt attracted it?"

Amy shifted her weight, changing the pressure of her body against his hip. "No, but it's why you bought the house next door. She had her own reason."

On the other side of him, Lucinda laughed gently at her daughter. "You make it sound like a person chooses to be murdered."

"I think she did," Amy said. "Probably not consciously, but her behavior was definitely dangerous. She put herself in the position of getting caught by the emotions of the men she played with, or at least one of them."

"How many men do you think she played with?" Devon asked guardedly.

"Leroy told me and Sharon there were at least three." Stampeding ahead as if to avoid naming names, she said, "In math, they taught us the simplest solution is usually the right one. So the most simple explanation is that she was killed by a jealous lover."

He felt glad his arms were on their shoulders because his knees felt weak. If he were alone he would have sat down and maybe hugged himself for warmth as he thought about how easily he had fallen into Natalie's web of lies. He had believed everything she told him simply because she was a widow who had killed her husband. Once she admitted that, it had been natural to think she was telling the truth about the rest of her life. But maybe she hadn't killed her husband; maybe that had been a lie, too. Had anyone killed Walter Wieland? Maybe he did die of natural causes following a massive stroke. As for Natalie's demise, maybe Amy's theory explained part of it in that, for whatever reason, Natalie felt guilty about Walter's death so behaved in a way apt to get her punished. Maybe she hadn't counted on the penalty being death, but in those kinds of games the limits are often broached. Devon had seen enough of that while working homicide. But beyond motive was method; to cut your victim's throat wasn't typical. And he couldn't dismiss as coincidental the close proximity in time to his arrival. His gut instincts told him Natalie's killer wanted him to watch her die.

So the key lay not in his connection to Natalie but to her killer. Of one thing he felt certain: he wouldn't be safe from implication until her killer was caught. If that wasn't enough motivation to get off his duff and kick some life into the investigation, he could try to salvage some of Lucinda's vacation by freeing them both from suspicion.

CHAPTER EIGHTEEN

I am Natalie Rowan Wieland, a widow aged fifty-eight years. I'm making this tape because I want the truth to come out. I don't care about my guilt anymore. What I did is far less reprehensible than what's happening to me. I'm leaving this record so people will know.

My troubles came to a head when the Bonners moved away, leaving their house empty. Its two acres stretch directly below ours, its yellow walls barely visible through the forest. Between scraggly junipers and bristly piñon, swatches of yellow shine like sunlight, making me feel as if my house is perched on a cliff surrounded by undulating fog that prevents me from seeing clearly. I thought about being in that bright sunny house many times before I garnered the gumption to sneak through the trees and take a look close up.

Peering through the windows, I saw that the entire front room was knotty pine, ceiling and walls, with an oatmeal colored Berber on the floor. The windows were long and narrow, throwing slivers of light to warm the seasoned old wood and glimmer softly on the round river-stones of the hearth. The next window down revealed the kitchen, knotty pine cabinets filling the walls beneath the knotty pine ceiling, a bisque stove under its hood, stainless steel double sink, black built-in dishwasher, the tubing for an ice maker lying on the floor where a refrigerator had once stood. Beyond the kitchen, a bedroom, more knotty pine, one wall of closets. I had to walk around the house to look through the window in the corner between the sunroom and the back wing of the house, shading my face to see through a rusted screen that a bathroom opened off this bedroom. That, and because it was integrated into the core of the house, made it the master, the other bedroom and bath having been tacked on long after the original construction in 1928. I knew those details of its history. What I wanted to be part of was its future. I coveted that house for its warmth. Mine, you see, is modern and white with brazen textiles owning neither charm nor character. Just slashes of color high on the walls so sometimes I fear the weavings will tumble into puddles of oil on the floor. I know that sounds like a hallucination; I haven't had a true grip for a long time.

Walter was insufferable. He hadn't always been so. In the beginning I thoroughly enjoyed his company. He showered me with jewels, sent fresh flowers to my home every week, and offered to pay my tuition at college. Even while I was pregnant, I maintained straight As. I loved anthropology and was planning to study for my master's when Caroline died. She drowned in our pool when she was only three. A nanny was supposed to be watching her. I was taking my final exam in pre-Columbian ceramics. By the time I received my grades—straight As again—I no longer cared. I came home from Caroline's funeral and didn't leave the house again for nearly six months.

Walter conducted a sort of confrontation one night. In the same way that alcoholics or drug addicts are confronted by their families, he sat me down and made me listen to how disappointed he was, how empty his life had become, and how only I could make him happy. So I rose to the challenge and did everything he expected. My heart wasn't in it but I don't think he noticed. Or maybe didn't care. As long as I performed as his comely wife he was content. With the passing of years, our marriage became more an arrangement of convenience. Of course, he was fifteen years older, so it shouldn't have been surprising that our sex life ceased long before I had any inclination to give it up. I handled that—I know how to use the bathtub faucet pounding at full force—but then he became critical and increasingly hostile, his jealousy dominating our conversations. When

Devon moved into the Bonner house, Walter became intolerable.

I wasn't watching Devon but the house. I had grown accustomed to taking comfort by sitting in the yard and daydreaming about living protected inside all that knotty pine. I stayed out of the yard once he took possession. I rarely even looked that direction. Almost always, when I did, Walter caught me at it. He was seventy-two and not well. All that August through the monsoon season when it was discouraging to go out because of the mud, our home became a battering zone with verbal abuse electrifying the air. We bickered through autumn and quarreled as the falling snow turned the outside world as white as our sterile living room. Fearing I would shrivel into nothing if I couldn't smell a wildflower or soak up the warmth of a rock in the sun, I often sneaked out to hide in the boulders between our yard and Devon's. The huge smooth stones held the sun's heat so long that even an hour or more after sunset they would still be warm. I laid on those rocks many evenings, staking out a respite of silent solitude before returning to my role as the perfect wife of an unhappy bully.

Christmas Eve, in the middle of an accusing tirade—he felt positive I had spent the hours I was gone in Devon's bed—he had a stroke. Devon was with Lucinda in Berrendo that week. No other neighbors are close. A few families live farther down the road from Devon, but he's a quarter mile from me, so they weren't anyone I knew well enough to call for help. I was left to the kindness of the enviably young and healthy EMS attendants, later the doctor at the hospital, a stranger, then Walter's lawyer explaining the terms of his will. If I wanted to inherit anything beyond Walter's pension, I had to keep him at home. If I didn't, his son would inherit everything.

So I brought him home. Although legally still a person, my husband had become no more than a body dragging various machines. I put him in what was meant to be the maid's room, a small cubicle beyond the laundry room, barely large enough to accommodate his bed and machines and one hard wooden chair for visitors. No one came. Not even his half-brother, Alex.

Not until Walter was dead. Then they battered my peace like bugs on a summer screen. Finally it was over and they were gone, the officious men: the undertaker, doctor, lawyer, insurance agent, and sundry police. I kept Gordon and Devon as lovers. I know how to take care of myself.

Lucinda clicked off the tape. She'd heard a noise outside. Either Amy was awake or Devon had come back, or perhaps Chief Bright was here with more questions. *I kept Gordon and Devon as lovers.* Wishing she hadn't listened to the tape, Lucinda slid it under her pillow and walked out to greet whoever was there.

Devon rang Natalie's doorbell, remembering waiting for the police here the night she died. He thought back to those minutes he had stood framed in this doorway watching her yard and driveway while she lay freshly dead upstairs. Turning around, he let his gaze scan the yard, searching for anything that might have been set awry, any possible indicator that another person had been anywhere near. The yard was an open expanse left in its *au naturel* state of wild grasses and embedded rocks. No one could have hidden there, neither themselves nor their car. The door opened behind him and he turned to face Alex Wieland in a red terrycloth robe.

"Morning," Devon said, repressing a smile at the man's knobby knees and skinny shins. "Hope I didn't wake you."

Alex shook his head and took a step back, gesturing for Devon to enter.

Inside the soaring living room, Devon couldn't resist looking up at the balcony and Natalie's closed bedroom door. He wondered if the room had been cleaned yet, and wished he could have examined the scene without her having been there. Distracted by her body, he had been unable to look away from it. His reaction to the whole scene had been uncharacteristically shocked, but the other times he'd walked into murder scenes he'd known where he was going and what to expect. Hers had been the first one he sailed into totally unprepared. So many things he might have noticed. Oddities that would take time to appear to someone only superficially familiar with the room, someone who had visited only at night when his purpose had not been to observe. He hadn't even checked the adjoining bathroom. What *had* he done? Covered her with a sheet. Picked it up off the floor because he couldn't walk away and leave her staring so gruesomely undefended. He wondered why the sheet had been on the floor. Had Natalie thrown it there, or her killer? What might have been lost by his picking it up and fluttering it through the air to cover her? Had the forensic team been thorough enough to vacuum the carpet? Or had that been done by the maid Alex hired to clean the room? Looking at the man watching him from inside the closed front door, Devon asked with a friendly smile, "How you doing?"

"Let's not pretend this is a social visit," Alex replied curtly.

"Okay," Devon said, wondering why not, since Alex had visited him a few days before. "I came to ask if you know the name of the nurse who took care of Walter here at home."

"Why do you want to talk to her?" Alex asked unhappily.

Devon could have broached his subject more gently, but Alex's attitude irritated him. "She's the one who found him dead."

"Are you sniffing around hoping to charge someone with murder?"

"I'm not the police," Devon said. "I have no authority to charge anyone."

"Then why are you poking your nose in where it doesn't belong?"

"Natalie was my friend," he retorted. "Whoever killed her planted the knife in my backyard. Chief Bright found it last night. I think that pulls me in pretty deep."

Alex stared a long moment. "What did it look like?"

"It had a wide blade, slightly curved like a scimitar." Devon watched him, thinking that wouldn't be a question he'd expect from the killer.

"You're certain it's the same one?" Alex asked urgently.

"Blood tests will prove it, but if not it's a helluva coincidence."

"It could have been deliberately planted as a decoy."

"Why?"

"As a tactic to delay the investigation. Perhaps the killer needs time to get out of the country, or is waiting for some other event that necessitates a certain counting of days."

"Such as?" Devon asked impatiently.

"Good lord, man. I'm simply posing possibilities. I don't have any answers."

"Do you think Natalie killed her husband?"

"I hope not. It would change his will."

"What do you mean?" Devon asked, feigning ignorance.

Trundling stiffly, Alex crossed the room and sat down hard on the white leather sofa. "My brother's will specified that his entire estate would go to Natalie, and subsequently to me, if he died of natural causes. If he died by anyone's hand, whether deliberate or accidental, his estate would go to his illegitimate son, Matt Keller."

"Do you know where I can find him?"

Alex nodded reluctantly. "Keller Construction Company in Alto."

Lucinda stood watching Sharon ride her bicycle back up the driveway. Her obligatory compliment on Lucinda's new hair color hadn't sounded sincere, and Lucinda was beginning to think she'd made a mistake. After learning Amy was still asleep, Sharon insisted Lucinda not wake her but ask her to come to the basketball courts when she was up. Listening to the silence of the house as Sharon rode away, Lucinda wished she had woken Amy and made breakfast while the girls chattered at the table. She seemed to be spending an increasing amount of time alone, despite having come to the mountains on what was supposed to be a holiday. With a sigh she returned to Devon's bedroom to play another tape behind his locked door.

I planned my escape for when Walter would finally be dead. I bought tickets and had cash for a trip to Italy. I bought two tickets, wanting to take someone but not having asked anyone yet, not feeling I could until he died.

But he wouldn't. I watched Devon work on his land, watched television, lusted after the young men in the soap operas, longed to leave the house for more than an hour or two, craved freedom. One night when I was drunk and had twisted myself into a rag of desperation, I ran through the forest intending to drown myself in the Magado. I ran into a tree and knocked myself out. When I woke up, I don't know how many hours later, I saw Devon fucking Lucinda in the rocks. She was sitting on one and he was standing between her knees; she was leaning back on her arms, her blouse draped open and her bare breasts round and firm in the moonlight. He was smiling—both of them had their eyes open and were watching each other—and he was smiling as his hips, half-revealed by the low slant of his jeans, ground rhythmically into her. I opened my legs and pretended he was fucking me. Watching him as intently as she was, I came with them, all three of us simultaneously, but I smothered my moan with my fist.

A secret, silent voyeur, I watched until they went back inside, then I pulled myself to my feet and walked home. I stripped myself naked on the patio and dove into the deep end of the pool. I swam the length of it underwater, climbed up the steps and crossed the patio, leaving wet footprints that the wind had already dried when I looked back from the sliding glass door. I walked to what had been the maid's room, the small cubicle behind the kitchen, barely large enough to hold all the medical equipment keeping Walter alive. I stood by his bed hating the blob of a parasite he had become. Gently I slid the pillow from under his head and firmly pressed it over his face. Abruptly, the indicator marking his pulse flatlined and ceased. I lifted the pillow and slid it back under his head. Studying his face, I couldn't see any difference. The change I had effected was in me. I walked out and closed the door, went upstairs and showered, slipped a white silk nightgown over my head, and fell into a deep dreamless sleep. The nurse woke me a few hours later to tell me he was dead.

The doctor declared the cause was natural, the nurse concurred, the chief of police accepted their version, the body was cremated, the remains dropped from an airplane circling Sierra Blanca, and suddenly I no longer have a husband.

Lucinda turned off the recorder. She remembered the time she and Devon made love on the boulders. It had been a magical moment, one of their most uninhibited sharings of intimacy. She felt invaded to know it had been witnessed. More than witnessed, shared surreptitiously by a woman starved for love. Worst of all was that Natalie had participated as a secret partner, then taken whatever strength she gained into her home and used it to kill her husband. Lucinda couldn't understand how anything so beautiful could have been twisted into murder. For herself, she denied responsibility, knowing she harbored no such impetus. But what did that say about Devon? Morbidly curious, she pushed the play button.

I tried to wait a circumspect length of time, but I had waited so long already. One night toward the end of March, after a day of constant snowfall and a long evening ahead in front of my fire, I impulsively called Devon and asked to borrow some wood as if I didn't have enough. I knew he was home because I hadn't heard his truck leave. So when an answering machine picked up, I left a message hoping he was standing there listening to it.

Upstairs, I changed into my ruby silk jumpsuit with a halter top. Underneath I wore neither bra nor panties. I redid my makeup lightly, knowing he would see me only in firelight, the kindest illumination on a woman's face. In the kitchen I was opening a bottle of merlot when I heard him arrive. I walked through the living room to the glass door, watching him as I approached. He held an armload of cut wood, his dark hair sparkling with droplets of melted snow, his tanned, handsome face wearing an amused smile. His jeans were snug over what I knew to be a high butt, his strong brown chest, whose muscles I had watched ripple many times while he rebuilt his rock walls last summer, was covered with a heather brown sweater, its low crew neck making his just-shaved face appear unusually vulnerable. I realized he was nearly twenty years my junior as I slid the door open and welcomed him in with sincere gratitude. Admiring that high butt I had coveted from a distance, I watched him gently drop the wood in the box by the hearth. When he stood up and turned around with the expectation of an invitation to stay shining from his face, I offered it along with a glass of wine, but he didn't drink. Going to the kitchen for my own glass, I thought about how succulent an alcoholic on the wagon might turn out to be, a man in proud control of his attributes.

While I was gone, he added wood to the fire so its leaping flames were throwing shadows across the ceiling as I returned. I sat on the sofa and watched those shadows high overhead, knowing I looked like a lithe flame myself, red silk on white leather. I looked at his smile of appreciation. Nothing more needed to be said. I set my wine down and joined him on the Navajo rug in front of the fire. I put my arms around his neck and kissed his mouth. For a moment he stood there without raising his hands or participating in the kiss except to receive it, which he did very well. Then his hands tenderly cupped my elbows, holding me as if I were fragile, as his tongue played on my lips, teasing me to want him inside me. I was so hungry, had endured so many lonely comes, that I curled beneath his hands in the fashion of his desire. I clutched him close, clinging as if we were suspended above an immense precipice and only the drive of his loins could diminish the distance to the other side. When we reached it, I fell as if into a pasture of clover, soft and fragrant beneath a lolling hot sun which I eventually recognized was the fire in the hearth. Awkwardly, he was still there. No longer the elicitor of sensual pleasures but merely my neighbor, naked on my rug.

"Thank you, Devon," I said politely. "May I call you again sometime?"

It took a moment but he wasn't dense. I watched him stand up buttoning his jeans, then admired his muscular chest as he leaned to lift his sweater off the floor. "Next time," he said, tongue in cheek, "I'm gonna charge you for the wood."

The machine clicked off and Lucinda sat staring at the reel that had ceased turning because the tape was full. As carefully as if she were handling artifacts of Devon's love, she removed the tape and returned it to the black velvet bag with the others. She had listened to three now, the first two and half of the fourth. Once she'd heard the end, the beginning and middle might become irrelevant, so she postponed knowing what, if anything, was revealed on the last half of the last tape. She felt excoriated hearing the widow's description of Devon as a lover, and didn't think she would ever be able to see him in moments of passion without remembering how he had looked in Natalie's eyes. Equally disturbing was having been watched with Devon in the boulders. Natalie had pretended he was her lover even then, had participated actively enough that they all three reached orgasm simultaneously. Lucinda thought she could understand how accidentally experiencing something desirable that had been withheld a long time could motivate a person to eliminate the cause of its being withheld. But to transform a moment of love—which it had been for her and Devon—into an impulse toward murder was a leap she could not understand. She shivered, fearing some degree of responsibility lay within Devon.

Then she remembered hearing Natalie apologize in the first tape: *Please tell Lucinda I'm terribly sorry to have involved Devon in my wickedness.* Lucinda emptied the black velvet bag into her hand and lifted the third tape from the others.

CHAPTER NINETEEN

Sharon loved the smack of a basketball slapped hard against a concrete court, the drum roll of a dribble across the key, the wind of the ball's velocity and its fluttering snag through the net, then the lazy bounce of its own inertia after dropping from the basket. Because the curve of the ball meshed with her palm, tossing it was like impelling a part of herself, inserting it into the world at her will. Catching it and walking away, dribbling steadily while retreating down the court, languidly bouncing the ball before her approach, then her energy coalescing, exploding as if pressured through the fissure of her arm, erupting out to release the ball. It sailed in a perfect arc to fall through the center of the basket, barely kissing the net as it spun by. This time she let the ball bounce three times before she moved to catch it. Turning with the intent to dribble down court again, she saw Leroy watching from the bleachers, closer than before. She turned and dribbled away. With her back to him, she again forgot she wasn't alone.

She thought of how much fun she and Amy would have in college come fall, and of Amy's parents who weren't married but might as well be. Sharon had never seen a couple so attuned, the way they were constantly checking in with each other, exchanging unspoken communications with a shift of an eyebrow or a shrug of a shoulder. She could see now why none of the local women had been able to make time with Devon. He wasn't much for being sociable, and Lucinda took all he had.

Sharon wondered what he thought about during the many hours he spent alone. He seemed almost a monk or a penitent, the way he lived so isolated except when Lucinda and Amy were visiting. Then he turned into this really sweet and supportive family man. The kind of husband girls dream about: modestly handsome, ravishingly attentive, and totally competent at handling the world, the only flaw being that he wasn't rich. At least Sharon hadn't picked up any hints of that. But he owned his own home and didn't have a job, so he wasn't destitute. She bounced the ball, wondering what her husband would look like, what his name would be, and what quality of his would make her fall in love.

Turning her back to the goal, she saw that Leroy was standing nearby. She caught the ball and held it tight against her breasts. "You're not s'posed to be on the court."

"Who says?" he asked, walking closer.

"What are you doing?" she scolded as she took a step away. "You're being silly."

He kept coming, wearing a smug grin and holding something down by the waistband of his jogging suit. She frowned as she took another step back. Knowing she was watching, he unwrapped what he held concealed in the loose folds of his sweatpants. Sunlight gleamed on the steel shank of a knife.

She turned and ran off the concrete court, across the wet field and through the gate in the chain-link fence surrounding the school, across the street and up an arroyo, its ground muddy beneath her sneakers, each step sliding before her soles caught traction. Uphill she ran, aiming for Salado Peak, the gentle slope where graduating high school classes painted an S near the top. Hoping he couldn't keep up, she was climbing now, jumping from rock to rock half the time, the school and village shrinking until they looked like toys on a game board. She was breathing hard but not gasping like he was. She could hear him,

182

closer than she had expected. In a ploy for time, she turned and watched the top of his head below her. When he looked up, she threw the basketball hard straight at his face. He ducked, and it sailed past him to bounce uselessly down the mountain. She ran on. He hadn't stopped when she had and was gaining on her. She could hear his grunts of effort. Striving for one more surge of energy to outrun him, she hammered her feet without mercy and felt herself pulling ahead. Her heart was beating fiercely enough to crack her ribs when she found herself flat up against a cliff. Only five feet high, it was easily scaled.

She was in another canyon leading higher. Now she ran in the bliss of being unable to hear him. Thinking she had won, she let her pace slack off until she found a comfortable rhythm between the thud of her feet, beat of her heart, and rasp of her breath. The canyon narrowed, then abruptly stopped. All around her were steep cliffs of crumbling shale. When she tried to climb one, the rocks fell apart beneath her hands and she slid back to the bottom. Trapped, she turned to watch the narrow crevice affording the only way in or out.

Springing up from a gold strike in the 1870s, White Oaks had boomed and fizzled, then flirted with being a ghost town for most of the twentieth century. A few eccentric residents kept the town alive until, in the 1990s, it began evolving into an artists' community. Like everything else in life, however, artists had changed from when Devon was young. Then the term conjured up visions of beatniks and hippies, passionate poets possessed by their work. Now an artists' community was a retirement village. The people had all worked serious, rewarding careers in other parts of the country. They came here because land was cheap enough that they could coast for the rest of their lives on their fat bank accounts and occupy their days throwing pots or weaving tapestries or painting pictures of barns and calling it art. Devon guessed maybe he was a little jealous that they had such golden parachutes dropping them into old age—it wasn't something he'd ever have—but he also felt the people were a bit self-indulgent. How many hand-thrown pots did a country need?

White Oaks lay in a treeless bowl between Baxter Mountain and Carrizo Peak. Cedarvale Cemetery was just off the road to the right about a mile west of town. Local notables were buried there, and every summer the town had a festival that included actors impersonating characters who rose from their graves. The county's violent past, once a source of shame and a major reason for its backward economy, had become its biggest tourist attraction. Sites claiming relics of outlaws and sheriffs were the most popular. Relics of artists and writers took a distant second. Politicians and bankers wouldn't have been on anyone's list of attractions if most of them hadn't also been outlaws or sheriffs earlier in their careers. The West had been conquered by those willing to use guns against their fellow man. As simple as that explanation seemed, it wasn't far off from describing what America was doing now in the Middle East. Devon felt angry when he thought of foreign policy, the current administration in Washington, or the fat cats in Santa Fe. The political arena was so far from any semblance of desirable that he could only stay sane by pretending it didn't exist. He knew that was the classic stick-your-head-in-the-sand mentality, but he was afraid if he let himself dwell on it he would join an armed militia. He had the skills they wanted: he was adept with guns, had killed and could do it again. He was also pretty good with his fists, but his best asset was reading people, knowing when they were lying, picking up clues from something as slight as the tic of a muscle; civilized skills good only at close range, not the long distance aim of a sniper. So his best asset would be useless and he'd be mediocre, which most of them were, willingly subsuming themselves under the command of madmen.

He coasted to a stop in front of the No Scum Allowed Saloon. In the past, he would have gone in for a beer and to pick up local gossip before making his call. Now he didn't drink, and his low-grade depression made conversation a high-energy activity. He sat with the engine idling in his old truck, his gaze scanning the broken foundations of dozens of abandoned and cannibalized homes for any hint of a street sign or clue as to where he might find the retired nurse and now eclectic artist, Wendy Reinecke.

The directions said to turn left two blocks past the saloon, but he couldn't discern anything denoting a block. He eased his truck forward and passed the first left—a mere track through the prairie grasses—about a hundred yards down the road. The distance to the second was at most half a block, more like a quarter, but it was the second left so he took it. Ahead a house with a shed stood surrounded by abandoned foundations. The house was small and low, plastered adobe painted a deep blue, the metal roof white, the doors and windows inset two or three feet so they seemed swallowed by shadows. The shed was a Quonset hut with a swamp cooler suspended high on its curve. When he parked in the yard and shut off his engine, he could hear the rhythmic turning of a pottery wheel from inside the hut. Studying the terrain through his dusty windshield, he thought the treeless prairie looked bleak. He had grown up in El Paso so was no stranger to forbidding landscapes, but if someone had asked his opinion right then of this town's fate he would have answered it should be left to the ghosts. He smiled wryly, wondering if Amy's psychic abilities were contagious. Whatever he was picking up had an extrasensory source, because what lay before his eyes was a bucolic scene complete with the sound of a workman perfecting his craft. Work woman. He was here to see a retired nurse.

The impetus that had inspired him to begin this journey was gone. He felt as if he could sit in his truck, in the warmth of the sun, listening to the slap of the potter's foot on her wheel, the hum of its revolutions, all day. He wondered if the noise was part of the appeal, the song of the wheel a meditation of sorts; wondered how he could cure himself of this depression that left him stranded like flotsam after a flash flood. Recognizing he was immobile when he should be moving, he couldn't muster the initiative to open the door of his truck and walk across that bright sunny yard to the studio where the woman was working. Back when he'd been on the job, twelve-, fifteen-hour days weren't unusual. Now he had trouble concentrating for more than an hour at a time. It was a habit, that's all. If he was properly motivated, he could pick it up again. He felt comfortable sitting here in the sun. The questions he wanted to ask the retired nurse wouldn't be pleasant, so it was natural that he tarry a while to enjoy something—anything—in the course of his day. Sighing, he opened the door and stepped into the lizard dry dust of the yard.

The potter's wheel stopped. She must have heard him. He walked toward the hut, watching her emerge in the doorway. She was hefty, short dark hair, no makeup, her sausage body enclosed in a canvas apron splattered with slip. Her hands were red with a peeling skin of drying clay, her eyes a surprising blue. He forced a smile and introduced himself. She felt his aversion and didn't smile. Reaching down into the pit of himself for the gumption to pull off a successful interrogation, he met her eyes with a plea for leniency as he explained why he had come. She pulled a dingy towel from her apron's pocket and wiped her hands while he spoke, glancing up at him occasionally, holding his eyes with hers, blue and frank with curiosity, then looking down again to rub the red off her hands with the soiled towel. She interrupted with neither comment nor question but let him fill the few silences that fell within his soliloquy. Finally he ran out of words and stood humbly waiting for an answer.

Reaching behind herself, she turned off the light inside the hut and closed its door. "Come into the house," she said. "You look hungry and I've got a pot of posole on the stove."

The hominy stew was flavored with chunks of pork and floating flakes of red chili. Without asking, she poured a glass of soy milk and set it by his bowl, then stood by the stove heating corn tortillas on a black griddle. She had left her apron at the shed, and her hefty body encased in tight jeans and a tucked-in, sleeveless yellow blouse wasn't unappealing. She looked like an advertisement for Rosie the Riveter or an Angelina Jolie character, women beyond being shocked or embarrassed.

After taking his first bite, Devon realized he hadn't eaten since the night before. Somehow food slipped his mind unless someone put it in front of him. The last thing he remembered having was Lucinda's green chili stew. Chicken and tomatoes instead of pork and corn, flour tortillas instead of the small yellow ones Wendy was serving. And not a glass of soy milk but a bottle of O'Doul's, cold and beading on the table, the prospect of sex ahead, his bedroom at his back. He turned in his chair and looked at the wall behind him, lime yellow, reminding him of the colors in Mexico. Then he looked at the woman again. She had finished with the tortillas—a small plate holding a stack of them was now on the table—but she stayed by the stove as if for protection.

"Come keep me company," he coaxed. "Talk to me while I eat."

She sidled closer and chose the chair across from him, setting it well away from the table so he could see all of her above her knees. She stuck her fingers in the pockets of her jeans and nodded silently to his compliments on her cooking. But when he brought up Walter Wieland, she hitched her chair closer.

"She never went near him," she said. "I could tell nothing had been disturbed since I'd left." Her face softened. "Not that I blame her. His heart monitor was the only thing moving in that room. It was a blessing when he passed."

"Do you think he might have been helped along?"

"Wasn't my place to make such a determination."

"But in your professional opinion as a nurse?"

"Nurses don't sign death certificates."

Devon smiled. "You've obviously thought about it, though, 'cause your answers come so quick."

"Living out here, spending most of my time at the wheel, I have a lot of time to think, Mr. Gray. But that doesn't mean I'm a blabbermouth. If you decide to stay in these mountains, you'll soon learn there's no quality better admired hereabouts than minding your own business." She put her hands on her knees and leaned forward as if about to stand up. "Anything else you want to know?"

Devon nodded. "The name of his doctor."

I called him over and we had a delicious time. [Natalie giggled.] He's very accommodating when it comes to games, and quick to catch my intention. I hate conversation during sex. The words are never right and usually stupidly repetitive. Silence is best, a soundtrack running in each partner's mind, a score and script that needs to coincide only on the physical plane. I believe some young blond once called it the zipless fuck. Devon is excellent at delivering his honed, masculine body into the hands of my fantasies. And he never pushes my head down toward his groin. I have never liked fellatio; finally I've met a man who doesn't ask it of me. Of course that means I can't fairly expect cunnilingus, but he's wonderfully adept with his hands. Best of all, he can sustain our fucking as long as I want him to, and the ecstasy of coming together with our eyes open watching each other is dependably cathartic.

Just thinking of him entering and leaving my home in the dead of night makes me want him. For days I'll imagine he's a satyr prowling my yard, watching for an opening to slip inside. I guess it was an easy jump to imagine he's a burglar stealing through the dark to my bedroom. I enjoy hiding under the covers, holding my breath, because for those few moments I truly am frightened. My imagination conjures degenerates and psychopaths just beyond my sheet. But it's always Devon's warm, naked body sliding in beside me, his hands caressing me as his breath plays on my skin like the dapple of sunlight through tall pines. He's always clean, always smells fresh, always strong, taking command while submitting to my silly games. Some nights we drop the pretense more quickly than usual. Then it's the core of he and I coupling with neither the roles of our games nor any baggage carried over from our daytime personas. Neither of us are honest in the real world, the one beyond my bedroom, but some nights we're honest between my sheets. Losing self-consciousness, we plunge from hunger toward satiation, touching places whose existence both of us had forgotten for far too long. Sometimes I find myself sobbing against his shoulder with the flood of sheer release. Murmuring animal sounds of encouragement, he doesn't stop fucking me but brings me back to riding pleasure in his company. After he did that a time or two, I began letting him linger before sending him out in the cold alone.

Lucinda turned off the third tape and sat hugging herself on Devon's bed. Though she had never cried during sex, she could easily imagine how he would react. An expert at delivering comfort, he could soothe a woman, as he had Natalie, while satisfying himself. It was a skill she supposed he had learned as a detective, women being most obliging when they were also most vulnerable. Holding them while they cried and answered his questions wasn't too different from comforting them during sex. The strength that demonstrated, however, wasn't charitable but selfish. Again she thought he could be a saint or a sociopath, and it bothered her that she claimed to be in love with him yet didn't know at which end of the spectrum of decency he lived. As if the tape recorder gave off an electric shock when touched, she reached out a finger and stabbed the play button.

At first I only had one glass of wine in the prelude leading into foreplay. When we started moving to my bedroom and he began staying later, I sometimes took the bottle upstairs and finished it in bed. Last night was one of those nights. I'll try to describe it verbatim. Talking about Walter, I said, "You can't understand what I went through, how horrible it was to see his skin turn chalky and his eyes glazed dull and his mouth only a hole to put tubes in. They fed him and he defecated and urinated and someone cleaned it up. Wasn't me. But just knowing about it destroyed the last semblance in my mind of the person he had been. You know, all that meanness before his stroke? He was so jealous and he would pick, you know? God, he tested my patience. But now the doctor says he had a brain tumor and that's what made him mean. I wonder why neither of us ever considered it could be a medical problem. Suddenly his behavior changed and we just assumed he was unhappy. You've never been married, have you, Devon?"

"No," he said, watching me without judgment. Both of us were naked under my flowered sheet. At the far end of the room, a breeze lifted the gauzy white curtain and dropped it softly against the barely open door. The moon shining through that fabric lit the room.

"Next time," I said, "I'm going to marry someone younger. Let him take care of me when I'm old and sick. That's the thing, when you're young, you think marrying an older man is sophisticated. He's so suave and has so much money, you think it's forever. But suddenly he's old and you're chomping at the bit. What marrying an older man really means is being a nursemaid for the last years of your marriage."

Devon chuckled. "Doesn't sound like fun."

"Fun?" I sat up and stared down at him rather belligerently, I'm afraid. He was watching me warily, his muscles tensed so I knew he could catch me before I did anything hurtful. I trusted him to have that ability. "I was in hell," I said under my breath. "I was in prison. I was being crucified daily by his suffering, his near corpse closed in a back room and still alive only because he had a strong heart. His brain was dead. Gone. No functions left. Would you want to live like that?"

Devon shook his head.

It was then that I told him. I whispered it, but he heard me. We were looking into each other's eyes, and I knew he had killed someone, too. He had been a police officer, I'm sure his killing was in the line of duty, but I could see the damage it did. Sharing that awful guilt was the real bond between us and probably explains the passion of our fucking, that both of us come from the same need to believe in our goodness against the stark fact that we have killed.

The tape continued to hiss, empty, for a minute more. The sound of the machine shutting off roused Lucinda from her slump. She walked to the window and looked outside. All the way to the road, the land lay lush and green from the gentle rain that had fallen in the night. Clouds still obscured the highest peaks of the mountains towering in the distance. Though invisible now, she knew the peaks were there, and she tried to believe Devon's love for her was as dependable despite being intermittently impossible to discern.

CHAPTER TWENTY

Amy was making "hot stuff couscous" for supper. Beyond the hiss of the vegetables simmering in the frying pan, the house was quiet, Lucinda alone behind Devon's closed bedroom door. Neither of them knew where he was. Adding the chopped pepper to the purple onion sizzling in olive oil, Amy suddenly felt dizzy. She sat quickly on the nearby stool and leaned her head over her lap as she saw again the vision of running footsteps on white ground. This time the loose soil wasn't snow but crumbling rock, and she realized the image was reversed. Black stones had appeared white, white sneakers black. Sharon's sneakers, her pale ankles and calves running on black rocks that crumbled into powder beneath her feet.

When Amy had gone to the basketball courts earlier, they had been empty, and when she went by Sharon's house, no one was home. Now she had this vision of Sharon in trouble, a vision she'd had before but never so intensely. Sharon didn't have a cell phone, and the ground she was running on wasn't any basketball court, so Amy had no way to find her. Slowly she stood up and began cutting the carrots, her knife mincing them into orange tidbits she scraped into the red pepper and onion. Turning her back on the sizzling pan, she lifted the phone off the wall in the corner and punched in Sharon's number.

The phone on the other end rang four times before Josh answered. To Amy's questions, he reported that Sharon wasn't home and he didn't know where she was. His mother would be back from the grocery store in an hour or so. Maybe she knew. He was in a hurry and had to go.

Amy listened to the dial tone for a minute before she heard her dinner sautéing behind her. Quickly she hung up the phone and picked up the wooden spoon to stir the red and orange fragments in the extra virgin olive oil. She began cutting the zucchini into tiny chunks, listening to her knife on the cutting board, the whisper of the sizzling oil, a blue jay jeering from beyond the window.

Sharon was in trouble. Amy felt certain of it. But without knowing where to look, a search seemed pointless. She remembered the advice Devon had given her in Berrendo: "Gather information until you have something solid to build on. Until then, let the chaos be." When she could allow chaos to run through her mind unhindered, she sometimes caught threads of the truth she was seeking. In this instance her initial thoughts had been influenced by her erroneous conclusion that the footsteps were left by someone running through snow. At the least, that had put the event half a year in the future. Now she knew the person was running through black rock, which could be coal or shale. At one time, there had been a coal mine near Salado. She wasn't sure where exactly, but someone would know.

She scraped the zucchini into the pot and stirred it with her wooden spoon. She also now knew for sure that the running person was Sharon. Previously she had associated the vision with her but hadn't seen her so clearly depicted in the actual scene. She had thought it might be someone close to Sharon who was destined to be irrevocably hurt, as had happened to her two years ago. She warned herself not to predict other people's lives by what had happened to her. Similarities were superficial, the depths as unique as stalactites.

Adding teaspoons of cumin, curry, and red pepper flakes, she was seeing cliffs of black shale. Where had she seen anything like that? It felt like a nightmare, the way the loose, brittle stone crumbled beneath even the slightest weight, becoming an avalanche that dragged everyone with it.

Devon didn't have an electric can opener. She found that amazing as she worked to turn the manual one around the top of the garbanzo beans. Dumping them into the vegetables, she scraped the can out and banged the spoon against the side of the pan. She tossed the can in the trash, stirred in a quarter cup of cilantro, put the glass lid on the frying pan, and turned the fire down to its lowest flutter. She washed and dried her hands, then knocked on the closed bedroom door.

After a moment, Lucinda opened it. "Supper smells good."

"Thanks," Amy said, looking past her to the bed where a micro tape recorder and several tapes lay beside a small velvet bag, all black on the blue comforter. "Are you recording your diary?"

"No," Lucinda said; a tad defensively, Amy thought. "What makes you think I keep a diary?"

Amy shrugged. "Sharon's in trouble. My visions are getting more intense."

"Do you think there's something you can do?"

"Look for her, I guess. I called her brother and he sure doesn't care. I don't think anybody in that family cares much about her."

"What families show others isn't always the same as what they share among themselves."

Amy nodded because she knew that, but she also knew Sharon had grown up fighting for every bit of recognition she achieved. "I'm going looking for a coal mine. Do you mind finishing supper? Just let the veggies simmer a few more minutes, then mix 'em with the couscous and put 'em in the frig."

"We can do that later," Lucinda said. "I'm going with you."

Devon sat in the private lobby for a suite of offices in the county medical center, waiting to see the doctor who had pronounced Walter Wieland dead. He was alone in the room, a bland space decorated in beige and dull pink, its one window blocked by a ponderosa swaying in the wind. Directly in front of him was an open door to an office where a woman worked at a desk. The nameplate beside her door read Sally Gere, MD, APA. She was petite, her black hair cropped in a mannish cut, her face gently made up and softly feminine. When she looked up, Devon smiled and asked, "What's APA stand for?"

"American Psychiatric Association," she answered, her voice professionally soothing.

He winced. "You're a shrink?"

She nodded.

"Can I ask you a question, off the record?"

"Are you a journalist?"

He shook his head. "I'm waiting to see Dr. Tanner about a death certificate he signed."

"So you're a police officer?"

He shook his head again. "A neighbor of the deceased."

She tapped her pencil's eraser on the desktop in a staccato rhythm before asking, "What question did you want to ask me?"

"If a man's depressed but doesn't want to take drugs, what would you advise as a remedy?"

"Is he depressed or sad?"

"What's the difference?"

"Depression is a treatable malady. Sadness is an unavoidable part of life."

Devon nodded. "I guess this guy's both."

"I would advise him to identify the things that are making him unhappy, change the ones he can, and adjust to those he can't. Like the Serenity Prayer. Have you heard it?"

He nodded.

"Other than that, a routine of exuberant exercise should get the good chemicals flowing in his brain again. If it doesn't, he should discuss an antidepressant with his doctor."

"Thanks," he said. "I wouldn't've bothered you but I figured anybody who'd leave the door open is inviting conversation."

"The ventilation's poor," she said. "There's not enough air with the door closed."

He thought another time he would've asked her to walk outside with him and stroll beneath the soughing ponderosas. Now his increasingly familiar lethargy sank his bones deeper into the chair and numbed his tongue so he finished the conversation with a smile that she received by ducking her head and scribbling in her charts again.

A few minutes later, Dr. Tanner's door was opened by a tall, bald man in his sixties. "Mr. Gray?" he asked, extending his hand. "I'm Richard Tanner."

"Devon Gray," he said, shaking hands.

Seated in the doctor's office with the door closed, Devon noted the inadequate ventilation and marveled that a hospital would be designed with such a flaw. "I won't take much of your time," he said, studying the doctor's thin, pale face beneath the shiny bald pate, the kind blue eyes and tenderly folded mouth. "I'm a neighbor of the Wielands, Natalie and Walter, and I was curious about Walter's cause of death."

Tanner leaned back in his chair. "His death certificate is public record."

Devon distinctly remembered Chief Bright telling him only an interim report had been submitted. "I thought it hadn't yet been filed."

"It's illegal to bury a person without one."

"He was cremated."

Tanner shrugged.

"I'll be blunt with you," Devon said. "Mrs. Wieland told me she killed her husband. I need to know if that was true."

"And you're representing who in this matter?"

"No one. Myself." He shrugged. "She told me a lot of things, that being one of 'em. I need to know what was true and what wasn't, to sort it out 'cause it's got me stymied. Whoever killed her might have planted the murder weapon in my yard. He's trying to pull me in, to implicate me, maybe even frame me, and I can't figure who he is or why he killed her until I know whether or not she killed Walter. I thought maybe something would've tipped you off if he didn't die of natural causes. Course that still wouldn't mean Natalie did it. She could've been covering for someone else. But the other day it occurred to me that maybe she lied and nobody killed him. Can you tell me the truth?"

"Falsifying a death certificate," Dr. Tanner said softly, "could cause me to lose my license."

"What did you write? Cardiac arrest? That just means his heart stopped. We all die of that, don't we?"

Tanner nodded. "His heart was badly damaged by his stroke."

"Nobody helped it stop, that you could tell?"

An air conditioner kicked on in some distant part of the building, sending a faint draft of cool air through a high vent. Almost inaudibly, Tanner said, "He was smothered. Probably with a pillow. I found the rachis of a goose down feather in his throat."

They stared at each other for a long moment in the cooling room.

Devon asked, "Would he have put up much of a fight?"

Tanner shook his head. "I doubt he was even aware of it happening."

"So Natalie could've done it?"

"A child could have. Now that you know, Mr. Gray, what will you do with the information?"

"I'll keep it to myself," he promised, standing up.

"If necessary," Tanner said, rising too. "I could deny this conversation took place."

Devon smiled. "I'll do my best to keep us out of a courtroom. You can count on that."

Sharon squatted with her back against the cliff, watching Leroy block the narrow crevice with his fat, heaving body. He was leaning over, his hands on his knees, blowing hard, his red face dripping sweat. She could feel a fine film on her own face, but she'd been here long enough that she'd caught her breath. She remembered the other times when she had tried to talk to Leroy, reason with him, insert some sense into his thinking. This time she felt too disgusted to say anything. She only had to get past him, then she could easily outrun him. She'd done it coming up the mountain; going down would be a breeze. Except she meant to go down the other side to Amy's rather than home. Once she got past Leroy.

She wondered if he had dropped the knife or if it was hidden in his sweat suit somewhere. His hands were empty fists clenched on his knees. Wanting to move before he caught his breath, she picked up a handful of stones and began throwing them at him hard enough that they must have stung. He glared at her, ducked his head to miss one, then stood up. She did, too, peppering him now with sharp chunks of shale. "Quit it!" he yelled. She lifted her empty hands, inviting him closer. He grunted and sprinted straight at her. She feinted one way then dodged the other, feeling his fingertips brush the back of her blouse as she escaped through the fissure.

Sliding down the mountain, she was going the wrong way until she caught hold of a juniper branch robust enough to stop her. As if it were a rope, she swung her weight around the tree and landed slightly closer to the crest. She climbed now with her belly flat against the cliff, inching her way up the craggy precipice. Not daring to look up or down, she didn't know how far she had yet to go. Finally her fingers grasped roots. She pulled herself up and rolled away from the edge. Staring up at the blue sky, she held her breath to listen for Leroy. Like a distant bull blowing dust, he could be heard at the bottom of the cliff. She rolled over and peered down. He was climbing, laboriously and clumsily, but making progress. Beside her lay a rock the size of a baseball. She picked it up with both hands, centered it over him, and let go.

It fell as if pulled by a magnet into the crown of his head and bounced off at a crooked angle. He hung suspended a moment, the top of his scalp sprouting bright blood that seeped through his dirty dark hair. His fingers lost strength and he slid on his belly, his face tilted toward her but his eyes blank. At the bottom he crumpled like an accordion before toppling onto his side. She considered climbing down to see if he was still alive. He could be faking; it could be a trap. She didn't think so, but it was possible. She argued against going for help, not knowing what she would say. As it was, it might seem he had fallen while climbing. There might not be any evidence she had ever been here. She wondered if she had left fingerprints on the rock she dropped on him, then remembered her basketball was somewhere on the other side of the mountain. It might be in plain sight or have fallen into a crevice and be impossible to spot. She would have to go look to find out. Staring at Leroy, unable to detect any breathing, she suddenly felt sick. She turned away to look at the mountain of pine forest sloping down toward the Magado and discovered she felt better. Taking several deep breaths, she started walking toward Devon's.

After a few steps she began to doubt that anyone would be

home. She had asked Amy to meet her at the ball courts. How long would she wait? And would she go home or somewhere else when no one was there? Maybe Lucinda would be at Devon's. Sharon could imagine telling her about Leroy. She had to tell someone. Even if he was dead, she couldn't leave him to the coyotes overnight. And what if he wasn't? What if he was slowly bleeding to death or dying from internal injuries that could easily be fixed in a hospital? She must tell someone no matter what. Even if it put her in jail? Even if she lost her athletic scholarship?

She was sweating again by the time she crossed the creek, skipping across the boulders surrounded by the lazily running water. She trotted up the bank and through the knee-high sunflowers to the road. Lucinda's blue Chevy was in the driveway. With tears blurring her vision, Sharon ran toward the gate in the unpainted picket fence. She pulled it closed behind her, hearing the latch click as she ran up the steps. The door was closed. Not seeing a doorbell, she knocked. Peering in the windows, she thought the light in the knotty pine living room seemed to hover as if with a haunted presence. To the naked eye, however, no one was home. She retreated down the steps and jogged around the house to the deck and back door. It, too, was locked. She looked uphill at the pink adobe of the widow's house gleaming through the darkly shadowed forest. Here on the deck it was warm. She sat at the redwood table and leaned back against the wall. It, too, was warm, having baked in the sun all day. That was enough for now. She would sit here and let this heat soak into her spine until someone came home and helped her with what she knew she had to do. The widow's house shone like mica through the forest, drawing her eyes again and again. Faintly she heard a radio and remembered that Mr. Wieland's brother was living there now. She stood up and followed the well-worn path through the forests' wild grasses to the edge of the widow's manicured backyard.

A fat, pink man was swimming laps nude. Not wanting to approach a naked man, Sharon stood half-hidden behind the slender white trunk of an aspen, its trembling leaves whispering above her. The man kept his head down, water washing across his face as his elbows rose and plunged, dragging his flabby butt the length of the pool. He kicked off at the deep end and plowed toward her again, his breath a bellows behind the rhythmic splashing of his arms and feet. At the shallow end he stood up. Exposing her to a full frontal view, he slicked his hair back with one hand, opened his eyes, and saw her.

"Are you the maid?" he barked.

His genitals reminded her of a huge slug slung across a pair of pale, hairy mushrooms.

"Speak up, girl!" He climbed the steps, the slug bouncing between his thighs, and waddled to a table holding a red terry-cloth bathrobe he promptly put on. Tying the sash, he faced her again. "Did Mrs. Sterling send you?"

Sharon stepped out from behind the tree, able to face him now that he was no longer nude. "She isn't home."

"Isn't she?" He studied her a long moment, then belatedly smiled. "I was beginning to think you weren't coming."

She shook her head, confused, but he had turned away and was walking toward a half-open sliding glass door. When he stepped behind a white loose-weave curtain and disappeared, she hesitantly followed him and found herself inside a soaring room. All the lines rose as if in a church. One whole wall was covered with slivers of bleached wood pointing skyward. Even the hearth, because the chimney tapered toward the roof, seemed to disappear in the distance like railroad tracks to eternity. Sharon consciously closed her mouth to hide her awe.

"All this, of course, needs dusting," the man was saying, "but I want you to start in her room. Do you know which one it is?"

Sharon shook her head, noting two brown leather suitcases at the bottom of a spiral staircase. "Are you leaving again?" she asked.

He followed her gaze, his lips pursed as if he were sucking on an invisible straw. When he looked back at her, his eyes wandered down the long line of her legs. "My passport finally arrived and I'm flying to Europe tomorrow. Would you like to come?"

"I don't know you!" she said, surprised.

He laughed. "No, of course not. Well, come along. I'll show you where the cleaning supplies are kept."

Chapter Twenty-One

Keller Construction Company was a parking lot of graders, dump trunks, and pickups below a cliff sporting a flat-roofed adobe house. Devon's old truck made the climb reluctantly and heaved to a stop on the level lot. The one-hundred-eighty-degree view was of mountains layered to the horizon. Standing at the side door of the house, Devon could also appreciate the ability to oversee the machine yard below. The door was ajar. From inside, he could hear a man speaking. Devon pushed the door open and saw the man talking into a cellphone. Around thirty, the man was tall and muscular with dark coloring. Devon could see an echo in the facial structure, an angle of the cheekbone he had noticed in Walter's portraits that gave his smile a surprised lilt. Keller motioned Devon in with a similar smile.

The room had been designed as a living room, with a kiva fireplace in one corner and expansive windows to take advantage of the spectacular view, but it was being used as an office, several tables cluttered with blueprints and scattered papers, empty coffee cups here and there, some with the fuzz of mold in their depths. Keller was talking about pipe lengths, insisting on the longer choice and apparently having difficulty getting whoever was on the other end to agree with him. Finally he said in exasperation, "I'll be there in half an hour."

Devon turned around and smiled as Keller put his cellphone back in his pocket.

"What can I do for you?" Keller asked, his light brown eyes

patient and curious.

Devon introduced himself and explained that he had been Natalie Wieland's neighbor.

Keller's eyes flashed hot with pain. With a quick blink, he shuttered them behind a manly denial. "So?"

"I don't have any right to ask," Devon said apologetically, "but how did you feel about Natalie?"

"I liked her a lot," Keller shot back. "Why *are* you asking?"

"I liked her, too," Devon said, trying to find common ground.

"That's what I heard," Keller muttered, his eyes hard.

"What, specifically?" Devon asked gently.

"I heard you were two-timing her with a woman from Berrendo."

Devon shook his head. "That's not how it was."

Keller dropped his shoulders with a short sigh. "No. Course not." He looked around. "You want some coffee? I could wash a coupla these cups and brew a pot."

"No, thanks," Devon said. "I came here hoping you could help me find the answers to some questions that've been bothering me."

"Like what?" Keller asked, guarded again.

"Are you familiar with your father's will?"

"I didn't read it. He left everything to her. What else matters?"

"And now her house belongs to Alex Wieland?"

"If he was her heir."

"You ought to read the will," Devon said. "I think the estate belongs to you."

Keller squinted at him a long moment. "What's your stake in all this?"

"I got pulled in 'cause I live next door." Devon smiled playfully. "And maybe 'cause I was a cop a while back, my nose caught the scent of a trail I couldn't resist following."

Keller laughed. "You're talking about the unnatural causes bit, aren't you?"

Devon nodded.

"The lawyer read me the will after my father's funeral, but my mind was wandering and I kept losing what he said. Figured someday I'd go back and read it word for word. The odd part is his putting that clause in prob'ly meant he suspected someone would kill him, but he hadn't had his stroke when he wrote that, so I don't know who he had in mind. Far as I know he didn't have any enemies except maybe Alex. They hadn't gotten along for years. After Walt died, all that seemed less important. Me and my dad weren't close but we got along okay. I don't have any hard feelings toward him. Some fathers are just as distant when they're living in the same house with their kids, so I didn't figure I was much worse off than most everyone else when it came to happy childhoods. I liked Natalie a lot. Even if I *had* inherited the house, I wouldn't't've kicked her out. It was her home. She deserved to keep it."

Devon waited for him to go on, then prodded, "And now?"

"I don't know Alex Wieland. I hear he's already moved in. Seems like Natalie oughta be buried 'fore he takes over like that. I got the funeral all set to go soon as the cops release her body."

Devon winced. "Why are they holding it?"

"Damned if I know. Cause of death was pretty obvious. They didn't need to do an autopsy but they did anyway."

Devon nodded.

"What an awful way to die," Keller moaned, his face raw. "You were there?"

"It happened fast," Devon said, "and the shock probably kept her from feeling pain."

"I hope she got that mercy at least." Keller squashed his emotions beneath his professional mask. "Have you found out what you wanted?"

"Yeah. Thanks for talking to me."

Keller spread his hands in frustration. "You gonna tell me what it was?"

"That it's unlikely you killed her."

"Why would I? I hadn't even seen her since my dad's funeral."

"And you never questioned the cause of his death?"

"He'd been brain dead over a year 'fore he stopped breathing. His finally letting go was a blessing for all of us."

"Mom, do you believe in my visions?" Amy asked as she drove her white Focus along Schoolhouse Road.

The green open meadows were cross-fenced with barbed wire and cedar stakes, the houses mostly modulars or double-wides. Corrals of horses with rustic stables filled the corners of every yard. The road was gravel, well-traveled, though no school had ever stood anywhere near. Chester had imparted that bit of information when they asked at Brewer's for directions to the old coal mine.

"Take Schoolhouse Road north off 380," he'd said. "Our schools've always been t'other side of town, but somebody moved a schoolhouse there from Bonita fifty-sixty years ago, so that's how come the road's got that name. Take it 'bout a mile and three-quarters and turn left on Coalora Road. That'll take you smack dab straight to it."

"There it is," Lucinda said, seeing the road sign ahead.

"You didn't answer my question," Amy said, taking the turn.

This road was dirt, muddy from last night's rain. At times she drove half off into the weeds to miss deep puddles.

"Of course I do," Lucinda said, holding on as the car bumped over the ruts.

"That's no answer," Amy said, her eyes on the road. "There's no 'of course' about it."

"No, of course not. I mean . . ." She stopped, wondering why she was floundering so badly about answering a simple question. Looking at her daughter, she said, "Yes, Amy, I believe in your visions."

Amy glanced at her warily then returned to concentrating on the rough road. "What's that mean?"

Lucinda sighed. "You don't give your mother much mercy. Can't we talk about this another, more quiet time?"

"Apparently not," Amy said, "since it's never come up before."

"Okay," Lucinda said, collecting her thoughts as she looked at the road ahead. A hill hid its final destination and made its ultimate length impossible to estimate. "I believe you're a highly creative person, and that you're attuned to thought waves most of us ignore. You perceive them as maybe more important than the ones we concentrate on, and you interpret the world according to what only you see combined with your high degree of creativity and come up with predictions that turn out quite often to be true. Not always. There's a degree of error in your cogitations, but I do believe there's something valid in your method." She leaned back and stared ahead at the swampy road, hoping Amy would be satisfied with that answer.

Amy was quiet, maneuvering through an especially wicked mud slick. "So you think it's a method?" she asked, safe on the other side.

"What do you call it?"

"A revelation," she answered too quickly. "The voice of God, I suppose."

"That's dangerous, Amy," Lucinda said, struck with worry. "It's one step from there to declaring yourself a messiah and getting burned at the stake. That still happens, you know. These days it's metaphorically and symbolically, but the destruction is equally effective."

Amy's wide blue eyes flashed with surprise. "Don't you think that's cynical, Mom?"

"No. It's rational self-defense."

Amy laughed. "I'm starting to get used to you as a blond, but I don't know if I could ever get used to you as a hard-bitten, tough-as-nails moll."

Lucinda flipped the visor down and used the mirror to tug her hair over her slowly healing wound. "I shouldn't have dyed it. Nobody likes it."

"What did Devon say when he first saw it?"

"That it may look better in daylight."

"Ouch."

Suddenly the car fishtailed on a mud slick. Amy gave it gas and the rear wheels bit into the mud and dug deep. "Shit!" she cried, throwing the transmission into reverse and spinning her wheels. Forward and back, she rocked the car until the mud sucked the tires to a dead stop. She turned off the engine and they sat listening to bubbles pop in the soup around them.

"Metaphorically, symbolically, and realistically," Amy said, "we're stuck."

Lucinda rolled her window down and leaned out. Both wheels were submerged beneath the shiny chocolate-brown mud. "We're very stuck," she said, settling back in her seat.

"There's a house," Amy said. "And damn if it that isn't a tractor! Wait here, Mom, I'll go see if he'll pull us out."

"I'll go with you," Lucinda said.

"No need for both of us to get dirty."

Amy was out the door before Lucinda could object further. She watched her daughter stride through the deep gunk toward solid ground. It was only a few steps, but they were achieved as a triumph. She turned around and grinned. Lucinda gave her a thumbs up and Amy marched off toward the farmer's tractor.

Lucinda watched her until she was a tiny matchstick person among the corralled horses and cows surrounding the house.

The door opened, but Lucinda couldn't see the person on the threshold. Gesturing at her muddy jeans, Amy didn't go inside. The door closed again and she turned with a grin and waved at Lucinda, who raised her hand above the car to wave back. After a moment, the tall skeletal farmer came out pulling on a cap. Lucinda watched them walk to the tractor. He fiddled with its innards a few minutes, climbed into the seat, adjusted a couple of levers, and turned the ignition. Even from so far away, Lucinda heard the tractor's irregular huff. The farmer held a hand down for Amy. She rode behind him, hanging onto the back of his chair as the two tiny front wheels turned, then the huge back ones shed mud as the machine crawled closer along the wet lane.

Its noise growing louder until Lucinda could hear nothing else, the tractor emerged onto the road full size. She could see the farmer's face now: long and lean, a blond beard going white, pale blue eyes beneath the brim of his gimme hat from the Lincoln County Mercantile. He nodded at her just before the tractor came so close he was hidden behind the car's roof. Here he paused to let Amy off. Lucinda reached across and opened the door so Amy could climb directly from the tractor into the car.

She put the transmission in neutral and leaned back out the window. "Okay!" she yelled up at the farmer. With a stench of diesel, the engine roared as the tractor pulled ahead. Amy put her seatbelt on as the tractor stopped and backed up. The farmer left his chair and came to the rear where Amy had stood. On his knees, he leaned to pick up a chain that seemed permanently attached to the tractor and fasten it onto the car's bumper. He climbed back into his seat and punched the gas. With a roar from the tractor, the car's wheels spun as it was yanked from the sucking mud.

The farmer didn't stop as Lucinda and Amy expected him to. Their car was towed a mile up the road and still the tractor didn't stop. They exchanged wary glances, beginning to worry. Amy tooted her horn and waved at the farmer. He appeared not to have heard. She blasted her horn longer. This time he waved but didn't turn around. She looked at Lucinda.

"Can't see as we have much choice," Lucinda said, "unless you want to climb onto the hood and try to unhook the chain."

Amy looked out the windshield, contemplating the task. "You're kidding, aren't you?"

"I wouldn't let you go if you wanted to."

"Good."

They both tried to relax enough to enjoy the odd ride, but unspoken between them was the knowledge that they weren't any closer to finding Sharon than they had been at home. Finally they saw the black macadam of Highway 380 ahead.

"He's taking us to the pavement!" Amy exulted.

"Yes," Lucinda said, relieved the farmer had turned out to be a good guy instead of the maniacal rapist she had been trying not to envision. It was the state of the country, she supposed, that she had lost faith in her fellow man, but her first inclination was to lay it closer to home. There was something mean about this mountain community, a legacy from the past, she conjectured, when cruel kingpins held the reins of political and judicial power as well as exercising the effective use of violence. There was a song Amy had played in junior high. The Tucson band was called Green on Red and the lyric Lucinda remembered was the flat-out statement that the West had been won by cheap labor and the mighty gun. The truth of that denied any romantic fantasy of heroes on horseback rescuing schoolmarms in long skirts, although Lucinda wasn't so jaded she couldn't concede the truth of that, too. Economically poor people— farmers like the one now pulling their car to the highway—had always lived by measures of honor and dignity that were capable of surviving any threat except total devastation of the social order. She had read enough pioneer memoirs to know courtship did occur and people were rescued, men as often as women, but the honor and dignity that sustained the poor's identification with culture were constantly degraded by the exploiting elite until those qualities became mere remnants of a battle flag preserved only in the minds of common folk. Still, even such scraps held a spine straight and kept sober eyes on the political machine.

The clanking of the chain made her realize the tractor had stopped and the farmer was unhooking their car. He came around to Amy's window, wiping the mud from his hands with a red kerchief he'd pulled from his overalls pocket. "You gonna be using these roads much," he advised, "you best get yourself some four-wheel drive."

"I'm just visiting from Cruces," Amy replied cheerfully. "Thanks so much for your help."

He nodded, stuffing his kerchief back in his pocket. "Where was it you was going so far out that road?"

"To the old mine," she said. "We're looking for a friend, Sharon Barela. Do you know her?"

"Angela's girl? Sure, but I ain't seen her out at the old mine anytime I can remember. And I can tell you for a fact nobody's been out there since last night 'cause there weren't no tracks through the mud in front of yours."

Amy glanced at Lucinda with a chastened smile. "We should've thought to look for tracks."

Lucinda nodded. "Guess we're not pioneer stock."

"You ain't from around here, that's plain," the farmer said. "Good luck to you ladies, and you stay on the pavement in your little rig here on out, huh?"

They both promised they would and both thanked him again, then watched him ride his tractor around them and return toward home. Slowly Amy pulled onto the highway, mud being slung off her tires sounding like hail hitting the pavement. "I should've asked him," she said, "where else in the county the ground's covered with black soil."

"There's the lava flow at Valley of Fires," Lucinda suggested.

Amy shook her head. "That doesn't seem right. I'm gonna go home and call her again. If I drive over there, her mother might get worried that you and I both are looking for her."

"Yes, she might," Lucinda said, proud of her daughter's sensitivity. "On the other hand, if Sharon truly is missing . . ."

"Her mother will figure it out soon enough, and we'll have to tell the police. At least someone will. I hope it's not me. I don't like Chief Bright, do you?"

"No," Lucinda said.

Chapter Twenty-Two

Sharon cried alone in the dark. Cramped in the small closet, she couldn't stop berating herself for walking into it in the first place. All the way to the kitchen, following the fat, pink man's butt jiggling under his red terrycloth robe, she had tried to formulate an explanation of why she was there, but the words wouldn't come together in any way that made sense. The fat man opened the closet and said there was a mop in the far corner, and she'd leaned in to get it, thinking she could do that much for him before explaining why she had come. But she looked back over her shoulder at the last minute. Seeing a white telephone on the counter, she met his small, piggy eyes and said, "I want to call the police."

The fat man frowned. "Hand me that mop first," he said.

She'd had to step over the threshold to reach the mop, and when she did, he put his pudgy, damp hand flat on her back and pushed her all the way in. The door slammed, leaving her in the dark as she listened to the lock catch. Startled, she groped and found the knob but it wouldn't turn. She kicked at the door, pounded it with her fists, and yelled for him to let her out. "I'm not the maid!" she uselessly confessed. Not that it made any sense for him to lock a cleaning lady in a closet. She shoved against the door, putting the force of her athlete's body behind her thrust, but gained only a sore shoulder. Sliding to sit down, she hugged her knees close to her breasts and cried. After a while she was quiet, but nothing else had changed. The house beyond the door was as silent as if no one were home. She sniffled, feeling sorry for herself. She worried for Leroy, too, hurt and abandoned in the mountains, maybe dead or dying, and she longed for Amy's clairvoyance to pinpoint the exact location where a rescue party was needed. But she had never truly believed Amy was psychic, and for as long as she'd known Leroy, he'd had rotten luck.

Chief Bright came to see me. I don't like his teeth. They're all even and equal, a perfectly aligned row that seems malicious somehow. And the way his cheeks puff into little balls when he laughs makes me suspect puffy balls are emblematic of his character. His professed purpose for the visit was to check on the well-being of a member of his constituency, but it wasn't long before his true desire manifested itself in his crotch. It was so obvious, I was embarrassed, but he just kept talking and grinning and balling his cheeks, all the time standing in front of where I was seated so his crotch was at eye level, more or less.

He began on a pathetic note, using the worn-down-at-the-heels rant about a police officer's life being on the line every day, that he never knew if he would see tomorrow, and that he lived in constant readiness to make that sacrifice for the good of the citizens who trusted him to keep the peace. I suspected he spelled it p-i-e-c-e in his mind.

"It's fortunate you're not married," I said. "So if it happens, you won't be leaving a widow and orphans on the dole."

He laughed, rocking back on his heels so his crowded trousers were thrust closer to my face. "Did you know 'dole' is an English word that Americans picked up from television?"

"Do you watch much television?" I asked.

"Nope," he said. "But I like to read a good dictionary."

That made me laugh in spite of myself. "Why don't you sit down?" I said, wanting his crotch out of my face.

He didn't choose a chair as I'd hoped but sat on the sofa quite close though not quite touching. Leaning near, he asked confidentially, "Do you enjoy playing games?"

I remembered the last time I trembled under the covers while waiting for a pretend-burglar in the person of Devon to find me.

Bright laughed with a conniving whine. "Have you ever wanted to fool around with a bad boy, Natalie?"

He was so disgusting, I felt myself being turned on by the masochism of submitting. "I thought cops're good boys, Gordon," I said.

He slid a little closer and began unbuttoning my blouse, deliberately doing it real slow. "We could turn it around. You could be a bad girl. Would you like that?"

"What would happen to me?" I asked, my breath so ragged I was barely able to whisper.

He opened my blouse, letting each side drop, so my breasts in their lacy white bra fluttered with my breath. "I could handcuff you to your bed and have my way with you. Would you like that?"

"You wouldn't hurt me?" I had the useless courage to ask.

He shook his head. "I'm the good guy, remember?"

So we came up here and I took my clothes off and he handcuffed me to the headboard. He had two sets of cuffs so my arms were spread wide as if I were trying to take flight. At first I raged against him when he raped me. That's what it was. I had changed my mind and didn't want it and would've stopped him if I could, but he gagged me so I couldn't scream. Probably no one would've heard me anyway, unless Devon happened to be walking outside. Bright took no chances, gagging me. I hated him fiercely that first time. Then he went away. Left the house. I heard his car leave. I laid there naked and soiled and handcuffed so I couldn't get up. He wasn't gone but fifteen minutes, he told me later, but it felt longer. I heard his car, then the front door, then his footsteps on the stairs, along the balcony, finally in my room. He acted surprised to find me like that and quickly unlocked me, ran a bath, carried me to it, and washed me as if I were a child. I fell into that role. It was what I craved right then, to be cherished and succored. He dried me with a fluffy towel and carried me to bed. The bed was fresh and clean—while I had soaked alone, he had changed the sheets—and he smelled that way, too. When he came inside me, I welcomed him in gratitude for the kindness he had shown. He was gentle; nothing like before. And though I knew I couldn't cry rape because of my acquiescence the second time, it was so sweet and I was so hurt I lapped it up like a kitten off his boot.

After that night, he felt he had a carte blanche right to enter my home. Sometimes he wouldn't knock but I would turn around in the kitchen or come out of a bathroom and see him standing there puffing his round little cheeks over his even white teeth. The first time it happened, I ordered him out. He laughed and said he knew about Walter, that the doctor had told him and they both agreed no good would come of indicting me for murder, but if it should happen to accidentally become public knowledge, then according to the stipulations of Walter's will, I would lose my house, wouldn't I? He sounded so stickily sympathetic, but because I had allowed him intimacies before, I couldn't deny him now. Away from him, I saw how manipulating he was, and I despised myself for giving in, but when I was with him, the combination of his legal power and decadent desires rendered me helpless. Often our evenings began with me on my knees much closer to his offensive crotch than I had been that first night. From there we ascended to my bedroom and the handcuffs and the period of abandonment as I lay soiled by his attentions. I often wondered what would happen if Devon stumbled onto me in that condition, but he wouldn't come without an invitation, and it was almost as if Bright knew my schedule before I myself did. Though he wasn't as good about predicting when Alex was visiting, probably because Alex and I have similar cars and in the dark or from a distance, if you couldn't see the plates, you wouldn't know which of us was going where. I wish I'd paid more attention and not dismissed it as frivolous, but Bright's reaction to the sudden appearance of my brother-in-law foreshadowed the future.

For a long time, although I saw Devon frequently when Lucinda was gone, Bright was ignorant of our affair. I had assumed he knew and didn't care. But when he grilled me about Alex, there was a meanness in his eyes that scared me. I tried to laugh it off by telling him about Alex's marriage proposal and how absurd I thought it was. Bright badgered me until I swore on a Bible that I had refused the proposal. Literally swore on a Bible. I didn't even have one in the house but he had a Gideon's in his squad car. He still didn't believe me, but the next time he came he had checked on Alex and learned I was telling the truth. Also that Alex stood to inherit the house after me as long as everyone accepted that Walter had died of natural causes. "So if necessary," Bright said with an insinuating smile, "I can make Alex into my ally in regard to you."

"What's that mean?" I wanted to know. "Do you think you own me?"

"Sweetheart," he said, sounding like a gangster in an old movie, "we're just playing here, okay? When I get bored, you'll be off the hook. Get it?"

I wondered how I could make myself so repulsive he wouldn't want me anymore, but it seemed whatever I did made him hotter. He liked me dirty, drunk, or semi-conscious from pills. All he wanted was a willing body who didn't want to be there. I fell into being that. No doubt because I felt guilty for what happened to Walter, at some pernicious level I craved punishment. And maybe, too, I thought I could come out the other end better off, having paid my debt, so to speak. If that turned out to be true, I was getting off a lot lighter than any sentence a judge would have meted out. Certainly a few weeks of sexual slavery were easier to endure than years in prison. That's what I had just escaped by caring for Walter. I didn't want to go back. But then one time Bright made Alex watch. Alex was furious at first and refused to do it until Bright mentioned the fact of my guilt, which I couldn't deny. After that, Alex sat glumly in his appointed chair and endured it as I did.

Lucinda watched the tape roll through a moment of hissing silence before she turned it off. There was more she had yet to listen to, but she dumped the recorder with the other tapes into their velvet bag she then secreted at the back of her makeup drawer in the bathroom. Catching sight of herself in the mirror, she thought her frightened expression made her look older. The blond hair was too pale; she missed the earthiness of her natural auburn. She looked at the Band-aid covering her wound and thought again how she had almost died. Natalie had died. After "enduring" the last weeks of her life, she had been murdered in her own bed. The place in the world a person felt safest. How many times had she snuggled deeper into the familiar groove in the mattress, pulled her covers like old friends closer around her? After a journey or merely a challenging day, nothing felt safer than being in bed at home. Yet it was precisely there that Natalie had been murdered.

And what a social salon her bed had turned out to be. At least two lovers visiting it regularly and one part-time voyeur. No, two. Besides Alex, there was Leroy. One willing and one coerced voyeur. One lover pretending to assault her, the other actually doing it. Did Devon bear less guilt because his was the pretense? Lucinda hated that he had been involved at all with that sordid quintet. His ignorance of the others might have excused him if the games he played with the widow hadn't been different only in degree from the ones Bright played, but Lucinda couldn't see that the evidence on the tape so far had identified any of the widow's lovers as being more likely her killer. She decided Natalie's mistake had been accepting Bright's punishment: once a woman gave a man *carte blanche,* nothing but submission could follow. From what Lucinda had heard on the tapes, either Alex or Bright could have killed Natalie: Alex because he blamed her for involving him in such a seamy scenario, or Bright because one of their games went too far. The games Devon played were so far below that flashpoint, Lucinda didn't suspect him of having harmed the widow, but the lesson

Natalie's death taught was to always maintain autonomy in a love affair. Lucinda wondered if her accident hadn't been a subliminal message to Devon that she was as helpless as the widow had been. She had to find a way to reassert the strength of her position vis-à-vis his, to assure both of them that she wouldn't be a needy dependent but an equal partner.

From the front of the house, she heard the screen door open and assumed it was Devon coming home. She met her own eyes in the mirror, wondering why she didn't share the tapes with him, why she was torturing herself by doling them out for listening with gaps of time between. After hearing one she always felt soiled and wished she hadn't listened, but like a teenager with a dirty book, she kept it hidden so she could privately indulge herself again. She wondered if maybe Devon hadn't felt like this about actually seeing the widow, this craving that got under your skin and made you itch for more. If so, it was nothing she wanted to share with him. She stood up a little straighter and walked out to welcome him home with a kiss.

The living room was empty. She walked through to the sun porch and saw Leroy's blood-streaked face through the window. Beneath the dried rivulets, he looked pale. Quickly she opened the door. "For heaven's sake, Leroy, what happened?"

"Is Sharon here?" he asked plaintively.

Lucinda felt a surge of panic. "We were looking for her earlier."

Amy came from her room and stood staring at Leroy. "Do you know where she is?"

He shook his head, his teary eyes bewildered.

Devon thought Matt Keller was too casual about not making a claim on his father's estate. Maybe he had enough money, owning a construction company and probably the real estate it operated from, and didn't want to become embroiled in challenging the will. But if Devon had suspected someone of murdering his father, even if no money were involved, he wouldn't let go until he knew the truth. A mitigating factor was Walter Wieland's coma. Releasing him from that after fourteen months couldn't be seen as anything other than an act of mercy unless the motive was money. But if Natalie killed Walter, neither Alex nor Matt could think he was improving his chances of inheriting the estate by killing her. On the other hand, either of them could have killed Walter as a favor to Natalie, not knowing the act disinherited her. If the killer didn't know that, he wouldn't have known Alex was the next beneficiary of Walter's will, which was an odd fact in itself given that Walter and Alex hadn't gotten along. The importance of that conjecture was canceled by the fact of Walter's murder, regardless of who had killed him. It didn't make sense for either Alex or Natalie to have done it, though experience had taught Devon that murders didn't always make sense. Acts of passion—jealousy or paranoia—often propelled people off precipices they hadn't anticipated and which, in retrospect, were illogical. In all probability, Natalie had killed her husband out of sheer frustration at his condition and her resulting confinement. If Alex subsequently killed Natalie, it could be because he was insanely jealous of a woman who had rejected him, which surely wouldn't be the first such murder in history, but it was unlikely the man would move in while her blood was still wet on the wall. Devon felt fairly certain Matt hadn't killed her. So who was left? Leroy? Or maybe, as Sharon had suggested, the killer had come from somewhere else, left no clues, and vanished. If Devon were the investigating detective, he'd look in her past for someone who carried a grudge, since no one local seemed an obvious suspect. But that belied his earlier suspicion that the timing of Natalie's murder had been arranged for his benefit. To cut someone's throat and get out of the house mere minutes before someone else arrived was due to either blind luck or intricate planning.

Turning into his driveway, he saw his house brightly lit. It was such an unusual experience that at first he felt alarmed. Then he remembered Lucinda was there and felt a surge of pleasure. All joy disappeared, however, when she came out the front door, her expression rigid with worry. He met her at the gate. "What's wrong?"

She smiled, her eyes softening almost to tears. "I thought I was hiding it."

He pulled her into his arms and held her tight, whispering close to her ear, "Don't ever hide anything from me. Whatever it is, we're in it together."

She broke their embrace and met his eyes. "Sharon's missing. And Leroy's here with a story you'll have to hear from him to believe."

Leaving the women at home, Devon drove Leroy to Sharon's house prior to again taking him to the hospital. Devon had listened to the kid's story with growing irritation. It seemed everything Leroy turned his hand to resulted in a disaster of lesser or greater magnitude. He had attempted to approach Sharon, which was how he told it, admitting he had a bottle opener in his hand that could have been perceived as a weapon, but all he wanted was to talk to her. When she ran, he did, too, hoping to catch her. In the mountains, it became a game. At least that was his version. He had seen the rock falling but hadn't had time to think what it meant. Since then he'd felt too confused, especially after learning she was missing, to know what to think about any of it.

When they reached the Barela home, Devon took Leroy with him to the front door. It was a modest house with a basketball hoop over the garage door. The driveway was slanted, though, and Devon could understand why Sharon preferred practicing on the school's courts. The woman who opened the door resembled her daughter in everything but height. Angela Barela was petite and pretty, with the same lustrous, long, dark hair as Sharon's, only Angela's was pinned up, not falling free from a ponytail. Her makeup, too, was that of a mature woman, the mauve shadow above her eyes suggestive of wearying wisdom. Glancing back and forth between Devon and Leroy, a spark of alarm flashed in the depths of her eyes.

Before Devon had spoken, she asked stridently, "Do you know where is Sharon?"

He shook his head. "Leroy saw her in the mountains a coupla hours ago."

Angela glowered at Leroy. "Did you leave her there alone, Mr. Gentleman?"

He hung his head, revealing the blood matted thick on his wound.

Angela gasped. "How you get hurt?"

"A rock fell on my head," he mumbled.

"Probably Sharon throw it at you, no? Probably you were chasing her with bad ideas. Is that what you were doing, Leroy?"

He shook his head, then shrugged.

She looked at Devon, her dark eyes hopeful.

Belatedly, he introduced himself.

"I know who you are," she said.

He wondered what that meant. Carefully he explained that Leroy had shown up at his house looking for Sharon, that he was taking the boy to the medical center to be treated but had stopped here hoping Sharon was home.

"She was s'posed to be home at four o'clock," Angela said. "She's three hours late, no? I called the police but they said she's not late enough for them to look."

"Did you talk to Chief Bright?" Devon asked.

She shook her head. "That new one, Officer Reese. He said she's prob'ly with friends having a good time and will be home in a while. But Sharon don't do things like this. When she's s'posed to be somewhere, she gets there on time. Being late's not like her, and I'm worried, Mr. Gray. Thank you for stopping. If you see her, please tell her come home, no?"

Driving the winding curves of Highway 48 south, Devon thought Angela Barela was a typical Hispanic housewife, obedient to authority and modest in her demands. The house behind her had seemed empty, and he felt sorry that she was alone in her worry. Thinking of Lucinda and Amy, who were worried, too, he would have much preferred being with any of them than driving a troublesome kid to a hospital for the second time. He glanced away from the moonlit road long enough to catch Leroy watching him.

"Awesome of you," the kid mumbled, "to do this for me again."

"I was just thinking the same thing," Devon said.

"Guess you prob'ly think I'm more trouble'n I'm worth."

Devon laughed gently. "Everyone's worth the trouble when they need help."

Leroy nodded. "I'd like to tell you something, Mr. Gray, if you promise not to get mad."

Devon looked far ahead to where the moonlit highway ran like milk around the edge of Angus Hill. A few cars were coming down, their headlights vanishing and reappearing from behind the curves. He thought their intermittent lights were like his life, flashing between safety and fear, comfort and threat, progress and lost ground. Knowing the road between them was a sliver between a cliff and a precipice, he concentrated on the luminous center line when he coaxed, "What is it you want to tell me, Leroy?"

223

The kid sniffed loudly and looked out his side window a moment, his face reflected back at Devon like a ghost riding on the running board. "You know that knife in your yard?"

"I remember it well," Devon said.

"I found it in the ditch alongside Hope Garden Road, you know the one to the cemetery?"

"Yeah?"

"Only, see, it used to be mine."

"Did you put it in my yard?"

"I'm getting to that part," the kid said impatiently. "I want to tell you this other part first."

Devon took his foot off the brake and let his truck pick up speed as they crossed the Bonito River bridge. Ahead lay Angus Hill, an eight-percent grade climbing a mile and a half to the crest. "I'm listening," he said, watching his tachometer slowly rise.

"My dad died in Desert Storm," Leroy said, his voice gaining strength as the truck's engine worked hard enough to drown him out. "The Marine Corp sent his stuff back. They called it a locker but it was a metal trunk full of stuff. Inside was this Turkish knife. I liked it and thought it'd be mine someday, but when my mom remarried, she sold all that stuff in a yard sale."

Devon winced. "Too bad for you," he said sympathetically.

Leroy shrugged. "Old Man Spivits bought it. He was so old, he'd been in World War Two! I paid attention and saw that he was the one who bought the trunk. I thought maybe I could buy it back from him but he wanted fifty dollars for the knife. Wasn't fair. He only paid twenty-five for the whole lot, but he was mean and wouldn't come down."

Beyond Leroy's window, the world fell away in a three-hundred-foot drop off the side of the mountain. Only a low guardrail separated the road from thin air. "What'd you do?" Devon asked.

Leroy sniffed again. "Old Man Spivits was a drunk. He got arrested lots of times for raising a ruckus in the village. The last time it happened . . ." Leroy turned on the seat to watch Devon. "He died in his sleep in the drunk tank."

Devon was beginning to catch the kid's drift. "Did he have the knife on him when he was arrested?"

"Yeah," Leroy said. "So it ended up in the evidence room. It wasn't evidence, but being as nobody claimed the old man's body or asked for his belongings, it just got stuck there."

"No pun intended," Devon said. "How'd you get it out?"

"I didn't! I told you I found it on the cemetery road. It was just laying there in the ditch. I wouldn't've seen it if there hadn't been a bright moon that night. I saw it shining and went down and saw it was my dad's knife."

"When was that?"

"Real late Friday night. I was on my way home when I saw it."

"Where had you been?"

"Out at the house on Diamond Peak."

Devon sighed, feeling sorry for the kid so lonely he spent his Friday nights alone in an abandoned house. But he stifled his compassion to stay on focus. "By Saturday afternoon, the knife was in my yard."

"I put it there Friday night. Walking home, I looked at it under a streetlight and saw it had blood all over it. Looked like blood, anyway, and what else would be on a knife? It was fresh, too, 'cause some came off on my hands. So then I was worried that 'cause I'd handled it and got blood on me, I'd look guilty if anyone found me with it. Walking by your yard, I got the idea to plant it there. I figured unless you'd done whatever had happened with that knife you'd get out of it eventually, but in the meantime you'd go through a lot of hassles and I kinda wanted that to happen 'cause of the way Sharon's got the hots for you and won't look at me twice." His voice rose to a squeaky plea. "I know it was stupid, Mr. Gray, and I hope you're not mad 'cause I told you."

"I'm glad you told me, Leroy, but your jealousy's misdirected. There's nothing going on between me and Sharon."

The kid sighed. "She won't ever like me now no matter what."

"Were you wearing gloves when you handled the knife?"

"No."

"So your prints are on it. Did you think of that?"

"I only thought about the trouble it was gonna get you in."

The road crested the hill and rolled flat between a sudden strip of lights. Devon looked at the kid in the neon glare. "If it comes to that, will you testify in court to what you just told me?"

Leroy looked out the window at the closed stores with their empty parking lots under amber lights, all of it surrounded by the dark forest sprinkled with patches of moonlight. "It ain't gonna happen, 'cause you know as much as me who took that knife from the evidence room."

"Who do you think took it?" Devon asked, thinking there were probably half a dozen possibilities.

"You know when you caught me looking in the window at Sharon?"

Devon nodded, remembering his delayed intention to question Leroy as the neighborhood's peeping Tom.

"I used to do that at Mrs. Wieland's house, too. She hardly ever closed her drapes, you know, and she swam without any clothes on a lot, at night, too, with her house all lit up behind her. You must've seen her from your yard sometimes."

Devon repressed a smile at the pleasant memory. "Yeah, I did."

"I saw you, too," Leroy said softly.

Devon braked for the red light at Cree Meadows. "Saw me

doing what?"

"Coming and going, mostly going real late at night, sometimes still buttoning your shirt when you came out her door."

Devon stifled a surge of anger at being spied on. "Who else did you see?'

"That man living there now. Mr. Wieland's brother, I guess."

"Half-brother," Devon said. "Anyone else?"

Leroy sniffed softly. "Chief Bright. I saw him lots of times."

"Did you tell him you put the knife in my yard?"

"No, sir. I just told him it was there."

CHAPTER TWENTY-THREE

The possibility that Chief Bright could have killed Natalie and been playing with him all this time nagged at Devon through the tedious hospital admission process. When the clerk, the same young woman who had admitted Leroy after he fell through the floor, asked if she should again charge the Salado Police Department, Devon nodded, halfway hoping she would call and make him talk to the chief. But she simply wrote down the account numbers and sent Leroy to triage. The nurse there briefly examined his head wound and admitted him into the emergency room. Devon followed, wanting to hear an encouraging diagnosis before he left. To his surprise, the attending physician was the same Dr. Tanner who had attended Walter Wieland's death.

As he examined Leroy, Dr. Tanner kept glancing at Devon, but they didn't speak until the kid was on a gurney en route to X-ray. Dr. Tanner nodded for Devon to follow him the opposite direction down the neon-bright corridor decorated with colorful prints of Navajo rugs. Reminded of the rug in front of Natalie's hearth, Devon felt a prick of pain puncture the paralyzing numbness of his depression. Natalie had been so animated as she emerged from the forced hibernation of her husband's coma; now she was a cold corpse in a morgue somewhere inside this same building. His knees melted from beneath him and he sat down hard on the black, fake leather sofa. From above him,

Dr. Tanner asked if he was all right. Devon told the doctor he was fine.

"I won't know the boy's condition until I see the X-rays," Tanner said, sitting a scant stretch away, "but his eyes are clear and he appears lucid, both of which are good signs."

Devon nodded, remembering the boy he had twice brought in to be examined. Leroy had first fallen through the rotten floor of his father's abandoned house, then had a rock dropped on his head by the girl he was in love with, which added up to pretty bad luck for a kid on the threshold of life. Devon looked at the doctor and saw Tanner studying him as if he were the patient. "I'm surprised to find you working ER."

"I do it on rotation twice a month," Tanner said. "We're a small community and there aren't a lot of us to cover the bases." He paused, as if calculating a risk. "That's how I happened to attend Walter Wieland. It was my shift on ER. I wasn't his regular doctor."

A notch clicked in Devon's mind, something he hadn't thought to pursue but was now provided. "I was under the impression you attended him at home."

Tanner shook his head. "The EMS technicians did what they could—which was nothing, he had expired before they arrived—then brought him here."

"And you pronounced him dead?"

Tanner nodded.

"Was Chief Bright anywhere around?"

"It wasn't until the next morning that he spoke with me in my office."

"What'd he say?"

"Just inquiring into the death of someone in his jurisdiction. I told him the same thing I told you the other day. He and I agreed justice would best be served by maintaining silence. Are you now going to break that and put everyone concerned in jeopardy?"

Devon shook his head. "I agree with your decision."

Tanner dropped his shoulders. "Thank you." He smiled half-apologetically. "I've amended the death certificate. The revised cause is homicide by suffocation. The state coroner's office told me Chief Bright will be notified by mail in a week to ten days."

"That'll change things," Devon said.

"Since the widow's deceased now, too, I don't see what."

"Once she's suspected of killing Walter, it's a logical next step to think her murder was motivated by revenge."

"Who would avenge the death of someone brain-dead?"

"I don't know," Devon said.

Tanner nodded at a nurse beckoning him from the end of the hall. "Don't overlook the possibility," he told Devon, "that any connection may be inconsequential."

That wasn't likely, Devon told himself as he drove down the mountain alone. Natalie had killed her husband for the obvious reasons. If not a repercussion of that, what other motive would anyone have to kill Natalie? There was Amy's jealousy theory. As far as he knew, Natalie had three lovers. Since he hadn't killed her, that left Alex and Chief Bright as suspects. Devon winced, thinking back to when he had assumed he was her only lover. His ego had made him an idiot. But berating himself for it now wouldn't help. He had to look to the future, figure his wisest plan of action from here. Unable to believe Alex had the cool to pull off a most difficult m.o., he was left again with Bright. Devon thought back over their encounters since Natalie's death. The take-out lunch, the tug-of-war over Leroy, Bright missing the planted knife when he arrested the kid for peeping at the girls, then finding it on an informant's tip. The informant being Leroy, whom Tanner had kept overnight for observation. Mild concussion was the diagnosis.

Devon was glad the kid had been admitted, because any way he tried to figure the scenario, Chief Bright came out as a dangerous antagonist. For one thing, if the chief was guilty, he'd be only too happy to pin Natalie's murder on someone else. Devon had no alibi and only a feeble excuse for being on the scene. His witness that the alleged murder weapon had been planted on his property was a teenager with a loose screw, a boy who had fondled the knife enough to obliterate any prints but his own, so the fact that Devon's weren't on it wouldn't mean much. It almost seemed he was being framed, but he couldn't figure who would bother. He didn't have any enemies in this county. Yet a case against him was coming together, his freedom salvageable only on the testimony of a boy Bright would just as soon be rid of.

Devon was sweating by the time he turned into his driveway. Inside the dark house, presumably asleep, was a woman trying to deny that her love for him would drag her into one murder after another. It wasn't what he wanted to give her. He had tried to leave Lucinda, but when she followed him he had welcomed her. He remembered thinking as he watched her walk through the gate, This must be what happiness feels like. It had been decades since he'd felt anything remotely comparable. Believing he would have to be something other than a lonely human to refuse being nestled in the heart of a family—the buffer it provided offered the only protection he knew of from the cruelty rampant in the world—he now told himself to face that alone, leave without going inside, abandon the house and everything in it to be disposed of at public auction. Because if he went in, either Amy or Lucinda would wake up and he would have to explain why he was packing, where he was going, and what he hoped to find at the end of nowhere.

On the other hand, he could gather the blessings of their

beauty one more time, maybe enough to sustain him a while, send them back to bed, and make his escape better prepared than if he left empty-handed. And, too, he could find out what they had learned about Sharon's whereabouts—hopefully put his sympathy for Angela Barela to rest—and leave knowing at least someone was safe. Would Amy and Lucinda be in jeopardy without him? Unable to imagine why anyone would want to hurt them, he couldn't understand that about Natalie either. She had been a good woman driven nearly mad by loneliness and isolation, but she was coming out of it. Or so he had thought. That was when he'd also thought he was her only lover. So she wasn't isolated by loneliness. She was two-timing three men, and one of them had killed her. If it was Alex, he had to be a cold-blooded s.o.b. to move in when her blood was still on the wall. Though he didn't like the man, Devon couldn't bring himself to believe that of Alex, but enough suspicion floated around the half-brother-in-law that he couldn't leave Amy and Lucinda alone right next door. He had to send them back to Berrendo without letting on that he meant to leave too as soon they were out the door. He disliked being duplicitous but their safety meant more to him than any self-appeasing sense of honorable honesty.

This period of penance is becoming wearisome. God, I hate possessive men. Their world view is limited to I-me-mine and the rest of the pronouns don't exist except in relation to his almighty I.

He bruised me tonight. First time. I have the imprints of his fingers on my arms from when he shook me. Didn't feel them at the time, just my neck wobbling like it'd break clean off. He was pissed, he said, 'cause last night when he was going over to talk to our neighborhood peeping Tom's stepfather, who lives a couple houses down from Devon, he was driving by Devon's yard and saw him walking through the boulders toward my house. Our illustrious chief of police claims he was about to come inquire if I needed to be rescued when he saw me greet my guest on the patio. My enthusiasm, he said, made Devon's welcome evident.

At that point I hadn't yet realized how angry Bright was. I had assumed he wouldn't care. It's not like whatever's going on between us is any kind of romance. I was more curious about what would happen to Leroy. It was frightening to look out from my dark house and see him watching in such a posture as to make me think he'd been there a long time. I would think back over what he had seen me do before I turned the lights off, whether it might be embarrassing, but ultimately whatever I had done was under the assumption of being alone. Protection against the infringement of privacy is guaranteed in our constitution. I think. Anyway it should be. I don't like peeping Toms and I expect my chief of police to protect me from them, but still in all I was concerned for the boy. "What's gonna happen to him?" I asked.

"His stepdaddy promised to take a belt to his butt next time they see each other. That's the best I could get."

"Pretty poor," I said, "when it comes to solutions."

"I'd beat the shit out of the kid myself," he said, "if I thought it would help, but right now I want to know how long you've been inviting your neighbor into your bed."

I smiled, trying to tease, and asked, "Which neighbor?"

He slapped me. He'd never done that unless I was handcuffed in bed and it was part of the game. I told him I'd had enough and didn't want to see him anymore. He laughed and asked how I planned to keep him out. He was standing by the sliding glass door, and he pulled his gun and smashed the butt down on the latch. Then he grinned at me like what he'd done was real clever. When I told him I could get it fixed in the morning, he said the only locksmith in the village was in the hospital and the next closest was backed up with a week of work.

"So you've made me defenseless," I said. "Why do you want to do that?"

"I've just made it easier for your menagerie of lovers," he

answered. "Maybe I'll send a few more your way. I get men in the drunk tank lots of times that I'd let loose if they had somewhere to go."

I didn't know what to say. I just stared at him. I hadn't known such despicable people existed. I mean, I'd known, but I hadn't met one face to face. On first glance he looked like a Boy Scout, and I guess he must seem that way on paper, too, having been hired as chief of police. But his core is bad. I know that now. I'm thinking of using those tickets in my bureau. I could arrange with a Realtor to rent my house and just disappear in Europe for a few years. Alex will try to move in as soon as I'm gone if I don't rent it out. I don't think I could regain possession once he gets settled in, and I certainly don't want him for a roommate, so I have to act to find an overseer immediately. A lawyer maybe. Why not Walter's? It's all the same estate.

The machine clicked off at the end of the reel. Lucinda watched the glow from the red light dissipate into the darkness. Only the last tape remained to be heard all the way through. It had ended with the widow's flat statement that Bright had something evil planned followed by her plea for Devon to hurry and arrive before the tape was spent. What Lucinda had heard after that was the hiss of silence, but she hadn't listened all the way to the end. More might be recorded, maybe even the murder. She rolled over in bed and faced Devon's empty side, remembering this was how it had started. After having left home a day early and driven two hours to be with him, she first had to wait in his empty house and then to wake in his empty bed. Both times he had been with Natalie. Where was he now? Chasing her killer, he'd said, or at least searching for clues. Lucinda couldn't help wonder if he wasn't a detective by definition and incapable of expanding himself to include being a husband, too.

Devon sat in his truck parked in his driveway. He had killed his engine and coasted to a stop to diminish the noise of his arrival as much as possible, apparently successfully because no lights had come on in the house. He wondered if that meant Sharon had been found. She had probably returned home unharmed, having thoughtlessly failed to tell anyone where she was going. Most cases of missing teenagers ended like that. It was possible, however, that she thought she had severely injured Leroy and had run away rather than face the consequences. Some women didn't believe they had a right to self-defense. He wondered if Natalie had been one of them. Except for those gruesome few seconds when he watched her die, the last time he'd seen her was in the café.

Most mornings, after he'd been laying rocks a few hours, hunger for food and a desire for companionship urged him to shower and drive to the café in town. Sitting alone in a booth among the almost exclusively male customers—mostly cowboys in starched shirts and scuffed boots—their conversations hummed around him while he read a newspaper and the waitresses—single mothers with big butts and broad smiles—showered him with attention. He was a social animal, after all, his energy chafing against idleness dripping like a broken faucet waiting for someone to bang it with a wrench or disconnect it all together. That morning he had glanced up from his *Ruidoso News* to see Natalie standing just inside the door looking lost. He laid his paper down, watching her eyes search the room for someone to latch onto. She was quivering with fright, almost hyperventilating, perhaps approaching full-blown hysteria. Ever the gentleman, Devon stood up. She caught the movement and met his eyes. When he smiled and gestured for her to join him, she jerked her gaze around the room to see who else was watching. Seeing that nearly everyone was, her eyes on Devon were frantic. He smiled again, this time with a teasing light, throwing her a challenge, a dare as if between children: *if you're worth anything, you can do it.* She walked like oil on rocks across the stained linoleum to his booth, where she slid in while he sat down. They smiled across the Formica and newsprint between them, and from the suggestive way she licked her lips, he knew he'd made a mistake.

He reasoned she was his neighbor, that was cause enough to greet her in a friendly manner, offer to share his booth when the only other seating was at the counter. The village, though, would connect them now. No getting around that. She was biting her lip, watching him. He smiled with encouragement. "How about some breakfast?"

She opened her purse and rummaged through what looked like a couple dozen blue tissues. Without looking up, she said, "I don't seem to have any money."

"My treat," he said.

Her head bobbed up over her open tissue bin. She squashed them back inside and snapped the purse shut, watching him all the time. "What'll I have?"

Standing behind the counter, the waitress was watching him. Half the people in the room were. "Menu," he said, mouthing the word without sound. She jerked into action. He guzzled his coffee, figuring on getting a refill while she was there. The large, glossy menu covered the table before he put his cup down. The carafe of steaming hot coffee tipped its contents to give him his refill as the waitress asked Natalie, "You want coffee, hon?"

"Please," Natalie whispered.

The waitress turned a cup right side up in its saucer, filled it to the brim, and left.

Natalie stared at the menu as if it were a Rosetta stone of undecipherable secrets. Suddenly she laid it aside and met his eyes. "I've been here before. The food's mediocre, at best."

He nodded. "Only show in town, though."

She sniffed. "You could've come to my house. I make excellent omelettes."

The waitress brought Devon's plate of *huevos rancheros.* "What'll it be, hon?" she asked Natalie.

"One pancake, please," Natalie said.

The waitress left.

"You mind?" Devon asked, picking up his fork.

Natalie shook her head, then looked around rather than watch him eat. He watched her, noting her makeup was meticulously done. So despite her apparent fright when she'd come in the door, her arrival hadn't been impetuous. Had she come looking for him? Or was it someone else she'd been trying to spot with her frantic gaze? Or maybe she was simply surveying her fellow villagers to see if in their eyes she wore a scarlet M on her breast. No one seemed to be sheltering those thoughts. As far as Devon could tell, the cowboys' attention aimed at Natalie was sympathetic curiosity at her first appearance in public after her recent widowhood.

Her pancake arrived with a plastic pitcher of syrup. Natalie stared at the melting slab of margarine as the waitress asked, "Anything else, hon?"

Devon met her eyes and sent her on her way. Natalie watched the slab melt as he cleaned his plate, wiping up the last streak of chili with a scrap of his last tortilla. "You gonna eat that or just watch it melt?" He sipped his coffee.

"Do you want it?" Defiantly.

He shook his head.

She poured a thin line of syrup in a circle around the margarine, then cut a sliver of pancake and put it in her mouth. She set her fork down and leaned back as she chewed. When she had swallowed, he asked, "How was it?"

She shrugged. "I saw your girlfriend arrive at your house."

He caught on to at least part of her motive for coming to the café—Lucinda wasn't due until tomorrow—but he had no clue as to why Natalie thought that news was so urgent. "So you felt you had to come tell me?"

She nodded.

"Thanks," he said, looking for the waitress to bring his check.

Natalie leaned forward and whispered, "Can I see you to-night?"

The waitress came. "Anything else, hon?"

"Just the check," he said, watching Natalie.

The waitress stood there, writing it down, adding it up, eyeing the pancake with one sliver missing. She laid the check face down in front of Devon, took his empty plate, and skedaddled. He turned the check over and reached for his wallet.

"Will you come after midnight?" Natalie whispered.

He laid money on top of the check and met her eyes. "Can't promise."

"But you'll try?"

He nodded. "Let me walk you out." Not that he wanted her on his hands, but he didn't trust her alone in public. He wasn't sure what he expected her to do, just that it could get messy and he was a tad too close.

A week later, after sitting in his driveway staring at his dark house a while, he started his truck and drove back toward the village.

Chapter Twenty-Four

It was after midnight and the police station was empty except for Officer Reese at the desk. He recognized Devon and smiled a welcome to his lonely shift. In his early twenties, Reese had a honey-blond crewcut, placid brown eyes, and a body fit for the ring, his biceps so buff they seemed about to break through the seams of the starched sleeves of his dress shirt. Devon accepted a cup of coffee, not because he wanted any but to increase the camaraderie between himself and the officer. While Reese was pouring it, Devon noticed the duty log open on his desk. After they were both settled into chairs with their feet up on opposite sides of that desk, blowing on the steaming coffee to cool it enough to drink, Devon casually said, "Mrs. Barela called my house earlier looking for her daughter, Sharon. Did the girl ever come home?"

Reese shook his head. "I'd be worried, too, if she was my kid, but the chief said teenagers pull stunts like this all the time and we gotta wait twenty-four hours 'fore treating her like a missing person."

Devon nodded. "Did you have a guy named Spivits die in the drunk tank a while back?"

"Yeah. Ticker quit while he was asleep. Easy way to go 'cept he wasn't home."

"Any relatives ever collect his property?"

Reese stood up and crossed the room to an old gray file cabinet. He squatted to open the bottom drawer and find the log he wanted. "Nothing here," he said. "I can check the storeroom if you want."

Devon smiled. "If you wouldn't mind."

"Feels good to move," Reese said with a laugh, disappearing around a corner.

After a second, Devon heard a door open at the end of the short hall. He stood up and walked around the desk to flip the pages of the duty log back to the Friday night Natalie was killed. The time slots were littered with penciled notations:

6:15 Barking canine; officer sent.

7:21 Domestic dispute; man arrested, trans. to C.D.C. by chief.

8:37 Horse running loose on 380; animal control sent.

8:45 Chief called in from C.D.C.

8:54 Forced entry reported, appt for investigation in a.m.

9:50 Tourist requested directions to Tularosa.

10:10 Prowler reported; officer sent, phones to R.P.D.

11:15 Officer back at desk.

12 a.m. shift change.

1:05 Barking canine; officer sent after switching phones to R.P.D.

1:25 Officer back at desk.

2:50 Speeder radar from office, state police called.

3:10 Homicide reported, officer sent, switched phones to R.P.D.

5:55 Day dispatcher arrives. Resume phones from R.P.D. paged chief.

6:10 Paged chief.

6:20 Paged chief.

6:32 Paged chief.

7:00 State Officer M.A. Wilton arrives to head investigation.

8:15 Chief resumes command.

Hearing Reeves close the door and start back, Devon sat down and picked up his coffee cup.

"Nothing there," Reese said. "Why're you interested?"

"Leroy Culler told me Spivits bought his father's stuff at a garage sale. I was just wondering if any of it was still around."

Reese sipped his coffee standing by the desk. His gaze fell on the duty log open to the Friday before. He met Devon's eyes. "Something happen a week ago you're curious about?"

"That's an understatement," Devon said.

"Yeah, I guess." Reese looked at the log, sipping his coffee. "First murder we have in this village and the chief's tied up in 'Zozo booking a wife beater into county detention. Bad luck, wouldn't you say?" He closed the ledger and sat down.

"Do you know what time he left the CDC that night?"

Reese picked up the phone. After a moment he said, "Yeah, Marty, Tony here. Listen, I got a gap in my log. Can you check yours and tell me when Chief Bright left your place last Friday night?" He smiled at Devon as they waited. "Thanks, Marty." He hung up and said, "Ten-thirty."

"So where was he?"

Reese shrugged. "I'll help you poke around as much as I can, but I ain't conducting any investigation of my superior without I get orders from higher up."

"Did you know he was creaming the widow?"

"Seems she was busy," Reese said, his eyes teasing.

"Do you think he could be pushed over the edge by a woman?"

"Do you know a man who couldn't?"

"Me," Devon said, then admitted sheepishly, "now that I'm sober."

The next time he parked in front of his house, a light shone from the kitchen. He looked at his watch in the glow from the dash and saw it was a minute or two after three. Quietly he let himself in. Watching him from where she sat at the dining room table, Lucinda was wearing a white cotton nightgown under her floral silk robe, open and its sash untied. The deep shadows under her eyes were either from fatigue or bad lighting, he wasn't sure, but her blond hair shimmered like spun gold. Though he couldn't believe she had dyed her beautiful auburn hair to look like a thousand other women wearing the same bottled color, he smiled and lied, "Your hair looks nice."

"You don't like it," she said. "I don't need any false compliments."

He shrugged. "I've yet to see it in daylight, it's just that I liked the old color better."

A bulb flickered out in the brass chandelier above her. When she looked up at it, the shadows under her eyes disappeared but her hair falling away from her neck revealed her naked wound as a red, puckered seam, and he suddenly understood why she'd done it. Gently he said, "It'll grow out again."

She met his eyes. "Where've you been?"

He went to the refrigerator for an O'Doul's, opened it, and came back sipping from the beading bottle. Starting with his visit to Mrs. Barela, then his trip to the hospital, and finally the police station, he recounted what he'd learned. She seemed to listen impassively, as if she didn't care, or as if everything he was saying was of no consequence. When he finished, he asked, "Did Sharon show up?"

Lucinda shook her head.

"Where's Amy?"

"Asleep, finally, but she'll be up again soon. She's terribly worried and feels bad because she can't intuit where Sharon is."

Devon snorted, feeling the beer's carbonation sting his nose. "If that were really possible, police work would be a helluva lot easier."

"Yes," she said. "How's Leroy?"

"He'll be all right. I wonder, though, if maybe Sharon assumed she'd killed him and ran away."

"That doesn't sound like her. She's pretty level-headed."

Devon stood up and set his half-finished beer in the sink. The first sips tasted good but, without alcohol, the beverage wasn't as rewarding as it had been. He pulled his shirttails out as he walked into his bedroom. On top of the blue comforter lay a tiny black recorder and several loose tapes beside a small, black velvet bag. "You been taping your life story?" he teased, facing her from within the room as he unbuttoned his shirt.

She stood up and walked toward him, slowly and deliberately, he thought, as if she were on stage and her movements significant to the plot. She turned off the dining room light, came into the bedroom, and closed the door. "It's Natalie's," she said.

He stared at her, stopping himself from asking if she meant Natalie Wieland, knowing it was an idiotic question. He looked at the tapes. There was one in the recorder, played maybe halfway through.

"That one was in it when I found it," Lucinda said.

"When was that?" he asked, watching her again.

"Two days ago," she said.

"Why didn't you tell me?"

"I wanted to hear them first."

He tried to hide his anger. "Have you?"

She nodded. "All except what's left of that one."

He looked at the tiny black splotch on his immense blue bed, then at her again. "Why didn't you tell me?" he asked again, having a hard time believing she would withhold anything so important.

She took a moment, then said, "I wanted to hear what she

said about you, to think it over before you and I talked about it."

"So?" he asked, feeling defensive. "What'd she say?"

"That the strength of the bond between you and her rose from a mutual need to believe in your goodness after having killed."

They stared at each other across the softly lit bedroom, the wind like a mouse at the window.

"What's that say about us, Devon? What's the strength of our bond based on?"

"Evidently not trust."

"Listen to the tapes," she said, her voice almost breaking. "I'll sleep with Amy tonight."

"Don't, Lucinda," he said, regretting his angry retort.

But she was gone before he'd finished saying her name. He watched the door close, then looked at the tapes on the bedspread, walked over and saw they were numbered. Not having asked if Lucinda used gloves when she handled them, he took a clean hankie from a drawer and sheathed his finger in the cloth as he pushed the rewind button. When the tape clicked to a stop, he took it out, put in the one marked No. 1, and pushed play.

"I am Natalie Rowan Wieland, a widow aged fifty-eight years," she said in the lonely quiet of his bedroom, a place she had never been. *"I'm making this tape because I want the truth to come out. I don't care about my guilt anymore. What I did is far less reprehensible than what's happening to me. I'm leaving this record so people will know."*

Listening to her describe with affectionate detail the interior of his house, he wished he had invited her in sometime. Plenty of opportunities had presented themselves, but he had shied away, protecting his privacy and preventing the awkwardness of having both her and Lucinda drop by at the time same. He had not known, however, that Natalie coveted this house, that it was her attraction to the edifice, not its occupant, that had caused the calamitous row between her and Walter. Devon also found it interesting that the only restrictive clause she mentioned in Walter's will instructed her to care for him at home if he became incapacitated. Nothing about her being disinherited if he died of unnatural causes. Devon grunted as if he'd been punched when he heard her say, *"I kept Gordon and Devon as lovers. I know how to take care of myself."*

"Apparently not," he muttered as he took the tape out. Knowing it must have hurt Lucinda to hear he'd been kept on as another woman's lover, he was glad he'd told her he'd been sleeping with Natalie, though it was small compensation for what he heard next.

On the second tape, she described herself as a rag of desperation, and he could hear her using those words, the pathetic self-deprecation that was only true when she believed it. Other times her ego was selfish and greedy. Like when she demanded he make her come and he would keep fucking into her for so long he forgot where or who he was and became only the pumping of his cock into a hungry pussy, sweat dripping from his chest onto the writhing breasts of a woman beneath him. Finally she would come and it would be like an earthquake ripping them apart. She would shove him off and twist her body tight to deny him access as she lay gasping and sobbing, her body quivering like a frightened fawn at the mercy of a hunter. Sometimes she wouldn't let him touch her again that night. He had to pull himself from the warmth they'd created, dress quickly, and slip out into the chill alone. He would shiver in the cold crossing both their yards. Standing on his deck looking at the fog shifting above the Magado, he had felt more dispirited than he could ever remember.

Feeling like a rag of desperation, she said, she ran through the forest intending to drown herself in the creek but had knocked herself out on a tree instead. When she came to, she saw him fucking Lucinda in the boulders. She watched—a silent, secret voyeur, she called herself—even coming when they did by imagining him simultaneously fucking her. After that, she said she walked home, took a quick skinny-dip in the pool, went inside, and smothered her husband. She said the machines abruptly fell silent. Devon wondered about that, but mostly he couldn't recall a time he'd had sex with Lucinda in the boulders when Walter was still alive. Careful not to give his neighbor a show, he had made love to Lucinda there only when he'd known Natalie wasn't home because he'd seen her leave. Walter had died in February when the snow would have made such an adventure uncomfortable at best, and anyway, Devon had been with Lucinda in Berrendo that weekend. So Natalie couldn't have witnessed it. It couldn't have inspired her to end her husband's life. Was she lying or confused?

He jerked when he heard her report that he had said "No." Surprised, he rewound the tape and listened again to her question. He wanted to defend himself by saying he'd come damn close to getting married a couple of times, had even lived with a woman once, but he was alone in the bedroom and the woman asking the question wasn't listening anymore. On the tape she reported that he had laughed before saying, "Doesn't sound like fun." Having missed what he was referring to, he was about to rewind when her voice exploded with anger: *"I was in hell! I was in prison! I was crucified daily!"* It dropped to a near whisper as she admitted confessing to him how she killed Walter. She had been convincing in person. On tape, she didn't sound sincere, though the next one sounded real.

She talked about Bright and the games he played, leaving her handcuffed naked to the bed as a joke. Devon wondered, as she did, what he would have thought if he'd stumbled onto her like that. But he always waited for an invitation, never even called her between their late-night visits. He was beginning to see how callous he had been throughout their affair. He had to admit that's what it was, though at the time he had convinced himself it was just casual sex, a relief valve for both of them, no emotions attached. Having been a detective who studied human behavior, he knew better than to think people did much of anything without attaching emotion to it. His vow to catch her killer proved he hadn't been uninvolved.

Alex, too, was drawn in at a highly emotional level. Forced to watch Bright fuck Natalie while she was helplessly handcuffed, he had endured that to protect her from blackmail. Natalie said, *"Alex refused to do it until Bright mentioned the fact of my guilt, which I couldn't deny."* Again no mention of the unnatural causes clause in Walter's will, only that she had killed him.

Next she talked about running away to Europe with the tickets she had hidden. Because she gave no dates in her monologues, it was difficult to match the events she described with what he remembered, but as near as he could figure she'd recorded that passage the day before their breakfast in the café. Something had happened the night between that spooked her into acting fast. Initially he had thought it was Alex's arrival, but he'd learned from Bright, and now had confirmed by the tapes, that Alex had been around a week or more before Natalie died. So it was something else that Alex did—maybe Alex— someone did that pushed her into that frantic visit to the café. Devon wondered if she had intended to ask him to travel with her, if it was that imminent invitation and departure that drove her killer over the brink. Amy was probably right in thinking the murder was motivated by jealousy. Bright had declared he was only playing and would drop Natalie when he got bored. Alex had declared he was in love with her, which certainly didn't prove he was innocent, but Devon had to come back to how cold Alex would be to move into Natalie's house with her blood still on her bedroom wall.

Something he had heard on the tape nagged at Devon. He rewound it and listened again to her asking if he had been married and his succinct denial. After that, she said, the breeze dropped the curtain against the open door. He pictured the room in his mind, seeing only heavy, dark drapes on the west wall. When he was there, the drapes had always been closed, so what he had assumed to be a window was actually a door. To where? He had never looked at that side of her house from the outside. If there was a door, it must lead to a porch.

He left his house and walked through the trees to Natalie's backyard, continuing around to the west side. A small balcony extended outside her bedroom. Within a low wrought iron fence, the floor looked to be about four by six. Not much bigger than a coffin, it would have provided a good place to stand and watch the sunsets. A good place for a quick exit, too. He looked at the ground around his feet but, in the dark, couldn't see any unusual disturbance. In the deeply shadowed wall beneath the porch, he discovered a lattice of dead vines curling up the southwest corner. Gingerly he stepped onto a crooked branch and tested it with his weight. The branch held. He carefully climbed higher until he could peer over the edge of the floor. The reddish wrought iron had spread rust in a splotchy pattern on the concrete. Or maybe it was blood. Natalie's killer must have been covered with it. If he had used this porch to escape, he had to have left some behind.

Devon looked down and saw where a branch had recently been broken. The white insides of its jagged ends hadn't been weathered more than a few days. It was as large around as the branch he was standing on, so the fact that it had broken could mean whoever had used it as a ladder was heavier. He looked at the door leading into Natalie's bedroom. It was still open a crack, though the ghostly curtain hung motionless on this windless night. Slowly he climbed back down and walked home, knowing the porch provided the only exit fast enough that her wound could still be throbbing when he had walked in. Surely her killer left blood in his wake. Devon wondered if Chief Bright had seen it, and if he had, what he'd been able to learn from the residue.

CHAPTER TWENTY-FIVE

Sharon felt something crawling on her arm. A second later she recognized the unmistakable eight-legged gait of a spider. She screamed and slapped at it, prompting a retaliatory bite near her shoulder. She slapped at it again and jerked to her feet, stomping and rubbing her bare arms as she shivered in a sudden chill. Lashing out, she beat her fists against the closet door, kicked it until her toes ached and the pain in her arm was a burn radiating heat. "Help me!" she cried, pounding on the door. Muscle cramps twisted her legs as a knot of pain dug into her stomach. She moaned and lost her bearings in the dark. Her legs trembling, she sat down hard and leaned her head against the wall. The darkness was spinning as if she were inside a child's toy. Outside were colors and voices and the good smells of cookies and cocoa, but here was only darkness, nausea, and fever. She hugged herself as her head floated disembodied in space, her ears burned, and she knew she was going to faint the second before she slumped unconscious against the broom.

She awoke to the smell of vomit and dust. Everything was so dark she at first thought she was blind. Then she remembered she was locked in a closet. Her head felt thick, her brain like mud. She touched a sore spot on her arm and felt pain ricochet to the bone, bringing back her memory of the spider. She wondered if she had killed it or if it still lurked in wait, watching her. Weakly she moved her foot to kick the door; the sound she made was a mere scratch. She opened her mouth to call again for help but only a dry croak came out. Her stomach hurt, she was sweating, and she began to shiver. Moaning, she rocked herself, being careful not to touch her swollen arm.

Lucinda heard Devon outside Amy's closed bedroom door. When he opened it, light from the kitchen penetrated the hall to enter behind him like an afterthought. Silhouetted in the doorway, his expression was unreadable. She sat up warily as Amy stirred and whimpered, still lost in a dream. "It's all right," Lucinda murmured, sliding from the bed. She settled the covers high on Amy's shoulders and leaned to kiss her cheek. "I'll be right back." Standing up to face Devon, she saw him retreating in the dim light on the far side of the hall.

She followed him, closing the door on her daughter's restless sleep. In the kitchen he had coffee brewing, though a glance at the clock on the stove told her it was past four. He stood with his hands in his jeans' pockets as he leaned against the counter watching her. She waited, wanting him to choose the topic. Finally he said, "You've had time to think about it. What do you want to say?"

Remembering back over the tapes, she folded her arms beneath her breasts and leaned against the dishwasher. "I guess what bothers me most is that you were playing the same games with her Bright was. He went a little farther, that's the only difference, a matter of degree not substance."

His words came at her like bullets: "You think I'm the same as him?"

She realized she had never seen him angry before. Irritated, impatient; not angry. "Who are you mad at?" she whispered.

"I trusted you. Why didn't you show me these when you first found 'em?"

"I told you why! Are you saying *you* don't trust *me?*"

"I didn't promise you fidelity, Lucinda. As I remember it,

you're the one who said we didn't owe each other that. Yeah, I played games with Natalie. She thought 'em up and got a kick out of 'em. It was all just fucking to me. I didn't care what fantasies she was spinning in her head." His dark eyes pierced into her. "I want to know what you heard on those tapes that set you against me."

"I'm not against you," she said, flabbergasted.

"You left my bed."

"I thought you deserved to hear the tapes alone, like I did."

He cocked his head as if to hear better. In a softer, more conciliatory tone he asked, "What else did you think about what you heard?"

"I think she set all three of you up equally, as if she knew this would happen. None of you are proven guilty or innocent, you're all just left dangling there like mice in front of her cat."

"That's a flattering portrait of my competence."

"Which I haven't shared much of lately. You disappear for hours and come home moody, sit in the swing or go for a walk, never have much to say and pay attention to me only when you want to fuck." She told herself not to say another word. From his face he was struggling to concede her point, but the argument against it was evidently strong.

In a flat monotone, he said, "I'm investigating a friend's murder."

"For who? Nobody's paying you. And as for my holding onto those tapes, do you think that was easy?"

He sighed. "No, I know it wasn't. Did you listen to the end?"

She hadn't and wasn't sure she wanted to. "Does it . . . is it . . . was the tape going when she died?"

He shook his head. "It ran out before."

"What then?" she whispered.

"Someone comes in but doesn't speak and she doesn't give us a name."

"What does she say?"

"No. That's pretty much it."

"Can you hear him doing anything?"

"Unhooking her. I'm pretty sure I heard that."

"Taking off the handcuffs?"

He nodded.

"And then the tape just stops?"

"Yup."

She watched him, seeing that his anger, though dissipated, was still there. "Why are you mad at me?"

"Where did you find them?"

"Under her bed," she admitted sheepishly.

"That time you left your hair in her curtain?"

"No, another time. I went to see Alex and offer to help with the funeral, thinking maybe I'd get to see the guest list. Remember how we wanted to see her address book? I was working on that angle. But he wasn't home, and you know how the lock on the patio door's broken, so I went in and looked, that's all. The drawer of her nightstand had been emptied and for some reason I looked under the bed." She shrugged. "I knew it was wrong to keep them to myself but I needed to know how it was between the two of you."

"What'd you find out?"

She took a deep breath. "A minute ago, you said she was the only one playing games. That for you it was just sex. Do you really believe that?"

He nodded.

"What is it with me?"

"Exploring love," he said without hesitation.

She mouthed the word without sound, then smiled and said, "That sounds nice."

He nodded. "In the morning, I want you and Amy to go home."

253

Stunned by his sudden decision, she could only answer, "Amy won't leave until she knows what happened to Sharon."

They stared at each other across the ten feet of dimly lit kitchen between them. Then he said with a whimsical smile, "Least we know she's not with Leroy." His smile was quickly replaced with a surprised expression. "Damn!" he whispered. "I bet she's with Alex!"

"What makes you think that?"

"She prob'ly came here after escaping Leroy. When she found nobody home, she went next door. You were gone yesterday afternoon, weren't you?"

She nodded. "Amy and I went looking for her."

He stood up straight. "I'm gonna call Bright."

"And say what?" she asked guardedly, neither trusting nor liking the chief of police.

Devon smiled as he picked up the phone. "That we heard screams coming from Natalie's house."

When her mother closed the bedroom door, Amy awoke from a vivid dream. She sat bolt upright and stared into the dark as she remembered pounding her fists against the lid of a casket she knew had been nailed shut. She didn't know how she knew, or why she called it a casket when she could stand up and even move a couple of steps in all directions. A very commodious casket, or a casket only in the sense that it would hold her corpse. She shuddered and turned on a lamp. Her mother had been here when she fell asleep; vaguely she remembered Lucinda kissing her cheek before leaving. Devon must have come home. Eager for news of Sharon, and not wanting to flaunt her breasts beneath only a nightgown in front of him again, she put on a thick green robe and pulled its tasseled zipper to the top. When she opened the door, she heard Devon's voice floating across the living room dimly lit from the kitchen.

"We heard a girl screaming inside the Wieland house."

Amy reached down and turned the bedside lamp off, then stood in the doorway, listening from the dark.

"Just now," Devon said. "That's why I'm calling." A pause, then he said, "Okay."

Amy heard him hang up the wall phone in the kitchen. "Bright wants me to stay here 'til he calls me back."

"Is he going to the house?"

"Says he'll have Officer Reese along and for me to stay put."

Amy took a step backward and eased the door shut. She unzipped and stepped out of her robe and quickly dressed in the clothes she'd taken off before she went to bed: jeans and a white eyelet blouse, socks and sneakers. In the bathroom, she rinsed out her mouth and ran a brush through the long swatch of her hair that hadn't been cropped short. The sapphire stud was still in her nose but she'd taken the ring out of her eyebrow the night before. She didn't put it back. Neither did she put on any makeup but walked out and into the kitchen with her face naked except for the sapphire.

The kitchen was empty, the door to the laundry room open. She walked through to the mud room and out onto the deck. They were standing close, his arm around her mother's waist, looking up at the widow's pink house barely glimmering through the dark trees. Devon glanced at Amy when she came out, then looked back at the house. Lucinda smiled and raised her hand for Amy to come closer. She snuggled into her mother's side, her arm around Lucinda's waist above Devon's as they all stared at the silent house.

"I had a dream about Sharon," Amy said.

Lucinda squeezed her shoulder, pulling her a tad closer, then patted her arm. "What was it, sweetheart?"

Amy described her dream of pounding against the lid of a coffin that had been nailed shut. She stopped when she felt her mother shiver.

"I can't imagine anything worse than being buried alive," Lucinda whispered.

In a tone of dismissing nonsense, Devon said, "We think Sharon's in Natalie's house."

"Why would she be there?" Amy asked, impatient with his lack of faith in her vision.

With a soothing softness, Lucinda said, "She might have come here while we were out and, finding no one home, gone next door for help."

"So you think she's over there with that cretin Alex?"

The house they were all staring at emitted no light or hint that anyone was awake or even home. Without explanation, Devon went back inside.

"He called the police," Lucinda said, "and asked them to investigate."

"I heard him," Amy said. "It's taking them a long time to get here, don't you think?"

"I'm going over there," Devon said, coming back carrying a small, black velvet bag.

He was down the steps and striding toward the trees before Lucinda reacted. "Chief Bright said for you to wait for his call."

Devon turned around at the edge of the forest. "Will you wait for me?"

Wanting to go with him, Amy looked up at her mother's worried frown and decided to stay. She squeezed her mother's waist, as a few minutes before Lucinda had squeezed her daughter's shoulder. "We'll be okay, Mom," she said.

Lucinda looked down and gave a little laugh, then looked back at Devon and nodded. As he disappeared under the dark of the trees, the women clung to each other. For seventeen years they had stood together against the vagaries of life. Only for the last three had a man made them feel vulnerable without him.

Sharon heard a noise beyond the door. Trying not to shiver, she listened hard but didn't hear it again. She tried to kick her leg but nothing happened. Her feet were numb, and she didn't think she could stand up. She was afraid the spider was still there and that she would poke some part of herself into its range and get bitten again. If the first bite hit her this hard, she doubted she could survive a second one. She wondered if spider venom became weaker with each bite, like snake venom did; wondered if there was an antivenin and if the hospital would have any; wondered how many people died every year from spider bites. She had read on the Internet recently that more people were killed by donkeys every year than died in plane crashes. Who would have suspected donkeys were so lethal? *Oh, jeez,* she thought, *I feel so bad, I must be dying.* She remembered a book she'd read, a story about Indians, and how when a young man was bitten by a snake, he remembered his father saying, "You won't die of a snakebite, you'll just wish you could." She almost laughed, remembering that.

She heard the noise again. It was a soft pucker of air, like someone had opened or closed an outside door, causing a chain reaction through the rooms that gently tugged at the closet door. Someone had come. Had they already left? She tried to move her feet but couldn't even tell where they were. Leaning forward she struck at the door, her hand slapping listlessly against the wood, her fingers sliding down in a whisper. "Please," she moaned. Forcing air through her swollen throat, she rasped, "Help! Help!" She fell silent and listened. Were those voices? Through several walls, far away, but men talking? Yes! Groping behind herself, she latched onto the straw of the broom and tapped its handle against the door in an erratic rhythm that she kept going, afraid if she stopped she would die.

Hearing footsteps on stairs just beyond the wall, she tapped harder, hearing the men walking above her now. "Please," she begged. "Help me." The men seemed to be standing directly above her. Surely they heard her. She tried to tap louder, tried to kick, to scream, but she only whispered and tapped with the volume of a computer keyboard. The men were retreating. "No!" she wanted to yell. As hard as she could, she beat the broom's wooden handle against the door. "Please," she sobbed, her voice a hoarse rasp through sandpaper.

Suddenly the knob turned and she was blinded by light. Then she saw dark, faceless silhouettes and felt lifting hands. One grasped her bitten arm and she screamed.

"Call an ambulance," she heard Devon say as she floated beneath the bright kitchen light. In another, dimmer room, he laid her on a sofa. She forced her eyes to focus on his face and say, "Something bit me."

He nodded. "Black widow. I saw it dead in the closet."

She managed to smile. "I wasn't sure I'd killed it."

"How long were you in there?"

"I don't know." She tried to think. "It must've been 'bout six o'clock." She looked at the small red spot on her swollen arm. "I felt I would die."

"You'll be all right. An ambulance will take you to the hospital but I think the worst has passed." He smiled. "Maybe you can visit Leroy there."

She remembered. "He's okay?"

"Mild concussion, is all. You'll probably both be released tomorrow. If you need a ride, give me a call and I'll come get you."

"Thank you," she said, reaching out with her good hand to touch the front of his shirt.

He caught her hand and kissed her fingers, then winked at

her just before he stood up and walked away. She looked around
the room, seeing Chief Bright and Alex Wieland sitting at the
dining room table talking too softly for her to hear their words.
Devon opened the front door for the EMS crew. She knew one
of them. His name was Donnie Welbourne and he'd been a few
years ahead of her in high school. "Hi, Donnie," she said. "I
think I'm all right now."

They put her on a gurney anyway and started an I.V. of what
Donnie said was calcium gluconate in her affected arm. As they
rolled her toward the door, Chief Bright came over and walked
alongside. "You feeling better now, Sharon?" he asked.

She nodded, craning her neck to see Devon talking into a
cellphone just beyond the open sliding glass door.

"Can you tell me what happened?" Bright asked.

"A black widow bit me. Devon said he saw it in the closet."

Bright nodded. "Why were you in there?"

She looked at Alex Wieland still at the table. The man wasn't
looking at her but at his hands. "He pushed me in," she said,
"then locked the door."

"Who did?"

"Mr. Wieland."

"Why?"

"I don't know!"

"What were you doing here?"

"I came looking for help 'cause of Leroy. Devon told me he's
okay now and I'm glad, but I didn't know that then."

"Did you ask Mr. Wieland for help?"

She shook her head. "He scared me so bad I didn't say
anything. Then he thought I was the maid and took me to the
closet. I don't know why he shoved me in and locked the door."

"I'll find out," Bright said. "You concentrate on getting well
and I'll see you tomorrow."

She looked up at Donnie as he folded the gurney into the

ambulance. "Will you stay with me?" she asked.

"All the way," he promised.

CHAPTER TWENTY-SIX

A door opened and Natalie whimpered. Footsteps muffled on the carpet came closer. The tiny clanking sound of the steel handcuffs hitting the brass headboard when someone released her. A rustle of bedcovers. "No," she said flatly, neither pleading nor desperate. The door closed, and the tape clicked off.

Devon looked at Alex studying his hands, then at Bright staring at the machine as if he could see past when it had stopped. Bright looked up and said, "That was me."

Devon nodded. "What time was it?"

"Eight-ten, eight-twelve, right around there. I was transporting a prisoner to CDC, had him locked in my car, so I didn't do more'n unhook her and leave."

"What'd she say no to?"

Bright's eyes were teasing. "Whether or not you'd been by."

"I didn't hear your voice," Devon said, resenting the chief's levity. He wouldn't have thought anyone who knew Natalie could listen to the tapes without feeling sad.

"I went like this," Bright said, closing his fingers into a fist and jerking his thumb in the direction of Devon's house. "She knew what I meant." He chuckled. "What would you've done if you'd found her like that?"

"Let her loose. I've got a handcuff key."

"Always keep it on you?"

"I would've gone back for it."

"And woken up Lucinda in all likelihood."

"Why do you think this is funny?" Devon asked.

"Her dying isn't," Bright said. "But the games she was playing with all of us kinda are, don't you think?"

Devon looked at Alex. "What do you think, Wieland?"

When Alex raised his head, tears fell across his cheeks. "I'm the only one who loved her," he moaned.

"Which prob'ly means you killed her," Devon said. He looked at Bright. "On an earlier tape, when she's describing how she smothered Walter, she says the machines simply stopped. According to the nurse, the only machine in there was a heart monitor. They beep every time the patient's heart beats. If Walter was smothered, his heart would've gone nuts and the machine would've sounded like a siren before it flatlined."

"So?" Bright asked.

"I don't think she killed him," Devon said, watching Alex.

Bright looked back and forth between them. "You think he did?"

Devon nodded. "As a favor to her."

"You can't prove it," Alex sniffed.

Devon shrugged. "Can't see as it matters much, can you, Gordon?"

The chief shook his head. "What we're interested in is who killed Natalie."

"What's this 'we' business?" Alex accused. "This man isn't a police officer or have any authority whatsoever. If this is an official inquiry, why is he here?"

"He's one of the suspects I'm questioning," Bright said.

"And I'm another one?" Alex asked indignantly.

"Chief Bright's as likely a suspect as I am," Devon said. "We both had ample opportunity. The problem is we don't have a motive."

"What about him handcuffing her to the bed?" Alex argued. "Doing those awful things while she was helpless."

"And making you watch," Bright teased.

"You're sick if you think I liked it!"

"On the other hand," Devon said, "Gordon took a long time delivering his prisoner." He smiled at the chief. "There's an eight-hour gap between when you called from Carrizozo and when you checked in again."

"How do you know that?" Bright drawled.

"I saw the duty log."

Bright shrugged. "The prisoner was a wife beater. I went back to the little lady and rendered her comfort."

"Was she willing, or did you handcuff her, too?"

"She ate it up," Bright said. "Why do you suppose Natalie would confess to killing Walter if she hadn't done it?"

"Maybe 'cause she knew Alex had," Devon said, "and she wanted to keep her house."

Bright turned cold eyes on Alex.

"Did you find any evidence," Devon asked, "on the balcony outside her bedroom?"

Bright looked at him with surprise. "We found some blood and knew that's how the killer got out, but nothing to pinpoint who he was."

"Except that it wasn't me," Devon said, " 'cause I was still here." He looked at Alex. "What did you have planned for Sharon?"

"Nothing," Alex answered plaintively. "That closet locks when the door closes. I don't know why. I didn't design this house. I certainly didn't plant any poisonous spider."

"She told me you pushed her in," Bright said.

"She came here pretending to be the maid," Alex whined. "Then as soon as she got inside, she wanted to call the police. I would've been on my way to Europe tomorrow."

"Leaving her in the closet to die?" Devon asked incredulously.

"I asked her to go with me!" Alex cried. "What was she doing here anyway?"

"She came to you for help," Devon said.

"So what?" Alex jeered. "I thought I was doing Natalie a favor by killing Walter. Instead I disinherited her. It wasn't 'til afterwards she told me about the unnatural causes clause in his will! After that, she said she killed him because she knew Bright wouldn't arrest her like he would me." He looked at the chief. "I almost would've rather gone to prison than watch what you did to her. She pleaded with me to wait you out, saying you'd get bored and we'd be safe." He frowned at Devon. "I came here that night to beg her for the last time to marry me, but she wouldn't. I watched her get ready for you instead, even to the point of stripping the top sheet off her bed. She sat there and arranged her negligee so prettily, ignoring me as if my role were to watch her with her lovers, as if I were no more than a eunuch. I was standing by her vanity, and her manicure scissors were laying there. They were small enough that I hid them in my hand as I leaned over to kiss her goodbye. She would allow me that if I didn't linger. This time when our lips touched, I stabbed those tiny scissors into her throat and slashed her artery. It's a simple maneuver if you know anatomy."

Devon shuddered. "What'd you do that made her come running to me in the café that morning?"

"I told her I wouldn't let her live without me." Alex reached out and flicked a crumb off the corner of the table. "Don't you think there should be a special law," he asked dourly, "for men duped by women into committing murder?"

"Maybe you can work on that in prison," Bright said, standing up. "Let's go."

Devon watched them walk out the front door, leaving him alone at Natalie's table. He looked up at the room where she had died, then at the Navajo rug in front of the hearth where they had first shared pleasure. He thought of Sharon and Leroy in the same hospital twenty miles away, and remembered he had promised to bring them home in the morning, which meant he should get some sleep. But he stayed seated at the table, feeling the weight of the house's unhappiness crowding close. He thought he could almost smell Natalie's blood enclosing him in an impermeable skin that threatened to keep him forever in this negative space, then he remembered Amy saying he held himself here by dwelling on it. Threading that thought into the eye of the right needle, he fell back on his old solution to insolvable problems: get out.

Lucinda felt melancholy, taking his shirts from the dryer and hanging them on hangers on the rack screwed into the laundry room wall. His hangers were black plastic, the kind you buy in discount stores a dollar a dozen. The clock in the room was a whimsical creation of a wire flyswatter, its net the face and the minute hand a black fly lurching around the circle. According to the fly, it was nearly dawn, though the sky outside was still dark. Each shirt she took from the dryer she draped on a hanger, straightened the shoulders, then closed the top button and one half-way down. The long-sleeved, rugged shirts had labels boasting such names as Northwest Territory, Sun River, Tribes, Woolrich, Union Bay. The dress shirts were from companies like Stafford and Cambridge Classics. There was an elegant gray gabardine from Brandini, a pale yellow linen by Merona, a denim from Bay Area Traders, and a brown corduroy by G. H. Bass. When she had done his laundry the first day she arrived, she had emptied only the hamper in the bedroom. This morning when she came in to wash a few things before packing to leave, she discovered another hamper stuffed with the shirts she was now hanging up. If nothing else, she reasoned, she had left him with a replenished wardrobe. It wasn't much to show for her summer vacation, but it was more pleasant to think about than the souvenir on her neck she was taking home.

His last words had been to ask her to wait for him. She recognized that as a double entendre, because he had literally asked her to wait in his stead for the call from Chief Bright, but of course there was an obvious and more romantic meaning attached to those words by convention. The question a soldier asks his girl before going to war, though if he truly wanted her to wait he would marry her before leaving. Devon had asked her to wait and to marry him. Although both times his actual words were ambiguous, she had said yes. What hadn't been open to misinterpretation was his flat statement that he wanted her and Amy to go home. Lucinda dwelled on that as she smoothed his shirts to fall straight on their hangers, suspecting it was the truth and the two invitations were mere effluences of his quixotic good moods. Remembering Natalie had said that what drew her and Devon together was their mutual need for affirmation after having committed murder, Lucinda knew she had nothing as dramatic to offer him. What she had was cozy and domestic, stable and reliable, but she didn't suppose a man who had chosen to work in homicide coveted such qualities. Because the fact remained that he was still embroiled in solving murders. Apparently he needed neither a badge nor any legal authority whatsoever to root out criminals where legitimate cops feared to go. She laughed at herself, thinking she should be hanging up capes instead of shirts.

The obvious question—would he ever stop—had an equally obvious answer: no. The next question—did she want to live with it—wasn't so easy. Superficially she could echo his no, she did not, but she did want to live with him. What she considered unfair was that in order to do that harmoniously she had to pay a huge price. While he lost only his loneliness, he gained a home, a nest, a sanctuary that she kept ready for his need. She gained fear as a constant companion, ghosts of murder scratching at her door. A string of them now: the corrupt cop in El Paso, the innocent schoolboy and his craven killers, a widow and her vegetative husband, each subsequent encounter threatening to shine a spotlight on the murder in El Paso. Yet she decided sharing his life forced her to acknowledge what was always true but usually forgotten: life was tenuous, love a gift with no guarantees. To live with that as a constant truth could be a blessing, if she had the courage to see it that way.

Hanging his shirts in his closet, she heard his footsteps on the deck, then crossing the mud and laundry rooms to the kitchen. A second later he stood in the doorway, looking tired but relieved, so she knew it was over. This time.

"You didn't have to do that," he said, nodding at the shirts.

She closed the closet door and shrugged.

"Alex confessed to both murders," he said. "He killed Walter to free Natalie, then her 'cause she spurned him. Amy was right. Jealousy was the motive."

"Amy was right about a lot of things," Lucinda said.

"She asleep?"

Lucinda shook her head. "After you called, she followed the ambulance so she could be with Sharon at the hospital."

He turned his back to the doorjamb and leaned against it as he stared into the dark living room. "I've known some callous men but nobody as cold as Alex Wieland. He thought nothing of leaving Sharon locked in a closet to die, and he moved into Natalie's house less than twenty-four hours after killing her there." Devon turned his head to look at her. "I don't see how he could've stomached it."

"Maybe he couldn't," she said, "and that's why he confessed."

Devon shifted his gaze to her open suitcase on the bed. "Is that what you're saying about sharing my life?"

She shook her head. "It bothers me that Natalie watched us make love then went home and killed her husband."

"It didn't happen, Lucinda. She admitted on the tape that she sometimes hallucinated. Anyway, we were in Berrendo when Walter died. Natalie may've seen us on the rocks last summer, but Alex killed Walter, remember?"

"Then planted the knife in our backyard?"

"No, Leroy did that, but the blood on it was deer blood. Seems some hunter lost the knife, or maybe threw it away 'cause it wasn't the kinda blade you'd want for cleaning game. It's anyone's guess who took it from the evidence room." His smile tugged at her heart. "Let's fly down to La Paz for the rest of your vacation."

She pictured a clean white beach beside a blue ocean, a lazy ceiling fan above a rumpled bed. "La Paz means peace. Is that what we'll find?"

He spread his palms wide in surrender. "I promise if I see a dead body, I'll turn around and walk away. Is that close enough?"

She laughed. "As long as it's not mine."

ABOUT THE AUTHOR

Elizabeth Fackler has published fifteen novels, along with short stories and poetry, nearly all set in the American Southwest. Her complex stories of deeply realized characters appeal to fans of psychological drama. She lives in Capitan, New Mexico, with her husband, Michael, and their two dogs, Pecos and Mitchum.